THE
LAST
VOYAGE
OF
POE
BLYTHE

ALSO BY ALLY CONDIE:

Matched

Crossed

Reached

Atlantia

Summerlost

The Darkdeep

ALLY CONDIE

THE LAST VOYAGE OF POE BLYTHE

DUTTON BOOKS

DUTTON BOOKS
An imprint of Penguin Random House LLC, New York

Visit us online at penguinrandomhouse.com

Library of Congress Cataloging-in-Publication Data

Names: Condie, Allyson Braithwaite, author.
Title: The last voyage of Poe Blythe / Ally Condie.
Description: New York, NY : Dutton Books for Young Readers, 2019. | Summary:
   Seeking to avenge the murder of her true love while on a dredge ship
   searching for gold, fifteen-year-old captain Poe Blythe becomes the
   architect of new defenses designed to destroy her enemies.
Identifiers: LCCN 2018042052 | ISBN 9780525426455 (hardback) | ISBN
   9780698135611 (ebook)
Subjects: | CYAC: Revenge—Fiction. | Boats and boating—Fiction. | Gold
   mines and mining—Fiction. | Self-confidence—Fiction.
Classification: LCC PZ7.C7586 Las 2019 | DDC [Fic]—dc23 LC record available at
   https://lccn.loc.gov/2018042052

Printed in the United States of America

ISBN 9780525426455

10 9 8 7 6 5 4 3 2 1

Edited by Julie Strauss-Gabel
Design by Anna Booth
Text set in Sabon LT Pro

FOR LAINEY, A STAR

THE
LAST
VOYAGE
OF
POE
BLYTHE

CALL TELLS ME HE SEES A STAR and that makes me laugh.

"I do." His voice is serious, his mouth against my ear.

I tip my head up. He's right. It hangs low on the horizon. "That makes six," I say.

"Seven," he says. "That *was* a star we saw the first night on the river."

"It wasn't." We've been arguing about this for weeks, ever since we left the Outpost behind and boarded the dredge to go upriver.

He laughs softly before he starts kissing me again.

Up on the deck, it's easier to hear past the sounds made by our hungry metal ship. But it's still impossible to completely ignore the constant throb and grate of the dredge as it moves along the river in search of gold, taking in rocks and stones, grinding them out. It tears up the rivers and leaves refuse and silt behind, ruins valleys, adds a smear of smoke to the sky.

"All of this, because the Admiral has a taste for gold," I say.

"I have a taste for you," Call tells me. I laugh because it's such a stupid thing to say, even though it's true, and I feel him smile.

"It makes no sense," I say. "What good is all this gold?" We all know that the Admiral wants to help the Outpost thrive. He thinks that getting more gold can help us do that, but I'm not entirely sure why. We've mined enough to last us for a while, and there's not really anyone to trade with anymore. We need so many other things. Cleaner air, more water, better medicine, ways to rehabilitate the land. All gold does is gild the time until we die.

"Who cares?" Call says. "If the Admiral didn't want it, we'd never get to be out here."

Call says things like this, but I've seen the expression on his face as he looks back at the devastation we leave behind. Churned-up riverbed, life choked to death so we can raise the gold.

Even though it shivers me to think of the ruin we're causing, I may as well count the stars while I can. Already, in two weeks out on the river, I've seen more than most people back at the Outpost will in a lifetime.

"*It was a good idea to come here,*" Call whispers. "*Admit it.*"

"A good idea," I say, teasing. "A good idea for us to spend our days in the belly of a noisy old ship loud enough to make us deaf. A good idea to spend our nights up here standing guard and ruining our eyes looking for things in the dark."

"A *very* good idea," he says.

Call had overheard some of the machinists in the scrap yard where we work talking about the dredge voyages. "It's not an ideal posting," the machinists told Call. "It's dangerous and you have to leave the Outpost." To Call, those sounded like promises instead of drawbacks.

"It's the only way you're going to see the world, Poe," he said to me. "The only way you're going to shake the dust of the Outpost from your feet."

And we both knew that signing on to the dredge was a way for us to be together, without settling down and having babies and working all day every day in the same places, doing the same things.

And then there's the biggest secret, the best dream of all.

We're going to escape.

At the turnaround point, we're going to leave. Run. Be free.

I have imagined it all. Blue lakes. Forest smell. The sound of something else alive in the woods, that isn't human and doesn't care that we are. We might not last long in the wilderness, but who knows. There's a chance we could survive.

I would rather be torn apart by something than wait for nothing. And it doesn't do any good to worry about what might happen later.

Instead, I think about now. I like now. A kiss on the top of the dredge under a smeary star sky with Call's hands touching me.

"Should we invite any of the crew to come with us when we go?" Call asks.

We've had this discussion before, too.

"No," I say. "Just us."

Call sighs in my ear, metal aches and scrapes against stone, the trammel inside the ship turns the rocks and sifts out the gold, water sluices against rock and metal.

And then the bell from the mining deck.

I swear because I know what it means. They need help with the dredge's main motor, the one that powers all the systems on the ship.

"Go on," Call says. "Then you can come back up here."

It's sliding past dusk and straight into night.

"Be careful while I'm gone," I say. "Watch out for the raiders."

"I do a better job watching when you're not here," he says, and even in the dim light I can see the twist of his smile.

"That's true," I say. "I won't come up again." I'm not joking. Perhaps we've been too giddy with freedom, with being outside.

"Poe," Call says. "It's all right. We haven't seen a single raider on this river."

Maybe they're dying off. Everyone knew it would happen eventually.

The Outpost is the only place you can last. The only place with dependable medicine and food and the protection of the Admiral and his militia. You give up some of your freedom for it, but most feel it's an easy trade.

Call touches my hand in the dark as I leave.

•   •   •

"There," Naomi says, right as the mining equipment kicks back in, a constant low growl and grind that becomes part of you, like a heartbeat. Powered by solar conduits and battery storage, the main motor runs everything on the dredge through power take-off systems. The mining system is the loudest. It's cobbled together from the dredge's original system because we didn't have the raw materials to replace it. The mining buckets move their belt, the trammel that sorts the gold from the rocks rolls, everything clanks and spins and grinds. Sweat trickles down Naomi's tanned face. She wipes her hands on a rag and nods to Nik and me. "Thanks."

"You're welcome," Nik says. We have to yell to be heard over the sound of the ship. Often we just read one another's lips. "Sorry we got you down here, kid," he says to me. In the lights below deck his face looks ghoulish but friendly.

"Any stars on the top deck?" Naomi asks.

"We saw one already tonight," I say. "You should come up."

Nik laughs. "You don't mean that. You and Call want to have the deck all to yourselves."

I roll my eyes at him even though he's right. But Naomi and Nik both follow me up the stairs, the pull of fresh air strong after having been down on the mining deck. As we climb, the smell of night breezes and even, maybe, of pine forests somewhere nearby, floats down to us. I breathe in. It's all worth it.

"Call," I holler, as I come up on the deck, but he's not

where I left him. I see several shapes moving in the dim lights that rim the base of the deck. Who else is up here? Some of the crew? "Hey," I say, stepping out onto the deck and then Naomi grabs my arm, hard, stopping me.

The shapes advance, evolve. As they come closer they turn from shadows into people whose faces I don't recognize.

Raiders.

"We want the gold," one of them says. "Tell us where it is. Now."

My mind races. My eyes hunt.

Where is Call?

He didn't have time to sound the alarm. Did he have time to hide?

"Tell us where it is," another raider says, "or we'll kill all of you and take it anyway."

I look at Naomi and Nik. Their hands are up.

"You can't kill all of us," I say. "You need us alive. You don't know how to run the ship."

"You two, take us below," the raider says to Naomi and Nik. "Show us where the gold is or we'll shoot you." He gestures in my direction. "Keep her up here."

The raiders train their guns on me. My mind wants me to stay alive. My heart is sick with worry about Call. But he's fast. He's good. He's probably hiding somewhere, waiting for his turn. Waiting for the instant he can pick them all off.

A moment passes.

And then I hear a terrible sound: the ship's motor shutting down. They're stopping us.

I sidle toward the edge of the deck. Are more raiders waiting down there in the water? Did Call escape? Is he standing in the river, silent, hoping I'll look over the edge? Waiting to catch me if I jump?

If he is, we could still get away. We could leave and not look back.

"Go ahead," says the raider guarding me. "Take a look."

I glance over the side. Spots of light on the water—raiders in boats, holding torches. There are at least three dozen of them down there in addition to the ones already on the ship.

How are there so many? They were supposed to be dying out.

Only twenty-three people live on the dredge. We can't handle an armed group this size. And we're too far up the river to call for reinforcements from the Outpost.

They've timed this perfectly.

Where is Call?

I'm frantic to find him.

The raiders herd the other members of the crew up the stairs and out onto the deck. I see Naomi, Nik. The cook, the first mate. The captain. The cartographer. The other machinists and the miners. None of our crew is armed. The raiders must have taken our weapons.

Call is not the only one missing. I don't see the second mate, either.

And then, last up the stairs, two more raiders, each carrying someone. *Good,* I think, *we injured some,* but then they throw the people down on the deck of the dredge and I see one's the second mate and the other is turned over, facedown, and neither of them moves.

I do. Across the deck I stumble, crashing to my knees next to the facedown man. I put my hand on a dark place on his back and it comes away bloody. Naomi makes a sound like a cry. They might shoot me in the back too but I have to know. I have to know what I already know.

I turn him over. And there he is, his face lit by the cool glow of the deck lights and the fire of the raiders' torches. His eyes are open, alone.

Call.

I put my fingers to his lips. His skin already feels cold to me.

"Get up," says a raider.

I don't.

Call was shot in the back. He didn't have a chance to sound the alarm. He was shot in the back and he was alone. What do his eyes say? Nothing. They say nothing. He's nothing. He's not here anymore.

Am I still here?

Can you be this hollow and not blow away on the wind?

I glance over my shoulder at the other crew members. My friends. Naomi and the captain and all the rest of them, and I think, *I wish you were dead instead of him. You and you and you. Everyone else on this ship. All of you. I'd trade all of you for one of him and it wouldn't pain me one bit.*

Someone else steps into my line of vision. A raider. I hear

the creak of his boots as he crouches down, but I don't lift my gaze from Call's face. His eyes.

"Do you know who we are?" The man's voice is rough as rock, or gold. Not the polished shiny gold that's been refined and purified. The heavier, dirt-burnished kind that we drag up from the river bottom.

"Raiders," I say.

"Drifters," he says.

I couldn't care less what they call themselves. I take Call's rough hand in mine.

My face is wet.

"We're letting you go," the man says. He doesn't raise his voice, but it carries well, and the ship is so silent. "We left food for you on the shore. It's enough to get you back to the Outpost if you walk fast and don't eat much." He leans close, so close I can feel his breath on my cheek and see the glitter of his eyes in the torchlight. "Tell your Admiral that we're done with you taking from us. Tell him this is the last time we leave anyone alive."

I reach into Call's shirt pocket. I look at the buttons, the fabric, instead of at his dead eyes. One of the raider guards grabs my shoulder to haul me back, but not before I've taken out the folding ruler that Call always kept with him.

"What's that?" the raider asks.

I don't answer. "Help me," I say to Nik. "Help me bring him with us." Even though Call's gone, I won't leave his body with the raiders.

"Leave it," says the rough-voiced raider. "Get on out of here."

Fury, hot-white and loud as a motor, sounds through me. "Naomi," I say. "Will you help me?"

She doesn't move. Her face is sad and sorry. She's afraid. They're all afraid. I'm not. The worst has already happened.

As they drag me away, I twist around and see that the raiders are dragging Call, too. His head lolls back. He carries none of his own weight.

He's heavy, and yet he's not here at all.

Out on the shore, the dredge is an enormous deep shape against the night sky, and then it's the sun, exploding.

"They've blown it up." The captain's voice shakes.

Heat washes over us. A few singed shards of metal come down into the water and glint-glance off the rocks we tore up earlier.

The wind shifts, and I see a whole spread of stars beyond the miry, polluted air. They vanish again behind the smoke from the burning ship.

Call is dead.

The raiders made Call nothing. Call who was everything.

I make them a promise, as their smoke and fire blot out the stars.

I will make you nothing too.

TWO
YEARS
LATER

CHAPTER 1

"WE TALK ABOUT YOU."

"I know," I say to the Admiral. He tells me this as we sit up in a room in the scrap yard's wooden office building, waiting for the rest of his advisers to arrive. The Admiral's Quorum—a group of four, three men and one woman—advise and assist him with running the Outpost. I've heard snatches of what the Quorum says behind my back, the stories they tell. Some good, some bad. Some true, some false.

They say I live in the Admiral's pocket.

That I'm actually afraid of the rivers.

They whisper about how I was a machinist when I first went on the dredge two years ago, and then came home with a weaponist's mind and thirst for blood.

Two days after Call died, while our crew was making the long trek back to the Outpost, I had my first "revelation." That's what the Admiral calls it. He tells the Quorum, "God tells her something in her sleep, and then she draws the designs for it when she wakes up."

My first one was about an armor for the dredge that kills any raiders who try to board. The other revelations have been about how to perfect it.

There are two problems with the Admiral's revelation theory. First, I don't believe in God, so he can't talk to me. Second, I don't think I actually sleep deep enough to dream anymore.

The Admiral and I watch the workers crawling over the dredge in the yard below. The ship came off the river yesterday, and it's been hauled inland to the scrap yard for repairs.

It's the hot-orange, simmering-sunset time of day, bearable only because of the knowledge that there are just a few hours left until the cool of night. The crew must be sweating as they repair the armor on the dredge. I know from working on the scrap yard with Call how it feels to have your clothes wet and dry and wet again over the hours of the day; your hands smudged black with dirt and oil; skin tight across your nose from the sun; eyes scalded and dry from looking closely at shining metal, fitted gears.

That's as much as I'll let myself remember.

There's a flurry of movement in the yard as the workers change positions. The dredge bristles with variations on front- and side-facing gears. Armor. When the ship is moving, its exterior crawls like an animal covered in parasites. The gears are strong enough to snap a bone like a twig, a hunk of iron like a tree branch.

For decades, the two dredges the Outpost owned were nothing but great metal hulks from a long-past time. They sat out at the edge of the city, along with all the other remnants and machinery too large to bother moving. When this Admiral took power, he began to repair things, to try and figure out a way to make the Outpost thrive instead of just survive. He brought some of the old relics to the machinists' scrap yard for cleaning and repair, including the dredges. The raiders burned one the night Call died. Now there's a single ship left to run the rivers for gold.

"Ah," says the Admiral. "Welcome." The others have arrived. General Dale, Bishop Weaver, General Foster, Sister Haring. They shake hands with the Admiral and nod to me.

My position at these meetings is always strange. I'm not part of the Quorum. I only attend meetings concerning the dredge. And the citizens of the Outpost consider me a peculiarity. Not a person. When we pass in the street, they smile and keep their distance. Which makes sense. I'm aligned with the people in power, and it's best not to disturb them. That's common knowledge in the Outpost. Everyone's got their work to keep them busy, everyone's got to scrape to keep alive. We mind our own business. That's what's kept the Outpost viable all these years, on our own, without another major city or settlement within hundreds of miles.

And I also understand why the Quorum hasn't taken me under their collective wing. I'm not officially a member of their group. I'm much younger than they are. And the Quorum may not have any qualms about the people I kill, but no one wants to be close to a murderer.

There's something off about her. I've heard it whispered. Not just lately. All my life.

"Thank you for meeting us here," says the Admiral.

"It's our pleasure," says Sister Haring. Her neat blond hair is pulled up in a bun. She's very beautiful. I don't like her at all. I don't like any of them, but I like her the least because she smiles at me the most.

"Please," says the Admiral. "Sit." The wooden table and chairs in the room are scarred with use. Stray stubs of pencil and bits of paper have been left behind from other meetings. This is how the Admiral likes it. I don't know where the Quorum usually meets, but whenever we gather here to discuss the dredge, the Admiral wants the room left as it is from when the people who actually work on the yard use it. He likes the workaday, part-of-it-all feeling it gives him.

Bishop Weaver takes his seat on the right hand of the Admiral. When I'm in meetings with the Admiral, he likes me to sit on his left.

The Devil's hand, people used to call it.

I wonder who sits on his left when I'm not here.

General Dale's eyes linger on me in his usual calculating way. Sister Haring smiles politely. I don't care what they think of or about me. My job is to design the armor for the dredge and keep both working. Not to talk to the Quorum, not to bother about what it is *they* do.

"I have good news to report from the most recent voyage." The Admiral leans forward, rests his elbows on the table. He's tall and broad-shouldered, with a square-cut sandy beard and piercing blue eyes. His skin is always a little pink, like he's been out in the sun working hard. His lips are chapped, the hair on his strong arms bleached by the sun. Years ago, when the time came to choose a new Admiral, the Outpost couldn't resist him. He has big ideas, and he looks like a man of the people. As always, he wears a blue work shirt, brown trousers, scuffed black work boots, a silk tie loosely secured around his collar like an afterthought. A casual gesture to his status.

I'm dressed exactly like him, except for the tie. And I wear my hair long, in braids.

I wonder what Call would say if he could see me now. None of this is what he would have wanted. Except he'd want me alive, and this is the way I've found to do it.

"The *Gilded Lily* performed perfectly," says the Admiral.

I hate the name they've given the ship. I don't think of it as *she*, or *he* for that matter. It's the dredge. It's a piece of metal. It's not alive.

"We took in twice the gold we expected," the Admiral says. His eyes light up the way they do whenever he talks about gold, and he cannot completely control the emotion in his voice.

It's the same thing that happens when he needs to address the people, but this is raw. Unintended. Caught in glimpses instead of put on for a sermon.

"*Ah,*" says Sister Haring, satisfied. Bishop Weaver raises his eyebrows, and General Dale smiles.

General Foster actually presses his palms together in pleasure. "Wonderful," he says.

"It was by far our most successful voyage yet." The Admiral waits a beat before speaking again. "Even though no raiders were killed."

The members of the Quorum each flicker with movement at this. An intake of breath, a folding of arms, a recrossing of legs. I feel eyes shift to me.

"No raiders died," says the Admiral, "because our machine's reputation is such that not a single one of them tried to board."

General Dale folds his arms. "*That's* interesting." Our eyes meet. There is a challenge in his. As if he thinks my armor isn't enough threat to keep the raiders away.

As if he's forgotten all the rust-colored stains on the armor when the dredge has returned from other voyages. All the ways my prickling, moving gears have ground the raiders into pulp when they tried to board.

"We saw raiders along the banks, watching and following," says the Admiral, "but none dared attempt an attack."

We saw. That's what he says. But the truth is that none of us in this room go on the voyages. The Admiral stays behind in his house on the bluff and I sit in my apartment down in the city. He thinks about gold and government and I think about killing and Call.

"It's time," the Admiral says. "We're ready to cull the Serpentine."

"Good," says Sister Haring, at the same time that Bishop Weaver says, "At last," his intonation like a prayer.

The Serpentine River. The biggest river in the area; the one with the most potential for gold. We've waited because it's going to be the most difficult to dredge. It's long and deep, and goes far into raider territory.

A small smile curls my lips, and I bow my head to hide my pleasure at the Admiral's decision. I hope the raiders find the courage to try and board the ship. So we can cut them down.

"To ensure that everything goes smoothly, Lieutenant Blythe will be on this voyage."

My head jerks up in surprise. He wants *me* to go?

That's not what we agreed, I want to say to him. I designed the armor for the ship in exchange for my life and for the lives of the others on the dredge on my first voyage. *My only voyage.*

We lost the ship, we lost the gold. We knew the Admiral might order our deaths, but my revelation about the armor saved us. It gave me leverage. Something to bargain with.

I look at the Admiral, at his clear eyes and the very straight line of his mouth. I work for him. I live under his protection. And I never, ever underestimate the danger of my situation.

"This is the most important voyage yet," the Admiral says. "I don't want anything to go wrong. I want the killing mechanisms to work."

"They'll work," I say.

"And you'll be there in case they don't," he says, a cool finality in his tone.

If the Admiral tells you to do something, you do it.

Or you die.

You would think that after Call died, I wouldn't care

anymore about dying. But I do. I saw him. I saw his eyes looking up and seeing nothing. I saw how gone he was. I knew he was nowhere else in the world or beyond. He was over.

The Quorum watches.

Why does the Admiral want me to go on this voyage, and not any of the others? Has he decided that he's tiring of me? Is this a trap of some sort?

That might be the case. It might not. Either way, I may as well make the most of the situation. "That's right," I say to the advisers. I hold each of their gazes in turn. Sister Haring is not smiling now. And then I meet the Admiral's eyes. "I'm going on the ship as Captain."

I have to give the Admiral credit. He doesn't even blink. All I see is a slight tightening of his lips that shows I've surprised him.

And that he's angry.

CHAPTER 2

THE ADMIRAL DISMISSES THE QUORUM and tells me to stay behind. The two of us are still seated at the head of the scarred wood table. Without the others, it feels very close. I keep my gaze on his face, on those ice-blue eyes, the freckles and age spots mingling on his skin. He's a force of nature, a magnetic presence wherever he is.

Ever since the Desertion generations ago, when the world drew back from us and we had to learn how to survive on our own, we've been led by Admirals. Some have been better than others. The older people say that the last Admiral almost ran the Outpost into the ground, and that this one has saved us all. "Not afraid to put in an honest day's work, even now," they say when they see him splitting wood out at the lumberyard or hauling goods down Main Street in his wagon. "Gets his hands dirty."

"So you think I'll make you Captain." The Admiral leans back in his chair and crosses his arms behind his head, one of his casual gestures that says *I'm nothing to be afraid of* and, at the same time, *You have everything to fear.*

"If you want me to go, you will," I say.

"*You* work for *me*." He brings his arms down and rests them on the table, drawing him closer. "You do what I ask. That's why you're alive."

I know all of this. There's nothing to say. I stare at the Admiral's hands. They are indeed dirty. Grease under his fingernails, in the lines of his knuckles.

"I wouldn't have thought you'd consider yourself a leader," he says. "You've always preferred to work alone."

"I still do," I say. "But if I have to be on that ship, no one else is going to be in charge."

I want as much control as possible if I have to go back out on the river. And the captain is the one person on board the dredge who gets a private berth. I don't want to have to bunk with anyone. Having my own space is a luxury I've become accustomed to over the past two years. Before then, I lived as most unmarried workers do, in the common quarters near our places of employment. My apartment is still near the scrap yard, but I've got my own bedroom, my own kitchen. Once I'm done with work for the day, I don't have to see or speak with another soul.

"Some of the crew might resent you," the Admiral says. "You're young. And you've been on a single voyage. A *partial* voyage, some might even say. Your excursion didn't complete a full pass of the river. And you came back without any gold."

I don't bother pointing out how much influence I've had on every voyage since. The Admiral knows.

"You do have more invested in the ship than anyone else," he says when I don't fill in the silence.

"Except you."

"Indeed." There's a turquoise ring on his right middle finger. He's worn it so long it looks like it's burrowed into his flesh, though the Admiral is not a heavy man and his fingers are lean. "Don't underestimate how much the raiders hate your ship."

"I won't," I say. I'm glad. I want them to hate it. And fear it.

"Good."

One of the Admiral's guards appears in the doorway, and the Admiral stands up.

"The ship leaves in seven days," he says. "Prepare accordingly. I'll have the manifest sent to you. So you can familiarize yourself with your crew." The Admiral smiles. A flash of very straight teeth. "*Captain* Blythe."

He leaves me alone in the room.

I feel something I haven't felt often in the two years since Call died. *Interest.* Why aren't the raiders trying to board?

I may not know exactly *why* the Admiral is consumed with pulling more and more gold from the rivers, but I do understand the power of obsession. Mine straightens my back. It keeps me alive.

CHAPTER 3

WE LEAVE TODAY.

From far enough away, jarred along in one of the Admiral's archaic, sluggish wagons, I almost can't see my ship on the river. With mountains behind it and a grassy river plain stretching out in front, the dredge masquerades as something it isn't, a natural part of the landscape. Sunrise and water can make even a dead thing look half alive.

But then we're closer, and I see the dredge for what it is.

I want to crawl all over the outside of the ship, making sure every gear works—touching the armor, polishing it. I've done this before the other voyages, the ones I didn't go on. But the Admiral didn't allow it this time around. He said he didn't want to risk me getting injured.

I don't like it. I wanted more time to check the ship.

I'm the first off the wagon when it slows. The Admiral's guards at the dredge know me; I lift a hand and they step aside.

"Don't let anyone else board until I say." They nod, and I climb on the ship. I'm the first on. And I'll be the last off.

That's what it means to be the Captain.

•   •   •

On my way down to check on the motor and the mining equipment, I pass the door that leads up to the ship's top deck. It's locked. Now that the dredge is armed, there's no reason to open it. Once the voyage begins, none of us will go above until we're finished. No one has been able to go up and look for stars since Call.

He often had trouble sleeping. Usually it was because he'd had the start of a dream that he didn't get to finish. He dreamed outside of himself, which I always thought was strange. As if he were watching things, rather than experiencing them, which was how it always was for me.

When we were young and living in the orphanage, every few weeks he'd find me at breakfast to tell me about a dream. He did the same in the scrap yard when we were older. And later, on the dredge. He'd tell me, *I saw a boy running, running* or *There was a man standing by a tree late at night holding a lantern* or *My mother was walking in a field and stopped to pick three flowers.*

"And then what?" I'd ask.

"That's when I woke up," Call said. "Finish it for me. Please."

Call liked me to come up with endings for his dreams. When I was younger and we'd had a fight, sometimes I'd refuse. When we were older and I loved him, he asked less, only when he absolutely had to know, and I never turned him down.

We became friends at the orphanage. Neither Call nor I had a story that was especially tragic. We were like the other children there in that we'd lost both our parents, and we were like the other children in that we didn't know exactly how. There are so many ways to die in the Outpost—working accident, childbirth, lung disease from the pollution that hangs in the sky from cities long ago and far away, any of the myriad illnesses we can't treat with the limited medicine we have. Still, we're told, it's less dangerous than being out in the wild.

I couldn't remember much about my parents—my father had never been around, and my mother died when I was three. Call had more concrete memories than I did. "My mother had sun-black hair, like you," he told me once when we were small.

"Sun isn't black," I said.

"It is after you look at it," he said, "when you shut your eyes. You see black and gold."

"And red," I said.

"Yes." He pointed to my hair. I pulled the ends around to look at them. He was right. In the sun, somehow, there were filaments of gold glinting along my braid.

"You're not supposed to look at the sun," I said.

"Sometimes you don't mean to," he said. "But you do."

I was jealous of Call—that he could remember his mother so well. Later he told me other things about her: that she had a quick temper, but laughed often. It was hard to reconcile that with Call, who was endlessly patient and whose laughter was rare and deep.

Call and I were both good at making things with our hands. And so, when the time came to leave the orphanage at fifteen, we got sent out to the scrap yard to work our way up, to haul and carry and do piecework for the machinists and learn from them.

The first time I slept after his death, I had the dream about the armor for the dredge. I was watching someone build it. It wasn't long before I realized it was Call. I kept trying to talk to him, but he wouldn't answer. He couldn't hear me. He looked right through me every time. Finally, I stopped trying to talk to him and paid attention to what he was making.

I always knew it wasn't real. I knew that Call didn't come to me in a dream to tell me to build the armor. I knew because it wasn't something Call would have ever wanted me to build in real life.

But I still finished it for him.

"Line up in front of me," I tell the crew assembled on the bank. "Don't worry about order or ranking."

Off to the side, the Admiral stands, watching.

The crew wears dusky-green uniforms like the ones we wore before; the hats are the same, too. Mine has a captain's insignia on it. I've worn my hair in braids to keep it out of my face, but now I wonder if they make the hat seem ill-fitting, make me look ridiculous.

The crew stands at attention, but their bearing as a group isn't perfect because most aren't true militia. It's a jumble of machinists, miners, and others pressed into the Admiral's service for this excursion. Most of the people in the Outpost don't pay much attention to the dredge voyages. People have so much work to do in their day-to-day lives that they don't spare a thought for the tasks of others. They trust the Admiral, and keeping the Outpost viable is a full-time job for everyone who lives here.

Generations ago, when people came to build the Outpost in this wild land where we now live, the Territory, they had support and supplies and contact with the Union that had sent them. The settlers had been asked to establish the Outpost as a jumping-off point for more explorations and because the Union had heard there might be gold to mine in the Territory. But after a few years, the Union sent word they were no longer going to keep up the Outpost. We were too much work, they said. Too far away from the rest of their provinces and cities. Too hard to protect. Too wild. We hadn't found enough gold to make us worth their time, and they no longer seemed to care about exploring. The Union ran the dredges ashore and stopped visiting or sending supplies. We were on our own. The first Admiral gathered in those who'd settled outside of the Outpost, for their own protection. The raiders are the descendants of those who refused to come.

"Name?" I say to the man in front of me.

"Owen Fales," he says.

"You're one of the miners." I've been over and over the names on the manifest. I know them all.

He nods. "Captain Blythe."

He's older than I am—thirties or forties—but seems soft-spoken. Perhaps he won't mind being led by someone as young as I am.

Down the rows I go. When I get to a young man with dark hair and blue eyes, my heart rises into my throat the way it always does at an unexpected reminder of Call. This man has Call's exact coloring and is handsome, too, but other than that they look nothing alike.

"Brig Tanner," he says.

"First mate," I say back, and he nods.

"Eira Clyde," says the girl next to him. She's very beautiful, with high cheekbones, dark hair. "Cartographer."

I raise my eyebrows at her. She's spoken before I can. She flushes, realizing the mistake, but doesn't break our gaze.

Is she insolent? Or merely inexperienced? I resist the urge to look over at the Admiral.

I'm sure that he'll have someone on board to watch me. To watch all of us. I wonder who it is.

I go through the names and positions. Officer Ophelia Hill, navigator. Officer Laura Seng, medic. Officer Cecil Clair, chaplain. Officer Corwin Revis, chief machinist.

Then a face so young it makes me stop. He must be my age, or perhaps even younger.

"Tam Wallace," he says.

"Ship's cook," I answer.

The excitement on his face reminds me of myself two years ago. He'll have heard about the myriad of miseries waiting for him on board the dredge—the grating noise and hard work, the boredom, the claustrophobia. He hasn't *felt* them yet. But if he's like Call and I were, he'll love the voyage anyway because it's an adventure. I feel a pang in my heart for who I used to be, for what I've lost.

"How old *are* you?" I ask.

"Sixteen."

A year younger than me.

"How did you become a ship's cook so young?"

Tam runs a hand through his hair, breaking the protocol of standing at attention when the Captain is reviewing the crew. He catches himself halfway through and drops his hand to the side. "I work at the meal hall where the Admiral dines. He gave me this assignment himself."

"If he likes your food, why would he waste you on the dredge?" I ask.

"He wants this voyage to succeed," Tam says. "People work better when they're well fed."

Young, malleable, talented but not in a way that's threatening to the Admiral, someone conveniently located in the kitchen, where he'll hear all the gossip. . . .

Maybe I've found the Admiral's watchdog.

Near the end, I see the one name on the manifest that I recognized, the one person I've *wanted* to see. My former boss, now my second mate.

"Naomi Moran," she says. Her hair, dark streaked with gray, is longer than I remembered.

"Second mate," I say.

"Captain Blythe," says a guard at my elbow. "The Admiral is ready to address the crew."

A subtle undercut. I was going to give my own message first; anything I say after his speech will be a letdown. I nod and the guard calls out, "The Admiral will speak to you now." They all turn in his direction like flowers to the sun.

The Admiral's wearing a suit coat and vest today. Even in the heat. I know the crew will love this. They'll see it as a sign of esteem. Perhaps it is. The Admiral looks as pleased as I've ever seen him.

"Come here, Captain Blythe," the Admiral says.

I take my place at his left.

"Captain Blythe designed the armor that protects our ship, our cargo, and our crew so well," the Admiral says. "I want this crew to accord her all respect in honor of the lives she's saved. Captain Blythe."

I stand stiff and awkward while the others salute. Will the Admiral's blessing help or hurt me on the river? It used to be that the crews were people like Call and me, who wanted to get out of the Outpost for a while. And the Admiral needed people to do the work and who didn't mind going. It worked out as well as anything could. But now things have changed. I can tell. I smell it in the cool-burned morning air, in the shift of the wind. In the way some of the crew makes sense and some don't quite seem to fit. The Admiral chose us all.

"This is the last river," the Admiral says. "The last voyage.

Your mission is important to the Outpost, to all of us. I wish you well, and I know you will succeed."

He lifts his broad-brimmed hat into the air and the crew cheers, all twenty-three of us. I raise my voice with the rest so I don't draw the Admiral's ire.

I've never liked being around people, but ever since Call, it's been worse.

The Admiral's eyes meet mine and he smiles.

We don't embrace or shake hands but she falls into step right next to me, our shoulders almost touching, as we board the boat.

"We're traveling on a ship of children and fools," Naomi says, low.

"You're right," I say. "What does the Admiral think he's playing at?"

"I don't think he's playing." Naomi's voice sounds rough like everyone's does when they get to her age. Like mine will sound eventually. "I think he has exactly who he wants on this voyage. I just don't know *why*."

CHAPTER 4

THIS IS THE MOMENT the voyage starts. Not when the Admiral gave a speech and people cheered. *This.* When the motor first turns, the ship moves, the armor whirs into gear.

I have a wave of memory—Call and I standing together on the deck of the other dredge, watching the trees and rivers pass by. It takes time and work to tear up a river the way the dredge does, so you can see almost everything. The ship is not fast.

Naomi and I are on the bridge, the small room at the front of the dredge. Here, we can steer the ship and watch the mining buckets coming up outside, a long loop of them rotating through on a bucket elevator. They're huge, weighing over a thousand pounds each, made of metal strong and durable enough to withstand scraping along the bottom of the river floor and hauling up rocks.

The windows of the bridge gave me trouble when I was designing the armor because they're a spot for a potential breach. One morning I woke up and the world went from dark to light with the opening of my eyes and I knew: *The ship needs eyelids.* The window armor can be retracted for viewing or extended over the windows for security.

Right now, they're open, and Naomi and I watch the river sliding slowly past beneath us. She gives me a thumbs-up. Everything sounds as it should, loud and sweet and terrible. I smile back. I think about what the Admiral said to me before we left. *Don't underestimate how much the raiders hate your ship.* But what *I* think is that the raiders shouldn't underestimate how much I *love* my ship. Or, to be precise, how much I love what it does.

It's a pale, twisted little thing compared to what I felt for Call. Maybe it's not even love, what I feel. I don't know.

But it's better than nothing.

I breathe a sigh of relief as I open the door to the captain's quarters. *Alone.* At last.

I can work with others when I have to, when I'm designing or refining the ship. I've been doing that for the past two years.

But this is different. I'm *living* with other people again. We're all stuck on board the dredge until the end of the voyage. Back when there were ocean journeys, they couldn't leave their ships because they were surrounded by water. Here, we're feet away from a shore, from land. It's enough to make you crazy, thinking about escape or climbing off and walking away. That's the strange thing about the dredge. In theory, you could leave. But in practice, it's not allowed.

None of us can leave. Not even the captain.

My quarters aren't much nicer than the rest of the crew's accommodations, except in one critical way—they're private. My space has a bunk, a desk and chair next to it, a tiny dresser. Everything is made of metal and bolted to the wall and floor.

There is a map of the Serpentine River Valley tacked to the wall. After I heave my bag onto my bed, I walk over to examine the map—the greens and blues and browns, the names of the tributaries and their valleys.

A knock at the door. I open it to find my first mate.

"I'm sorry to bother you," Brig says. "But is there anything you'd like me to do? Naomi's at the helm and she says she doesn't need me to relieve her yet. I've been down to the mining deck and everything seems to be going smoothly."

Right. Orders. I need to remember to give them.

"Call a meeting for me," I tell Brig. "During both meal times." We eat in two shifts so that there are always personnel to keep the ship going, and the cafeteria is the only area large enough to hold everyone. Except for the mining deck, I suppose, but it's hard to hear down there.

"Will do, Captain Blythe."

Brig salutes without irony. He's had militia training, I'm sure of it, though he's wearing the same uniform as everyone else. There's something sad and set about his eyes, an almost-gentle, resigned quality, though everything else is sharply defined—his hair combed with military precision, his broad shoulders straight and his posture upright.

He'd also make an excellent informant for the Admiral.

I close the door.

I go back to my bag and pull out my comb, set it on the desk. I take out some shirts. When I reach back inside the bag, my body goes still as my fingers brush against something unfamiliar. I know the feel of everything I packed and this isn't mine. Paper, soft and worn, folded into a large square.

I pull it out and open it up.

It's a map, a little like the one on my wall. Except this isn't a full map, just a piece of one. At the corners where it's folded, there are small holes. It's old.

But the message written on it is new. Scrawled in dark black ink that has bled into the fog-soft paper.

This is not your river.

Is it a threat? I run my thumb across the words.

Of course it is.

So. There may be someone on board who sympathizes with the raiders.

I fold the map back up and zip it into my bag.

You want to play cat and mouse with me? I think. *Good. Let's play.*

CHAPTER 5

"SO HOW LONG DOES IT TAKE to get used to the sound?" Tam asks me as I come through the dinner line in the cafeteria. The noise from the mining below is enough to rattle your teeth and shake your brain against your skull.

But Tam seems to be handling it well. He looks cheerful and calm, and he's not sweating, though the kitchen must be hellish hot.

"Soon," I say. "Never."

"Be careful." Tam puts a dish with a metal cover on my tray. "Don't burn yourself."

I take my meal to the table at the front of the room because that's where the captain on my other voyage always sat. He was an older man with a weary manner, but he was efficient and fair. I've never blamed him for what happened. He didn't kill Call.

That ship was the twin of this one, the layout is the same, but Call was never here. I make sure to remind myself of this every time I catch myself thinking of him, hoping against hope to see him come around a corner, through a door.

Someone—Tam? his kitchen assistant?—has set the tables with real napkins and flowers in heavy metal cups. The delicate blossoms shake with the constant vibration of the dredge. A petal falls as I set down my tray. I don't sit.

All eyes on me. I was the last to enter the room.

It's time for the first meeting.

"I'll make this short so you can eat," I say. "I know that for those of you who haven't been on board, the dredge can take getting used to, but that will come with time. There are some things you *must* remember. You cannot leave the ship. You may not go outside or up on the deck. If you do anything to compromise our mission, the consequences will be swift and severe."

A few heads nod, but most people remain still. According to the manifest, eleven of the crew have been on a dredge voyage before and the others have not. To work on the ship, they're required to have mining or machinery experience, or to be an expert in another area for which we have need. They also have to be able to swim and shoot. In my opinion, those last two aren't necessary anymore. Not now that we have my armor.

I make eye contact with a couple of men at the back who look greener than the rest. The ship's getting to them. The motion, maybe, making them sick. Or the noise. Or the heat of many bodies in close quarters.

I fold my arms. I'm sweating, but so is everyone else.

"Our job is straightforward. We gather gold and kill any raiders who try to harm us or interfere with our mission."

Someone raises a hand. "I heard that when we have to turn the ship around you might let us out to have a look."

"The instructions we were all given say explicitly otherwise," I say.

Disappointment crosses more than one person's face. Why did they think there was a chance? They all know the Admiral forbids it.

Maybe they think I'm some kind of rogue. Or that I'm weak, and they'll be able to push me around.

"I'll call meetings as needed," I continue. "For now, enjoy your dinner. It will be the one time that your seatmates smell as fresh as they do."

It's a poor attempt at humor, but they laugh. I sit down. I've done what's necessary. Stated the rules, demonstrated that I plan to adhere to them, shown that I am not *completely* cold and without camaraderie. You can't command a ship that way. I don't know much but I know that. I think I'm relatively safe from mutiny because no one wants to harm the person who designed the ship's armor and who can best keep it running.

Except maybe the person who left me that note.

I lift the cover off my dish and the smell instantly makes my mouth water. Around me, others are murmuring in surprise.

It's not stew or any of its incarnations, the usual mishmash of food put together and seasoned to disguise its age or toughness. It's separate, distinct, beautiful food—meat with wine-colored sauce, crisp salad greens, crusty-outside-and-steaming-hot-inside bread.

Heads swivel to the serving area but Tam has disappeared.

Naomi leans over to me. "Reminds me of that story about the children and the witch in the wood," she says. "Why is the Admiral fattening us up?"

I laugh, remembering. "This ship isn't made of candy."

"That it isn't," she says, and her face goes grim.

Maybe the Admiral is going to eat us. Isn't that how the other story ended?

"Excuse me," a man says, standing up. "I beg your pardon. If I could offer a few words as well."

Chaplain Clair. I remember him from this morning and from the manifest. A prickle of irritation rustles through me. I never said he could speak.

The chaplain is short, smaller than me. And he has a sweaty red face and a twitchy little nose and big patches of wet on the underarms of his uniform. I want to roll my eyes.

"You may speak," I say. "But keep it quick. We need to eat."

Right then, there's a clamor at the door. Heads turn and I see Brig pushing into the cafeteria with two crew members, both men. Brig and the man on the right are trying to restrain the one in the middle, who's struggling. Has there been a fight? No blood, that I can see. But the man they're holding has wild in his eyes.

"I'm sorry to interrupt," Brig says. "But he was trying to get off the ship. He came onto the bridge and tried to climb through the window."

"It's driving me crazy," the man in the middle says. Jonah

Miller, I remember, from the roll call earlier. "The noise. How *slow* it is. Just let me off and I'll walk back to the Outpost. We haven't gone far."

"We're not going to stop the whole dredge and risk the crew," I say. "Stopping makes us vulnerable. Once we're in motion, we stay in motion."

He casts his eyes around desperately, trying to think of another way out. "Let me jump off the deck," he offers, his voice tinged with hope.

"No one goes on the deck," I say. "And no one jumps."

"So there's no way off." His shoulders slump. "There's no way out."

"Of course there is," I say. "We could put you in one of the dredge buckets going back into the water and out you'll go into the river. We won't even have to stop. If you don't drown or get caught on any machinery, you can swim your way to shore and walk back to the Outpost."

His eyes go wide. My words have given him a new source of panic.

"If there's a way off, then there's also a way for the raiders to get on!"

He's trying my patience. "If they attempt to get on that way, they won't make it far," I say. It's true that the buckets dragging the river bottom for gold are large enough to hold a person, if the person were small and curled themselves up tight. But I've equipped the bucket line with the guillotine—an enormous blade that each bucket passes under as it arrives inside the ship. No one over the age of ten or so could make themselves so small that they wouldn't have *some* part sticking out—a head, an arm, a leg.

The room is silent.

"You can go out," I say. Bluffing. "I'll help you do it myself. But there's no way back on."

Jonah's eyes are still wild. Brig holds on to his arm. I tilt my head. "Get him out of here," I say. "Send him through the buckets. Off the ship."

Will Brig do it? I'm interested to find out more about my first mate. It's against the Admiral's orders. No one's supposed to leave the ship. Period.

But then Jonah starts to weep. "I'll stay," he says. "I'm sorry."

"Then get back to work." I nod to the other crew member who's holding Jonah upright. "You stay with him. Report any other problems immediately."

Brig meets my gaze as they start toward the door.

I wonder if he would have put the man off the ship.

I wonder if I would have.

Naomi stands up. "Permission to speak requested, Captain." She says it loud enough for everyone in the cafeteria to hear. Brig and the others pause in the doorway.

"Permission granted."

"I want to speak on behalf of those who went with you on your first voyage," Naomi says. "We never had a chance to thank you. For our lives."

"That's not necessary," I say. The bargain I struck with the Admiral—my armor design for the lives of the crew who lost the other dredge—isn't something I want brought up now. I motion for her to sit down but she doesn't, so I stay standing, too. Crew members are putting down their cutlery, leaning in to listen to Naomi.

"I went on the next voyage, you know," she says. "The first one with your armor."

Why is she telling me this now? In front of everyone?

"The raiders tried to board several times," she says. "We heard them, even with all the noise of the dredge. Screaming. Scratching. Pounding with fists and weapons."

Naomi pauses. "We looked through the bridge window when we absolutely had to to navigate," she says. "We saw a body fall down now and then. But we didn't go outside, of course, until we got back."

Everyone's still, listening to Naomi. All our beautiful food is getting cold. I can smell it. I'm hungry.

"When we got out and looked at the ship," she says, "it looked like it had rusted. There was so much blood. They spent days cleaning and oiling it so it could leave again."

A few of the crew members look at me with a hint of fear in their eyes.

I'm not sure what to say in the silence but right then I hear the door to the kitchen area swing open. We all turn to look at Tam.

He's carrying a cake. A ridiculous, towering white cake. Something so frivolous and rare in any circumstance, it's ludicrous to see here on the dredge. But somehow, he managed it.

Has he heard what we've been saying? Tam's eyes meet

mine over the cake. I'm only a year older than he is, but he's so young. He's who I used to be.

"Did I forget a wedding?" I ask, and I feel the tension in the room give, and some of the crew laughs.

"We're all married to this ship," Tam says. "To the *Lily*."

The crew laughs again, and as Tam brings the cake closer I realize it's the dredge. He's turned it into a confection. A fluffy, ornate cloud.

Tam has spoken lightly, but as he hands me a knife to cut the cake he makes certain to hold my gaze. In his eyes is a warning.

About what?

I shouldn't make the mistake of thinking Tam's like me, the way I used to be. He might be. He might not.

I plunge the knife into the cake, and then lick the cutting edge of the blade, careful not to draw blood.

"Get another knife, Cook," I say. I don't use Tam's name because there's no reason to—crew often refer to one another by our titles—but I still see a flicker of hurt in his eyes. "We might be in the belly of the dredge now, but soon it will be in ours."

The others laugh again and in a few moments I'm slicing into the cake, and Tam hands it around, accepting their compliments and congratulatory slaps on the back. "Save some for the other shift," he tells them.

When the bell clangs for the shift change, everyone stands up to leave. Besides Naomi and me, Chaplain Clair is the last one out. He never did have his chance to speak.

"What do you think he wanted to say?" I ask Naomi.

"I'd imagine it's something about the Admiral," she says. "How working for him is a great and noble endeavor."

I pause at the door. "So we've already had our first would-be deserter," I say. "Do you think there will be more?"

"Not after that," Naomi says. "And I've heard the crew talking about you. They say that the Admiral trusts you. That you're hard."

I suppose it could be worse. I gesture for Naomi to go through the door first, but she has more to say.

"You've changed." Her eyes are shrewd.

I press my lips together. Naomi wouldn't speak to another captain this way. Her tone is respectful but she's calling on our past, she's speaking of personal things.

"Thank you, Second Mate," I say. "If you'll excuse me. I need to prepare to speak to the next group."

"Of course," Naomi says.

Several people have challenged me today. The chaplain put himself forward to speak without an invitation. Tam talked to me as if I were a peer. Brig hesitated when I told him to send the man off the ship. Naomi assumes that she knows me.

I need to put an end to all of it.

CHAPTER 6

I MAKE MY WAY to the small platform down on the mining deck, where I can watch the machines work and the motor run. The two crew members standing up on the platform keeping guard nod to me. "You can go down for a bit," I say. "I'll take a turn."

"Thank you, Captain," one says.

I take their position at the watch.

This is the most dangerous place on the ship.

Everyone—the would-be deserter, the Admiral himself when I first showed him the plans—worries about someone getting on the dredge through the buckets. It's the first spot they picture a breach now that the top deck is secure and the windows on the bridge are armored. But the most vulnerable part of the ship isn't where the gold comes in. It's where the rocks go out—a rectangular protrusion called the tailings stacker that juts out the back of the ship. It's high above the river and a constant stream of *tailings,* or *slicken*—rock and debris—cascades out of it as long as the dredge is mining.

I thought for a long time about how to best secure the stacker. I gave it the same outside armor I used on the rest of the ship—gears and turns that move all the time, ready to chew up and spit out.

But after that, I was stuck. The stacker *has* to have an opening, needs to be constantly disposing of the slicken, or we'll sink under all the weight. Finally, I decided to trust in the sheer force of the tailings coming out and in the fact that my armor covers everything but the opening. Those two things, plus the height of the stacker from the river, means that anyone trying to board would likely die. And it wouldn't be a good death, to be cast out with the tailings and buried, still alive, in the refuse of the ship, body crushed under what we don't need, can't use, and drowned in the water besides.

There aren't really *any* good deaths if you try to board my ship.

I think about all the systems working together. The mining gear, the propellers that the ship uses for motion, the armor— the dredge is like a person, with each system combining to make a whole. There are ways to disengage the systems from the main motor, but we rarely have occasion to do that. And everything takes their energy from the solar conduits. It's efficient. My ship runs smooth.

This is not your river.

It's time to look into the matter of the note written on the map. I have another hour before I need to be up at the helm.

First, the logistics room. Maybe I'll find a map there with a piece cut out. Although it seems unlikely I'll be *that* lucky.

And I want to talk to the ship's cartographer, Eira Clyde. The young woman with dark hair.

In the hallway, I run into Brig. Since I'm the captain, most people step aside or flatten themselves against the wall. Not Brig.

"I'd like to talk with you," he says.

"Good," I say. "I need to speak with you as well. Go ahead."

I'm tall, but he's taller, and we both have to duck our heads under the dredge's low ceiling. It makes for awkward eye contact, which I like, because when we're sitting down or fully standing Brig can draw himself up to his full height and look down on me.

"That man who wanted to desert," Brig says. "Would you really have put him off the ship? He thinks so. The crew thinks so."

As is the case every time I've spoken with Brig, I can feel his charisma, his pull. He's handsome, but it's more than that. The timbre of his voice, maybe, and the way he looks you full in the eyes. Most people don't. They end up glancing away. There's a subtle force to Brig that makes me try to take up more space so he can have less.

"Of course," I say.

He nods, as if that's the answer he expected. I get the sense that there's something more he wants to say, but after a beat of our quiet and the ship's noise, I speak instead.

"When Jonah Miller tried to desert," I say, "why did you

bring him to the cafeteria, when you knew I was holding a meeting? Why didn't you lock him down in his room and keep him there until later?"

"I brought him in because I thought you'd want to make an example out of him," Brig says.

"I don't care about examples," I say. "If something bad happens, I want the least amount of people to know about it. I want everyone to keep quiet and do their work. It's loud enough on this ship as it is."

"Captain." It's not quite an acknowledgment. There's a hint of objection in Brig's voice.

"And I want you," I say, "to follow my orders. This ship needs me to run. It does not need you."

Call used to laugh when I'd threaten someone, another worker on the scrap yard, another child on the playground when we were small. "You couldn't hurt anything," he'd say.

"They don't know that," I told him.

"But I do," Call said.

Now, though, I think even Call would believe me when I say it.

"We must have similar concerns about this voyage," Brig says. "It would be helpful if we could discuss them."

"All I need from you," I say, "is to follow my orders."

Brig looks like he might speak again but I turn away, brushing his chest with my shoulder in the tight hallway as I pass by.

There is not nearly enough room on this ship.

. . .

When the time came for Call and me to move out of the orphanage and into the quarters out at the scrap yard, we walked there together, our packs slung over our shoulders. We stopped in our tracks at the same time in front of the huge mural painted on the cinder-block exterior of the dormitory.

The Outpost is full of murals. In some ways I liked them because they lent color to the buildings. But the lack of proportion in the people bothered me. They were all depicted in the same style—the men had impossibly large muscles and broad shoulders, the women had nipped-in waists and enormous eyes. The painted people stared at us as we went inside the dormitory.

"They're watching us," he said.

"They're jealous," I said. "We can move and they can't," and I stuck out my tongue at them, which made Call laugh.

We were still only friends, then, Call and I. It was over the course of the next year, when we walked past each other in the scrap yard all day long and sat together at dinner at night, that things changed. We'd always been close, but our new lives brought us closer. We had the same marks on our hands, same cuts from the metal. We told each other stories of our days, of the frustration we both felt at the work we were doing, how all we ever did was fix things, how we never got to *build* anything. We both felt like time was running out. We felt the urgency of our lives in a new way, that we should at least do something with them.

And we fell in love. I remember thinking how strange and right it was, that I could know that I wanted a different life and yet also know I wanted this person, same and new, with me.

CHAPTER 7

AS THE CAPTAIN, I'm entitled to go anywhere on the ship at any time, so I open the door of the logistics room without knocking. Eira turns, a pencil tucked behind her ear, another in her hand.

"Captain Blythe," she says. "How can I help you?"

"I need a map." I don't want to tell her about the note. After all, she's just as likely as anyone else to have left it. More so, in fact; she has the easiest access to all the maps.

"Of course," she says. The logistics room is tiny, lined with metal cabinets with long thin drawers. In the middle of the room there's a small, bolted-down table with a chair. "Which one?"

"I want the most detailed map you have for this part of the river."

"I think that map was placed in your quarters at the beginning of the voyage," she says.

"I'd like for you to look again," I say. "I'll help. I promise I'll keep things in order. I don't want to hamper your work."

Eira nods and moves over to one of the cabinets. I go to the cabinet next to her and slide open a drawer, leafing through the maps while keeping an eye on her as well.

The maps feel different depending on their age—soft, brittle, stiff, smooth, all different textures, like the land they depict. My favorites are the topographical maps, with bumps for mountains and slick blue plastic for water. The Union didn't skimp on the maps they sent with the first settlers, and the Outpost has taken great care with them ever since. The Admiral must trust Eira a great deal if he appointed her as the cartographer for this voyage.

"Here's one," Eira says, "but I don't know that it's any better than the one you have already."

I take the map from her and go to the table. She hurries over to sweep away her papers and drafting materials, but before she does, I see what she's been working on.

It's an artistic rendering of the dredge, and it's exquisite.

"You did this?"

She glances over. Her mouth draws tight. "Yes," she says.

"What is it for?"

"I'm afraid that you've caught me working on something simply because it gives me pleasure," she says. "I find the ship fascinating. And challenging, artistically. Your armor is particularly hard to draw."

I think she means that as a compliment. Looking at Eira's picture, I feel a twinge of jealousy. I've never been accused of artistry in my drafts or drawings. My work is accurate. Exact. Utilitarian.

"You're right," I say. "This map isn't quite as good as the one in my cabin. Let's keep looking."

We return to the cabinets. Even though the ship grinds on below us, I can hear the smaller sounds we make, the sliding of drawers, the rustle and flick of our fingers through the maps.

I get into a kind of rhythm as I'm going through the papers, and I almost miss the map that I've been looking for. I flip right past it and then have to stop and go back. A spot on the map matches up with the back of the note left in my bag. There isn't a piece cut out of this one but I'm almost certain it's a print identical to the one someone left in my bag. I recognize the contours and curves of the land replicated here, and the paper feels of a similar age.

I take it over to the table and spread it out, and when I see the whole thing, I realize I'm looking at a map for the Cutwater River, the one I dredged with Call. I didn't recognize it before, because the note only showed a bit of water and land.

They've given me a piece of a map that marks the place, or close to it, where Call died.

I laugh.

Eira looks at me, surprised.

I lift up the map of the Cutwater and, in doing so, I accidentally move her drawing of the ship and reveal another sketch underneath.

It's a drawing of people looking toward a golden sun. Some kneel. A few shield their eyes. And in front of the sun—almost as if it's pulling the sun along, bringing it to them—is the dredge, which also shines like gold. On its deck, among the armor, stands the upright figure of the Admiral.

It's a draft of a mural.

Eira's talent is undeniable in the dredge picture, but this drawing is different. It's highly stylized, like every other piece of Outpost art. Even the dredge, which she drew so beautifully in her other piece, is inflated and bloated, not intricate and accurate, like her other work.

Eira takes the mural draft from me.

"That's a commission I'm working on for the Admiral," she says, her voice perfectly level. She reaches for another paper, and as she pulls it away I see yet another drawing. It's a person, lined in, almost featureless in its conformity as the type of figure shown in murals. But I recognize the stance, the braids.

It's supposed to be me.

Eira's eyes meet mine.

"You're hard to draw," she says.

"Why would you try?"

She puts the drawing of the mural back down on the table next to the sketch of me. "Here's where you'll be," she says, pointing at the crowd. "I've left a spot to add you in once I get the draft right."

"As long as I'm not one of the people kneeling," I say, and she looks at me with a flicker of amusement in her eyes.

"Where will it go?" It seems that the sides of every building in the Outpost are already covered with murals.

"I don't know," she says.

It looks like every other mural, I think again, my eyes running over the figures.

Almost too much so.

Almost like a parody.

"Thank you," I say to Eira, rolling up the map of the Cutwater River to take with me. "You've been very helpful."

"You're welcome," she says. I'm willing to bet that after I leave she'll go over and note which map I took. She'll know I lied to her, since the Cutwater River is nowhere near here. I wonder what she'll think of me then.

I close the door and put the map under my arm. I can't be sure, but something about the way she drew that mural makes me think that Eira is *not* the Admiral's watchdog.

So. Does she sympathize with the raiders?

Did *she* leave the note?

CHAPTER 8

A KNOCK ON MY DOOR in the middle of the night. I twist onto my stomach, my woolen blanket tangling up in my legs, and reach for the lantern on the dresser. It glows softly in my hand as I answer the door.

"What is it?" I ask.

"Captain," Naomi says. "You're going to want to see this."

I dress quickly and pull on my boots. My hair is loose and I braid it as I walk, following Naomi down the tight, twisting metal staircase into the depths of the dredge.

The mining crew waits for me. Things have been going well enough during our first week on the ship. We've had no incidents aside from the one with the would-be deserter the first night. Some of the workers smile when I meet their eyes.

The news must be good.

"Look, Captain," one of the men says.

Even in the lamplight, even before the haul has been

through the trammel for sifting, I can make out the dull sheen and color of gold. I've never seen a haul like this. There's so much gold you can spot it among the rocks.

"How long has it been this way?" I ask.

"For the last hour," Naomi says. "We've taken on more in that time than in the rest of the voyage."

"And the quality's good?"

"Very."

The ship's chief miner, Noah Warren, holds out a map in front of me. "We're due to keep to the left soon," he says, and I look where he's pointing. We're nearing what's called a *braid*, when the river splits into several different channels before coming back together again miles later. "But our best guess is, that with the way the gold is deposited in the bed of the river, we're more likely to keep up this kind of success if we go up the channel on the right. We're requesting your permission to divert our course."

Noah has to shout to be heard down here, but something about the situation still feels quiet, intimate. Knowing that it's dark outside. The gold. All of us up in the night on the water. We're far enough down the river that our ability to communicate with the Outpost ended days ago. This call is mine to make.

I run my finger down along the map. I'm sure many are wondering if I'll stay loyal to the path the Admiral set out for us to follow. I wonder if the person who left the note is trying to lure us off course so the raiders can attack. Maybe this much gold is a trap.

"When do we need to decide?" I ask.

"I'd guess we have about two hours before we'll reach the fork," Noah says. "Give or take."

"Let's see how much more gold comes in over the next hour," I say. "If it runs out, the point may be moot."

"Should I wake you again when it's time?" Naomi asks.

"No," I say. "I'll stay up. But have someone take Brig's place at the helm. I'd like to talk with both of you about what we should do."

"I will," Naomi says. "Though I have no opinion to offer, myself. It's your decision to make."

That surprises me some.

I climb up to the platform in the mining deck again, dismissing the guards for a moment so I can think. I look out over the back of the dredge through the opening at the end of the stacker, making sure the night lighting is working. That was another dilemma—when it gets dark, do we light up this part of the dredge so that we can see who might be coming on? If so, we also make ourselves impossible to miss. The Admiral and I decided that it was better to keep the ship lit during the voyages. The noise gives us away, anyway. You can't miss the dredge coming up the river.

Footsteps behind me. Too heavy to be Naomi's, but not without grace. Someone who could make themselves stealthy, quiet, but who has chosen not to.

Brig comes to stand on my left, so that my line of vision includes both him and the stacker. "Naomi said you wanted to see me."

"Did she tell you about the gold?" I ask.

"Yes," he says.

It's hard for me to get the words out. It was easier to ask Naomi. "I've already talked to Naomi. Do you have an opinion about which part of the river we should take?"

"I'd stay with the course we were given at the beginning of the voyage," Brig says. "But I'll answer to the Admiral with you if you decide to deviate."

The first part of his answer doesn't surprise me, but the second part does. If this goes wrong, answering to the Admiral is no small thing. Is Brig serious? He looks it. One of the lanterns swings overhead with the motion of the dredge, and his features seem narrowed, then shadowed in the moving light. I don't know him well, and I know him even less like this.

I look past Brig to the stacker, but I can tell his eyes are fully focused on my face.

"I was glad to be chosen for this voyage for several reasons," he says. "One of them was because I'd get to see the armor in person. It's even more impressive than I imagined."

It's a compliment. I could thank him.

"Tell the guards to come back up to their post," I say.

Alone again. I find myself glancing for a moment at the metal plate hanging on the wall. There was one exactly like it on the other ship. The dredges are so old they predate even the Union. Those long-ago crews scrawled down codes on the plate for the bells they used to communicate over the noise of the mining equipment. One short ring means stop the trammel. Two short rings means start it back up again. Three means there's an emergency and to cut the motor and sound the main alarm throughout the ship. Call and I used to wonder about that.

"Shouldn't it be one short for an emergency?" I asked. "If a raider were cutting your throat, you'd want the signal to be quick."

Call shook his head. "You're so bloodthirsty."

It was a joke, then.

I could change the warning system now, if I wanted. I'm the captain.

With the threat of the raiders dispelled, the most likely emergency is that we'll need to stop the dredge because the ship has taken on something that could grind and break the gears, or because someone has fallen into the mining equipment on the inside.

The raiders aren't the only ones who can kill. One person could shove another into the machinery, send them out through the stacker along with the tailings.

Time's up.

The gold's still coming in fast.

Crew's quiet, eyes on me, waiting for my decision.

"We'll keep to the right," I say to Naomi. "Let Brig know."

She nods and heads up the stairs. I stay down with the crew. "May I?" I ask Noah, and he drops a few of the nuggets into my cupped hand. Their lumpy shapes remind me of tiny fossilized hearts, heavy and dead.

CHAPTER 9

GOLD, GOLD, AND MORE GOLD. In three days, we harvest more than any other previous voyage has on its entire run.

"You running out of places to put it?" one of the crew asks Noah as we break for lunch in the ship's cafeteria.

"We'll throw *you* overboard if we need more space," Noah jokes back. The atmosphere is so different from the first day of the voyage that everyone in earshot laughs. No one is offended, no one can imagine wanting to leave, not right now.

"If you run out of space, you can fill my room," someone else calls out. "I wouldn't mind sleeping on a pile of gold."

I have a moment of gladness because they're all so happy, because they're smiling, but it doesn't last.

This isn't our gold. It's the Admiral's.

"Think we'll sink under the weight?" Tam asks.

It's true that the motor is working harder—we have a heavy cargo and a long way yet to go. We may have to return early if we reach our storage capacity before we get to the planned turnaround point in the river.

And then what? Will the Admiral send us back out? Or will we have brought back enough for whatever it is he has in mind?

"We're fine for now," I say. "Have you been on the mining deck again?"

"Yes," he says. "They need the help. And you gave me permission to assist."

"As long as the food doesn't suffer."

"It hasn't," Tam says.

"That's true." I eat every bite of the meals Tam serves. My plate is always as clean as if it had been licked by a cat. "But when do you sleep?"

"I don't," he says. Then, hastily, "I do. Don't worry. I'm fine."

"Remember," I say, "the Admiral's not here for you to impress."

"I'm not trying to impress the Admiral." Tam looks at me. His hazel eyes have flecks of gold. There's something there. Is it worth mining deeper to find out what it is?

"It's interesting," Tam says. "The more gold we get, the more grim you look."

He's right. The wealth, the ease, the success of all this puts something inside of me even more on edge. I feel like the ship has changed form. Now it's not a sleek wild cat with claws and teeth at the ready, hair standing on end. It's plump and sated, curled up in the sun, waiting to be gutted.

. . .

When I walk into my quarters after supper one night, I know instantly that someone's been there. Nothing is ransacked but everything is slightly askew. The chair, not quite tucked in under the desk. The edge of my blanket, pulled out a bit from the bunk.

Someone wanted me to know they were here. Wanted to scare me.

Who could it be?

I have the only key to the room.

That's not true, I think to myself. *Clearly, someone else has another.*

Did the Admiral give someone a key so they could keep an eye on me? What else do they have keys to? The mining deck? The bridge? The firearm lockers on each level?

I fold my arms and look around, not touching anything, trying to memorize all the differences. Only when I'm sure I've noticed everything do I walk over to the bureau, which has a drawer ajar.

That's where they've put the note—on top of my folded shirts. It seems personal. I don't like it. This is an even bigger violation than putting something in my bag.

This is not your gold, the note says.

I crumple the paper in my hand.

Enough is enough.

I walk out in the hall to the nearest alarm box and pull the handle down. The ship begins to wail.

CHAPTER 10

I DON'T FLINCH.

It makes sense that I can handle the sound. Call died before the alarm, when the ship stopped. *That's* the sound that I don't think I'd be able to bear. For me, the sound of Call going gone is the sound of the ship going quiet.

The crew knows the protocol. If the alarm sounds, they're to report to their assigned spots in one of the ship's two largest areas—some to the cafeteria, some to the mining deck. Naomi's over the deck and Brig's in charge of the cafeteria. I'm supposed to secure the bridge, leaving Ophelia Hill, the navigator, in charge. Once I've done that, I call to my first and second mates on the ship's communications system.

"All here," Naomi says, yelling to be heard over the noise of the trammel down on the mining deck.

"All here," Brig says.

"Good," I say. "I'll come to the mining deck first."

Some of the crew are wearing pajamas—it was their shift

to sleep. They watch me, eyes wary. Do they trust me? Should they?

"The dredge itself is stable, and you are in no immediate danger," I say, "but there is a raiders' sympathizer on this ship." I hold up the crumpled paper. "This is the second note they've left for me. We can't risk anything on this voyage, particularly with everything going so well."

The openness I've seen on everyone's faces over the past few days has disappeared. Eyes narrow, faces go blank or angry or worried.

"I'm going to search the ship before they have time to hide anything," I say. "Everyone stays here until I give the all clear. Watch one another. Naomi, make sure that no one leaves."

Members of the crew shift their feet. Someone clears his throat. The goodwill we've had on the ship sifts out like the slicken and slips overboard.

"You should take someone with you when you search," Naomi says, leaning close to my ear. "So you have a witness to back up whatever you find."

She's right.

Who?

I look out at the crew. They are tired and gray-faced from lack of light. The trammel turns and the gold keeps coming in.

Tam, I think. Everyone likes him. Everyone *trusts* him. He was right about the food—it makes a difference in the morale on the ship. They'll believe the person who feeds them.

"I'll take Tam," I say to Naomi, and she nods.

Up in the cafeteria, Brig has his group standing at the ready. Tam's with them. I repeat the speech that I gave the crew on the mining deck. Brig's expression flickers, and I think I see a hint of anger there. And betrayal. I didn't tell him about the notes.

Because he's one of the suspects. He should know that.

Someone raises a hand, but I shake my head. "I'll answer questions later," I say. "Right now, time is what matters. I don't want to hold you here any longer than necessary. We have a ship to run." I face Brig. "Make sure no one leaves."

Brig lifts his chin in acknowledgment. "Yes, Captain."

"I need you to come with me," I tell Tam. "I want someone to witness the search, and I need my first and second mates to stay where they are for now." I nod to Brig. "I'll be back as soon as I can."

Tam's quiet as he follows me down the hall. I know from glancing at my watch that it's nearing dusk outside.

Dusk was the time Call liked best in the Outpost, when we'd finish up work at the scrap yard and have a few moments of our own. It's strange. I almost feel like if I could get up to the deck, I'd see him.

That makes no sense, I tell myself. *Call is dead. He's not on the deck. He was never even on this ship.* Never on this ship, never on this river.

Tam starts to say something and then stops.

"What?" I ask.

"Are we searching *your* room?"

I don't bother dignifying this with a response. I'm not going to go through my things in front of Tam. Besides, I've already searched my room. And I already know it's not secure.

"Don't touch anything. Just watch me."

"Right," he says. "What are you trying to find?"

"I'll know it when I see it," I say. I hope.

I didn't expect it to bother me to look through people's things. But it does. When you see what people bring, you learn about them.

Naomi has almost nothing besides the standard items issued to everyone on the ship. She has one faded book, a collection of fairy tales, which is unexpected. It seems a bit fanciful for Naomi.

Brig's room is more revealing. There are two packs of well-worn playing cards, some clothes that aren't standard-issue, several photos of him with people I assume are his parents—an older woman and a man whom Brig resembles. He also has a pocketknife. "I'll take this," I say, and I slide it into my pocket. "We're not supposed to have weapons on board. Brig knows that."

"It's just a knife," Tam says.

I raise my eyebrows at him.

"What?" he asks. "I have dozens of them in the kitchen."

"That doesn't make me feel better," I say.

We go on, from room to room.

Eira's belongings are immaculately tidy. She has an outfit to wear for when she gets off the ship, I suppose—a blue skirt, a white eyelet blouse, a pair of shoes that aren't practical in the least. A mirror, some ribbons. A set of beautiful colored pencils.

"We haven't found anyone keeping a journal," Tam says as we leave Eira's room.

"Not much time for it."

"I make time for it."

"You really *don't* sleep, then," I tell him. "What do you write?" I want to distract Tam. He's been paying close attention. I wouldn't be shocked if he's been keeping a list in his head of what each person has.

"I write about what happens," he says. "Don't you? Aren't you supposed to keep a record? Like a captain's log?"

"No," I say. No one ever told me to, anyway.

I'm starting to feel frustrated. What am I looking for, exactly? I thought I'd know it when I found it, but that hasn't been the case. And clearly whoever it is was smart enough not to hide something in their room. Anything revealing is probably hidden somewhere on the ship. Some secret spot. Perhaps on the mining deck, or in the cafeteria?

Should I have checked those places first?

Or it could be on their person. I'll have to search everyone individually.

I open the door and we go into the next room. Another typical one, shared by four people. Two bunks, two dressers, each with two drawers. No desk.

"This one's my room," Tam says. "I share it with some of the other kitchen crew."

I feel along the bottom of the beds, turn back the blankets. Slide my hand into the pillowcases, shake them upside down.

I open Tam's drawer. I have to pull hard. Whatever's inside is heavy. "What have you got in here?"

The drawer gives way and I stumble back and stare inside. Gold.

The whole drawer is filled with it. With the new, high-quality nuggets we've been dredging up the last few days.

I look at Tam.

For the first time since I've known him, his expression is panicked. "I didn't put that there," he says. "It's not mine."

A dull pain begins to throb against my right temple in time with my heartbeat.

Gold. Gold. Gold.

What was he hoping to do with it? What does this mean?

"Captain Blythe," he says. "Please, I—"

"Out," I say to Tam. "Now."

He puts his hands up and, facing me, makes his way out of the room. Is he afraid to turn his back to me? Should *I* be afraid? I wonder if he's hidden a kitchen knife somewhere.

"Walk in front of me," I say. "Don't give any reason to make this harder than it is. We're going to the cafeteria."

I need backup and Brig is the closest.

"Captain Blythe," Tam says, and I can tell he's fighting to stay calm. "I didn't take the gold. Someone else put it there."

We've come to the stairs. "Turn around," I say. "Walk down facing forward, or you're going to fall. Keep your hands up where I can see them."

Why would he steal gold? Why would any of the crew? It's heavy and bulky and surely he'd get caught when he tried to get it off the ship.

Is this why he's been so keen to help on the mining deck?

Has Tam been leaving the notes in my room?

A wail goes through the dredge. It's the alarm. Again.

I didn't pull it this time.

Underneath it is another sound, the sound of silence growing. The trammel isn't spinning. The motor isn't running.

The ship is slowing down.

The sound of ending, of something stopped that used to be moving—*that's* the sound that makes me sick.

I hear the *clang, clang, clang* of footsteps running up from the mining deck. Someone reaches the top, almost colliding with Tam before pulling up short.

It's Naomi.

The sight of her makes the dull pain behind my temple turn sharp. First Tam, now Naomi. I *know* I can't trust people. But can't they at least stay where they're supposed to be?

"I told you to stay down—" I say, but she interrupts me.

"Captain," she says, "it's the raiders. They've boarded the ship."

CHAPTER 11

"ALL CREW, TO EMERGENCY DEFENSE POSITIONS," I say into the speaker on the wall. For a moment, my voice overrides the warning siren. "There's been a breach on the mining deck."

I click off the override. The alarm continues to howl, warning us.

"Weapons," I say to Naomi.

"Someone smashed in the lock to the firearm locker near the mining deck," she says. "We'll have to get them from up here."

I'm tearing down the hallway before she's finished her sentence. "How are they getting on?" I call over my shoulder to her. Tam runs with me. Is he coming to fight with or against us?

"Through the stacker," she says. "Someone on board disabled the mining system."

"Who?" I ask.

"I don't know," she says. "As soon as the last of the tailings went out through the stacker, the raiders started coming on."

"How?" The tailings stacker is high above the river. They'd have to climb up my armor to get to it. I thought of everything. *Didn't I?*

We've reached the firearms locker. *We'll get the raiders. We have a procedure for this.* I unlock the door, and Naomi and I each sling as many rifles as we can over our shoulders. Tam reaches for one but I gesture to the door across the hall, one of the small supply closets. "In there," I say. "Now."

"You need me to help," he says.

"I can't trust you," I say. "Get in *now*. Naomi, cover me."

She does and I open the closet with the captain's master key. Tam backs inside, hands up. I slam and lock the door. It's taken a few seconds, ones we didn't have to waste.

If he was up here with you, he couldn't have been the one who disabled the mining system.

Unless he managed it when he was down on the mining deck earlier. Or has someone working with him.

I shake my head. *Think about it later. Act now.*

I hear some of Brig's crew coming down the stairs from the upper deck to join us. If he's followed protocol, he's sent three people up to guard the entrance to the top deck, two to keep the bridge secure, and the rest to the area of the breach. That's what's supposed to happen in the case of an emergency, unless I tell him otherwise.

Did I force the traitor's hand? Was my search through everyone's belongings what triggered this? Or was it already planned?

"Fall in," I say to the rest of the crew, and they do so without a word. Naomi and I pass guns along to them. The taste of fear is sour in my mouth. Any one of my crew could be in league with the raiders. Any one of them could shoot us.

We round the corner, the sound of our boots a rumble and a storm down the hall, onto the mining deck.

The door is wide-open.

The raiders have guns trained on *my crew.*

The alarm howls.

"Captain!" It's Naomi. And then she's pushing me back. "Don't let them get a clear shot at her," she shouts to the others. Crew from behind rush around to protect me.

Even now, the raiders keep coming in through the stacker. One after the other after another. The buckets hang still, the trammel doesn't turn.

But I know the ship so well that even under the sound of the alarm I can hear that the armor is still going. It's the last system working, running on the energy from the solar panels. The raiders have disconnected it from the other systems and left it functioning. Why?

Because they've found a way on. And they don't want *us* to try to get off.

How are they getting on? Did they learn to fly?

No.

The raiders coming though the stacker have something strange attached to them. Some kind of fabric that for a second I think might be wings, but of course it's no such thing.

They've made gliders.

The raiders shrug them off as soon as they hit the floor of the mining deck. They lift their guns in our direction. Their hands are bloody, and one of them sinks to the floor with blood blooming across his chest in a serrated pattern.

When I see this, I understand. It all notches into place, like the gears of my armor.

They must have gotten somewhere above us, and then dove in. With the mining system shut down, and the slicken no longer coming out, they could, if they timed it *perfectly*, glide to the stacker opening and climb in. They'd still get cut up on the edges of my armor, but it would be possible.

I'm livid with myself. I didn't think they could get us from above.

The longer we stand here, the more of them there will be.

"Listen," says one of the raiders. Do I recognize him from that night two years ago? I think I know his voice. That roughness, the edges of it.

His face is deeply tanned. His rifle is pointed right at me, held tight in his bloody hands. "We're taking prisoners, if you come peacefully. Put down the weapons, put your hands up. We're going to take the ship, but we don't have to kill you."

Liar. I've seen what they do. It's seared into my brain.

"You lie," I say. "I heard what you said last time. So did

she." I jerk my head over my shoulder to Naomi. "You said it was the last time you'd leave anyone alive."

There's a speaker on the wall near me. I slam my fist onto the call button and shout out, "We've lost the mining deck, Brig. Seal us off. That's my order."

He'd better obey.

I raise my gun. I will have to hit the mark perfectly to make the kill I have in mind.

I don't miss.

I've been responsible for many deaths before, but I've never dealt one with my own hand and I wonder if I'll feel sick later. A dark hole feeling in the bottom of my stomach says that I will. When there's time.

If there's time.

I blew apart the main control panel to shut down the armor.

I just killed my ship.

In the confusion following my shot, Naomi and the others and I push back up the stairs right before the metal door between decks comes down, sealing off the mining deck below us. Brig heard me. He did what I asked.

We're safe for now.

For a *very* short now.

"Get up the stairs," I call out to the crew. "Go to the cafeteria."

Some move without questioning. A few look at me, their

backs pressed up against the walls of the narrow hallways to let the others pass.

"*Go!*" I yell. "*Now.*" They obey, pushing their way into the crush of bodies surging for the cafeteria.

"Bring up the rear," I tell Naomi.

It takes two minutes to get us all to the cafeteria. These are minutes we will never get back and I hope I'm not wasting them. I climb up on a table and Brig shouts at everyone to quiet down.

"The raiders will break through the barrier," I say, "and there are more of them coming through the stacker."

"Why the hell did you shut down the armor?" someone calls out. "Now they can board at will. You've killed us all."

"No," I say. "They left the armor on so we wouldn't climb off. I shut it down so we could escape. We go to the upper deck, jump ship, and find one another the best we can on-shore. Then we'll regroup and take the dredge back."

"Or we could stay on board and fight here," someone says.

"No," someone else calls out. "We should give up our weapons and then try to sabotage the raiders later."

"You'd rather *surrender*?" The thought never crossed my mind.

"Did you find the traitor?" a third person calls out.

"I didn't have time," I say, fury boiling over and making me grit my teeth, spit the words. "*We* have no time. If you want off the ship, we go now."

Brig and Naomi both salute and I appreciate the gesture.

"Where are the machinists?"

Three people raise their hands.

"Brig, take them up," I say. "They escape first."

We're missing machinists. Corwin, our chief machinist, didn't make it through the mining deck door before Brig had to close it. That, especially, is a loss. The raiders will likely try to force him to repair the ship. But I can take the ones we have left, the ones who weren't working on the mining deck when the raiders boarded. I can make it as hard as possible for the raiders to get the dredge back in working order.

"We don't get a choice?" says one.

"No," I say. "Go. I'll cover you. I'll come last."

On his way out the door, Brig leans in to say something low in my ear. "*Be careful. You're the most valuable person on this ship.*"

He's right. Not just because I'm the captain, but because I designed the armor. Do the raiders know that?

If they don't, they will soon.

"I'm coming with you," Eira says. *Good.* She knows about the ship and the maps. I should have included her with the machinists, but it's even better that she's chosen to go.

Brig and Naomi herd the machinists and Eira toward the cafeteria door. I point at the rest of the crew. "Let's go."

No one moves.

We have no time.

"Come *on*," I say. "I'll cover you, and we'll all jump. We'll regroup and take back the *Lily*."

"*How?*" someone asks.

I don't know. I have been thinking moment to moment.

I have been thinking *live now* and *save the ship later.* I can't save the ship if I'm dead.

I hear sounds below. Raiders, coming for us?

"Maybe *you're* the traitor," someone says. "Maybe you're leading us to our deaths."

"I'm no traitor," I say. "And I don't surrender."

They all look at me. Faces and faces and faces and none of them want to follow my lead.

But I've got Brig and Naomi and Eira and the machinists.

Would Tam have come?

There's no time for him now.

I hear the raiders on the move below as I head up the stairs to the top deck. They've broken through. Brig and I shove open the door to the deck stairwell, and he leads the machinists in a scramble up the steps, Eira behind them. I nod to Naomi to go up, too, and then I fire a few shots down into the stairwell before racing after her. They're coming for us.

Brig waits at the top with the others. I throw him the key to open the final hatch out onto the deck. "As soon as it opens, run, and jump out into the river," I tell everyone. "Don't try to climb down. The armor isn't moving, but it's sharp. Jump clear of it. And if you try to climb, the raiders will have more time to pick you off."

Brig nods. "I'll cover you," he says to me.

"No," I say. "You and Naomi go first. I'll cover you all. We find each other in the woods to the west." Of course, that area might be riddled with raiders, but I don't think so. The way the raiders are boarding us means they're up higher than we are, on the bluff to the east of the river.

I push past the machinists and Eira in the stairwell so that I'll be able to cover Naomi and Brig when they jump. I look out across the deck, which is still and unmoving.

From up here I can see more raiders in the light of the setting sun.

Dozens of them, on a bluff, with their glider wings.

The outcropping where they perch is perfectly situated for them to fly down on us. And the wind is perfect, too. The elements have conspired against us, along with the traitor on board.

My mind spins, trying to catch on to an answer that will set all the gears into motion, that will help me understand how this happened. Who suggested we change course? Who said we should come up this part of the river?

Who is the traitor?

The raiders are poised. Waiting. Now that I've shut off the armor, they're going to descend on us like spiders on the wind. We have to get off before they realize the armor is down and start jumping onto the top deck. We'll never be able to hold off so many.

Our window is closing.

"Captain—" Brig says.

"*Go*," I say.

He and Naomi run at the same time, low and fast, Brig faster. He vaults over the side of the ship smoothly, even with the armor that bristles near the railing. Naomi takes longer, but she makes it over, too.

I don't hear any shots.

"*Go*," I say to the others. Eira nods to me and darts across the ship deck, careful around the armor. She climbs up, and then she's over.

"I can't swim," says one of the machinists, huddled down on the deck. We're almost out of time.

"You can," I say. "Or they wouldn't have let you on this ship. You'll be fine." I'm not good at this. I don't know how to plead and cajole. "I'll help you. Go."

"No," he says.

"We can't survive the raiders out there," another machinist says. "We can't survive the woods."

"You can." I lift the rifle, threatening them. "*Now.*"

Something in my eyes makes them flinch, but no one moves to leave.

I *could* shoot them. That's what I should do. I should slick the deck with their blood as they cower and waste time. If they won't help me, I should make it so they can't help the raiders.

On the bluff, the raiders are moving into some kind of formation.

They've noticed us up here. They've seen us jumping in the dusk. They know the armor is down.

It was only a matter of time, and time's up.

People will die today.

But not me. When I die, Call is dead.

"You'll help us when it's time to get back on," I tell the

machinists, and I put down my rifle. I can't risk it going off as I jump. I reach into my breast pocket for Call's ruler and hold it as tight as I can in my hand, swinging my legs over the railing and teetering on the bristly edge of my porcupine ship.

A group of raiders take their leap from the bluff a moment before I jump from the dredge. They glide down like bright dark comets from the sky, the cloth of their chutes glowing, their bodies silhouetted black against the lowering sun.

CHAPTER 12

THE TASTE OF RIVER WATER is strong in my mouth, and the edge of the ruler cuts into my hand as I crawl out into the long grasses near the bank. *I'll get up and keep running. Head for the dream Call and I had. Leave the others behind.*

For a moment, I'm tempted.

Then I hear the river slapping against the ship behind me.

And I can't help it. I look back.

One of the raiders stands up on the deck, silhouetted. My heart misses a beat. He's standing in the spot where Call used to keep a lookout on the other dredge. Against the orange blaze of the sky, the pink tips of the mountains, the night about to be new with stars, the figure could be him.

But it's not Call.

Because of these people, it won't ever be Call.

I will *never* run until I take them all down.

CHAPTER 13

WHAT A MESS I'VE MADE.

I laugh to myself under my breath.

I wish I'd held on to my rifle instead of leaving it behind on the deck. Maybe it wouldn't have accidentally gone off on the way down. Maybe the water wouldn't have ruined it.

I'm soaking wet. I wipe my hands on my sodden shirt and stick the ruler into my pocket, feeling around to see if the knife I took from Brig's room made it, too. It did. That's all I've got.

Night is coming down, and even though it's summer, I feel an edge to the air.

I wonder whether Tam is still locked up.

He didn't have a chance to explain. Everything went wrong and I left him on the dredge. But I did the best I could.

I should never have been in charge of this voyage.

I don't understand people. I only understood Call.

And my ship.

I can still get one of them back.

• • •

In the last of the light, I find footprints in the mud, heading deeper into the forest. Two sets, together, and the tread on the boots is like mine. By the size of them, I would guess Brig and Naomi, or Brig and Eira. Two of the crew have found each other and are walking together, which means they made it out of the river and to shore. Four of us jumped, and at least three of us lived.

That's something.

The dredge remains still, so I hear every sound I make as I follow the footprints north. They parallel the river but stay in the cover of the forest. How did the others get so far ahead of me so fast? I didn't waste *that* much time trying to persuade the machinists to come with me.

It's strange to walk on land after so long on the boat. Everything feels solid and slippery at the same time. Leaves move under my feet, but the ground itself doesn't shift. The air smells wonderful. Clean. From what I can tell, much of the scent comes from the green pine trees around me. *If only Call could have smelled this.* This is air for running.

Do it. Go.

That feeling again, so strong.

Something catches my eye in the darkening woods farther upriver. Lights, glimmering through the branches of the trees. They flicker and move, the way sunlight catches on ripples in a pond.

I leave off tracking the footprints and creep through the

trees. I don't know how to move through the brush fast and quiet at the same time so I have to settle for going slow. The branches scratch and water drips down my back. But the lights draw me closer. *Stars. I think they're stars.* A stick cracks under my feet. *Slow down.* But I have to see. *So many.*

Faster, faster through the trees.

The lights get bigger. Did I remember stars all wrong from when I was on the river with Call? These aren't high and cold, but close and low. It feels like I could pluck them, cup my hands around their warm, burnished radiance.

Too close, too gold.

Not stars.

I stop in the underbrush, stunned.

The lights are part of a village, which is up in the *trees.*

The houses bow out from the tree trunks like boats, like full bellies. People move inside like silhouettes, climb up on ladders from the ground. Aren't they worried about setting the forest on fire, with lamps up in the trees? What are they using to keep those lights aglow? There's no electricity outside of the Outpost. And how did they attach the houses to the trees? I creep closer.

The people call to one another, shouting out in voices that seem celebratory, happy. Are they raiders, too? If so, what have they heard from their associates on the dredge? Are they pleased with their victory? Do they know some of us escaped to the forest?

I need to try and find the others. I can't take the dredge back by myself.

It's fully night now, and I'm tired and cold. I finally tear my eyes away from the raiders' beautiful, impossible village and make my way back through the bush. I find a place to rest where I can still catch a flicker of light through the trees.

Curling up on the ground, I pull leaves and dirt over me. There's no danger I'll sleep. It's too cold and I'm too near the raiders for that. But, lying there alone in the dark, I make another promise to them.

You'll pay for taking my ship.

Chapter 14

DAWN FILTERS THROUGH THE TREES. The villagers are awake, calling out to one another. I stretch my cold limbs and stand up partway, keeping my head well below the brush but rising up enough that I can see their village in the light for the first time.

I wasn't imagining things.

The homes remind me of wasp or swallow nests tucked up under the eaves of houses in the Outpost. They're like the little ships we studied in machinery school, the kind that sailed by the power of the wind. Wooden frames bow out from the trees, their limber golden struts covered by canvas. The design reminds me of the gliders, and the peoples' clothes and the cadence of their words are familiar as well. They *are* raiders.

It strikes me as oddly cannibalistic, the way they make their structures out of wood and then adhere them to the struts' own unhewn counterparts. But it's effective. They've made what they need out of what's available.

When I designed the armor for the dredge, I was trying to protect us from the raiders without knowing much about them. I'm not going to make that mistake again.

The engineering intrigues me. I want a closer look. I want to know how they do it.

It must be hard to anchor the houses in the branches. As I edge through the brush, I see where the raiders had to cut away limbs from the trees to make enough space for the homes.

Why build up so high? Are they afraid of something on the ground?

My fingers are locked and cold and I blow on them, bowing my hands out like the tree houses so I can get more air in. I'm wondering whether I dare risk getting even closer when the village swings into movement.

Some raiders swarm down the ladders. Others lower bags and boxes to the ground. The canvas sides of the houses seem to breathe and billow, and then the cloth falls to the earth slowly, ballooning and undulating on its way down.

They're breaking camp.

Was there a signal? Did I miss it?

Once all the canvas has been removed, teams of raiders climb up the trees using ropes. They detach the wooden struts and lower them to people waiting on the ground. Once the backbones of the houses are down, the raiders dissemble them and wrap them in the canvas. Then they shoulder the bundles. Even walking, they'll be faster than the dredge when it's on the move.

I lift my head a little higher to watch them go, the green leaves in front of me swaying. I put out my hand to still them.

So *this* is how they follow us, how they have so many people. How they've lasted all this time, and the leaders of the Outpost were never able to flush them out entirely. The raiders have villages, *and* they live on the move.

A sound, behind me. I duck down and turn and see—

A girl. Dark hair, damp clothes. Slight. Staring right at the patch of brush where I'm hiding. The husky rasp of leaves against my ears and hair makes sounds like *see you, see you.*

It's Eira.

There's no point in hiding. I stand halfway back up, slowly. She followed my orders and jumped off the dredge, but is she a friend or an enemy? All it would take to reveal us to the raiders is a shout.

Eira's hair is tangled and her clothing dirty, her lips bluish. I wonder if she's as cold as I am, and where in the woods she spent the night.

She says something, but I can't hear.

Eira creeps another step closer. Hardly any sound. She's better at keeping quiet than I am.

Her mouth moves again and this time I can make out the words.

Captain. Come with me.

Behind us, I hear a groan and crash of wood and the raiders shouting. Something has fallen. A strut. A tree. I'd like to turn and see what happened, but I don't want to have my back to Eira.

Brig, she mouths. Again, I see the words she's saying but I can't hear them. *Naomi. This way.*

We all made it.

Will they help me get the ship back?

There's only one way to find out.

"How did you find me?" I ask Eira, as she leads me through the woods.

"*I came to get a better look at the raiders,*" she whispers, holding back a branch so it doesn't slap me in the face. It's a kind gesture, but almost futile—with so many branches growing high and low and thick in the forest, I'm already scratched up.

"How quickly did the three of you find each other?" I ask.

"It didn't take long," she says. "Brig and I came ashore at nearly the same place. Then he saw Naomi struggling and went back for her. She's hurt."

I look over my shoulder in the direction of the raiders' camp.

"How much farther?" I ask. I don't want to lose track of them.

"Not far."

"How bad is Naomi's injury?"

"It doesn't look good to me. But she says she's fine. It's her arm."

A few more moments and there they are, dirty, ragged patches sitting in the green and brown and gray of the forest.

"Captain," Brig says, standing up. There's a gash across the bridge of his nose. "You made it."

"I did," I say. "We all did."

The three of them had one another to stay warm during the night, but they look as cold and hungry as I feel. Naomi holds her arm awkwardly, and blood has soaked through her sleeve. Part of the bottom of her shirt has been torn off to tie around the injury. "I hit something in the water when I came down," she says. "I'll be fine."

"The wound's deep," Brig says.

"At least I'm not pouring blood anymore," Naomi says. "Let's get moving. We're too close to the raiders."

"I don't want to lose them entirely," I say. "We need them."

"For what?" Eira asks.

"To take back the ship." Brig's eyes meet mine across the heads of the other two. He knows that's the next step. Good.

"We have some time, not much, while they take down their village," I say. "But we can't lose them. They have information we need. And we're going to have to steal from them if we want to keep from starving. I don't have any food. Do you?"

All three of them shake their heads. *No.*

I hold out my ruler and Brig's pocketknife, the one I

confiscated when I searched his room with Tam. Brig raises his eyebrows when he sees it, but doesn't say anything. "What else do we have?"

"I've got these." Eira pulls a pen and pencil from her pocket.

"We're a fine group of soldiers," Naomi says. "We all left our rifles behind."

"The water would have damaged them anyway," Brig points out.

"We can draw and measure them into submission," Eira says, and Brig's mouth quirks up in a smile.

I study Naomi's face for signs of pain. I see resolve and exhaustion. She's the oldest of the four of us by many years. "Has anyone cleaned the wound?"

"Eira did a good job of it last night," Naomi says.

"Can you tell me how, exactly, we're going to get the ship back?" Eira asks.

"I don't know yet," I say. "I haven't had much time to think."

"You didn't imagine that your armor would fail, did you?" Eira's tone is matter-of-fact.

"Her armor *didn't* fail," Naomi says. "There was a traitor on the ship. They shut down the mining system, and the raiders got on through the stacker. Without the traitor, the raiders never could have boarded."

Mist curls against the dark-green backdrop of the trees. Our clothes—dirty, still damp—blend in, so it feels that the faces of the others are in sharp relief as they consider me, and one another.

"It's possible," I say, "that the traitor jumped with us."

"It's not me," Brig says. "I want to get home. I've got family there."

"So do I," says Eira.

"There's no way for either of you to prove that," I say. "We'll have to take your word for it."

"That's true." Eira doesn't sound offended.

"I don't have any family," Naomi says. "But these ships are my life. I've been on every dredge voyage. I want to see the last one through."

"I don't have any family either," I say.

Brig laughs softly. "I don't think any of us suspect you."

We all want to get the ship back, for one reason or another. Brig and Eira care about returning to the Outpost. The ship is Naomi's home, and it's my creation.

"Why did you lock Tam up?" Naomi asks.

The other two turn to stare at me.

"I found gold hidden in his room," I say. "Right when the alarm started going off. Naomi and I needed to find weapons and get to the mining deck. I wasn't about to hand Tam a gun when I didn't know who he was or what else he was hiding. He could have shot me in the back."

"The raiders will let him out," says Eira. "If he was the traitor, they'll be glad to see him. If not, he can surrender like the rest."

"If it *was* Tam, he was working with someone else," I say. "He was with me when the mining system went down."

If it wasn't Tam, who was it? How many traitors are there? The questions hang between us in the soft air of the forest.

"We'll have to be careful," Brig says, after a moment. "We don't want the raiders to know we're out here."

"They probably know it already," I say. "They must have communication with the raiders on the dredge. They have to know some of us jumped. Maybe they even saw it happen. And our bodies haven't washed up on the shore."

Just thinking about the water, the river, makes me restless to get back to the ship.

"We follow the raiders and figure out how to take them down," I say. "We'll figure it out." I've already got some ideas from the few hours I spent observing them, but I'm not ready to share. I put the ruler back into my pocket and keep the knife out, at the ready. "Brig, you lead. Naomi next, then Eira. I'll come last." I want to keep my eyes on all of them.

Eira shivers now and then as we creep back slowly through the brush, even with the morning sun finally slanting through the trees. But she doesn't complain. None of us do. Naomi looks over her shoulder and gives me a wry, tight-lipped smile, as if to say, *It could be worse.*

Brig's height means that he has to constantly duck and keep low where Naomi and Eira only have to bend their heads. He holds back branches and waits for Naomi to take them from him so that she doesn't get whacked in the face coming through the brush. There's a leaf in his hair, and my fingers itch to pluck it out. Not because I want to touch him, but because I want to put things right.

We should not be here in the forest, cold and hungry with debris in our hair. We should be safe, warm and fed, on my ship. Whoever did this will pay. Anger wells up inside me and I grip the knife tightly.

Brig said I was the one person he *didn't* think was the traitor. But I can't say I feel the same about him.

Or any of them.

CHAPTER 15

WHEN THE RAIDERS HAVE ALL MOVED ON, when we can no longer hear the sounds of them pushing through the forest, the four of us edge out into a clearing. *"Food first,"* I whisper.

The raiders didn't bother to hide the evidence of their camp. They tidied up and took what they needed, but there are footprints everywhere, drag marks in the dirt, fire pits blackened with burned wood. And compost piles. Flies buzz busily around them. We all fall silently to picking through the refuse, pulling out bits of meat, vegetable peelings, an apple core. The raiders' castoffs raise questions in my mind. *What kind of animals do they hunt? Where did they find an apple out here?*

"I miss Tam," Brig says, spitting a piece of something rotten onto the ground.

I try to push away the shame of eating from the raiders' compost pile. The faster I swallow their scraps, the sooner I can track them down. They will keep me alive long enough to defeat them.

"Let's go," I say after I've managed a few more bites. "I don't want to lose them."

"We could split up," Naomi says. "Two of us could stay here and scavenge what we can. Two of us could track them and come back for the others. We're faster than they are. We don't have anything to carry."

I've thought of this, too. I don't want to waste time, but it's true we need food and to learn what we can from the abandoned camp. But who do I leave in charge of whichever pairing I'm not part of? Out of all these people I don't trust, I suppose I suspect Naomi the least.

"Naomi and Eira will stay here," I say. "Brig and I will track the raiders and come back for you. Meet us where you slept last night."

Eira glances at Naomi. I'm counting on Eira to be too kind to say she doesn't want to stay behind. And I'm right.

"You first again," I say to Brig.

The two of us make our way down the path the raiders left when they broke camp. It's much easier than forcing our way through the brush. The raiders clearly know where they're going. This is their terrain.

Like the ship is mine.

A sound. A shout?

Brig doesn't seem to have heard it. I grab his shirt to keep him from going forward and he turns in surprise, his blue eyes sharp on me. I jerk my head in the direction of the river.

Another shout. And in the distance, the sound of water?

"*Careful,*" I whisper to Brig. "Let's get off the path. Head for the river. I think that's where they've gone."

We crouch low and move slow. Leaves and twigs scratch and brush against our clothes, our hair, our skin. My legs ache with the strain of keeping down.

And then I see the raiders. A teeming mass of them, gathered on a glimmering gray sandbar that juts out in the river.

How far are we from the dredge? I glance back downriver and there it is, silent and still. I force myself to look away, to swallow my anger.

Brig's lips move. He's counting. Trying to get an idea of how many raiders we're up against.

The sun glints off the water upriver, and at first I don't recognize what I'm seeing out on the sandbar. But as I watch, it becomes clear. Takes shape.

The raiders are turning their houses into boats.

They bend the lithe golden struts. They strap the canvas over the curves. Like they did in the trees, but this is for the water.

Brig looks over his shoulder and meets my eyes.

Their engineering is so efficient, so simple. But I'm not fooled. It takes a sharp mind—or many sharp minds—to come up with designs so clean and direct and yet so multifaceted.

Some of the raiders are already paddling downriver, in the direction of the still-quiet dredge; others help assemble more boats and set off upriver. I think they're going to rebuild the village in a new spot.

Brig and I make our way downriver from the sandbar in search of a safe vantage point to watch the operations on the ship, or even—I hope—to find a place to cross and get a better look.

As we creep along the shore, I watch from the brush, trying to figure out the way they're putting each boat together, frustrated once again that I can't see exactly how everything works. The canvas must be waterproofed to keep the rain out of their houses and to prevent the river water from soaking in and sinking their boats. But *how* have they waterproofed it?

These boats—with the canvas taking in the wind and their curves below the surface cutting through the water—they make movement possible. And what's more, the raiders have sun on their faces in the day and stars shining down on them at night. They're not locked up inside. They can see. They use the river instead of destroying it.

Learn from it, Poe, I tell myself. *That's how you take them down.*

Though most of the village is relocating farther upstream, a few of the boats are coming downriver and across the water to meet up with the dredge.

I'm encouraged by the ship's silence. The raiders seem to have been unable to start mining again. When I blew apart the panel, it's very possible that I damaged more than just the controls for the armor. The thought gives me hope.

I wonder why the villagers were camped a distance away in the first place. There are a few good reasons I can think of. If something went wrong, and we killed the raiders who boarded, we wouldn't have noticed the others in the village if they were farther upriver from the ship. And, of course, it would have been hard to pinpoint the exact place the dredge would stop.

Or there's another reason, one I don't even know enough to think of.

A few minutes later I see something, and my heart catches.

A footprint. Made by a boot like ours.

This print is smaller than Brig's, larger than Eira's and Naomi's, and not mine, because I haven't been on this part of the bank before.

Someone else made it off the ship.

Without a word, I pull on Brig's sleeve. When he turns, I point down at the print in the muddy bank threaded with grass. He raises his eyebrows at me.

Did someone else escape? Or did the raiders let them go?

Another fork in the road, another braid in the river. Do I want to follow this footprint to see whether there are more, or keep going toward the dredge to find out what's happening? What is the best way to get the ship back? I'm torn. I motion for Brig to crouch farther down in the weedy marsh while I decide.

We can't speak out loud this close to the raiders. I point at the print with one hand and in the direction of the dredge with the other, then shrug my shoulders. *Which way should we go?*

Brig catches my meaning. He thinks for a minute, his expression cool and thoughtful. Then, he points at the print.

That decides me. I point at the dredge, and motion for him to go.

●   ●   ●

"It's not that I don't trust you," I say, when we're concealed nearer the shore.

"It *is* that you don't trust me," Brig says, but his tone is mild. Amused? "But what if I'm saying the opposite of what I really think?"

"Could be," I say. "And maybe I've already figured that out." I'm not trying to be funny, but he smiles at me, fast and full, a flash. I feel the jolt of that smile, the unexpected moment of connection.

"I don't see a good place to cross," I say. This annoys me because I want to get closer to the dredge. We *could* cross, even a river this wide and deep, because there are chewed-up rocks and boulders behind us from our passage along the river, but we'd be totally exposed under the big, blue sky.

The two of us crouch down. As time passes our legs get tired and we kneel, sit, contort into different positions. Half crouches. Near kneels. Hiding with someone feels oddly intimate because you're attuned to their every breath and movement. I'm not used to holding still for so long and Brig must not be either, though I have to admit he's better at being quiet than I am. "How old were you when you had your militia training?" I ask him softly, pointing to the insignia on his shirt.

"Sixteen," he whispers. "Two years ago."

I'm also becoming deeply familiar with the landscape of this patch of ground where we've taken up residence. After the clean, man-made lines of the dredge, the amount of texture in the forest and on the bank feels almost ludicrous. Pebbles and rocks pressing against my flesh. Leaves and grasses intermingling with one another. The lap of water against the bank, the brush of wind across my skin, smells of pine and mud and ripeness.

"Were you part of the Admiral's guard?"

Before he can answer, we both catch movement on the river and fall silent. Raiders emerge from the bushes, carrying a boat. I wish we were closer so that I could see them better, see their faces.

I wonder what Naomi and Eira are learning. I hope they're being careful. That, if they're caught, they won't tell the raiders that anyone else is out here with them.

I wonder if whoever left that boot print is watching us. From the trees. From the bushes. From another place along the river. The thought makes my skin crawl.

The raiders on board my ship have lowered the gangway ramp so that the others can climb on. The ramp is made to meet up with land, but they're using it to bring in the boat, so they slide the ramp right down into the water. Their boat is small enough for them to pull it onto the gangplank after them, and in the absence of the grinding of the dredge, I hear the sound of the wood scraping along the metal.

Some of the raiders lean out to touch the unmoving armor on the side of the ship as they come aboard.

Don't touch it. It's not a pet to be stroked. It's a knife meant to cut you. Kill you clean and dirty.

They leave the gangplank out and their boat sitting on it.

The panic I've been trying to keep at bay licks at my heart.

We're so close. I have to get my ship back. What if we tried to board the dredge right now?

"How well can you swim?" I ask Brig.

"I'm not bad," he says. He looks at me, at the boat. "You think we can make it without being seen?"

At that moment I hear people calling out. Another boat has left the shore. And, up on the deck of the dredge, half a dozen raiders have gathered with their gliders. They're everywhere.

"Damn it," I mutter under my breath. *Slow down, Poe.* I want to be back on my ship but I need to take my time. Do it right so we don't get caught.

I study the dredge, my mind racing. We have to get back on before they get the armor going. But a single knife won't be enough against them. The raiders have our guns. I curse myself again for leaving mine.

What if I made some kind of trap that halted the ship, or smaller snares that caught the raiders as they move between ship and shore? What materials could I use? I am used to steel. This place is all tree and rock.

There's got to be a way. I'm sure I've missed something.

"What have you noticed about the raiders as we've been watching them?" I ask Brig.

"The children," he says.

"What?" That wasn't the answer I expected.

"There aren't many," he says. "Of course, maybe they keep them safe in the houses, but I haven't seen many little ones."

I didn't pay attention to the number of kids. I didn't even get a count of how many raiders I saw in the village. I was so taken with the houses they were turning into boats. By the mechanics of how they live, rather than the people themselves.

"I didn't notice," I admit to Brig. "I was focused on the houses. The boats."

"That's good too," he says. "You know what someone builds, you know them."

I feel a warm rush of satisfaction—that's true, he's right—and then a thought strikes me. If someone looks at the dredge armor, do they think they know me?

Well. That's fine.

They do.

CHAPTER 16

MY STOMACH ROLLS WITH HUNGER and my throat is
parched dry by the time we need to go back. Brig and I scoop
water into our hands from a stream that runs to the river; I
make a mental note that we need to find or steal something
that can hold water.

Brig leads the way back to our meeting-place without
error. In spite of myself, I'm impressed. There are spots where
it would've been easy to get turned around. Sometimes the
trees are clustered together—at other times, they form natural
corridors, the light streaming in soft between their branches.
Brig and I don't say a word.

Naomi and Eira are already back, sitting on the fallen logs.
They look up; their faces show relief when they see it's us.

"Did you learn anything?" I ask. "Did you find any food?"

"Well," Naomi says, "so to speak," and then someone
steps out from a tree behind her.

Tam.

Clothes still damp from the river, hands up so I can see that there's nothing in them.

"How'd you get out?" I ask. I keep my arms down and loose in case I need to reach for the knife. Tam and I face off across our tiny clearing, the others standing around us. Brig is at my elbow. To defend me? To help Tam take me down?

"The raiders found me," Tam says. "They let me out to join the others on the ship. We're all sleeping crammed eight and ten to a room." His face is bruised—forehead, nose, cheeks, chin—and his hands and forearms are, too. Did the raiders beat him? "The ship's not running, so last night I slid out through the tailings stacker."

"Didn't they have anyone keeping watch?"

"Yes," he says, "but I got past them."

His story seems suspicious. Easy. But the bruises on his body are consistent with injuries you'd get if you came out of the tailings stacker and landed on refuse and rocks in the water.

"I brought food." Tam tilts his head in the direction of a canvas bag on the ground behind him, near one of the fallen logs. "Stuff that doesn't get ruined if it gets a bit wet."

"Eira," I say. "Get the bag and show us what's inside."

She obeys, dragging the green canvas sack into the middle of our loose circle, closer to me than to Tam. She takes out the items one at a time.

He's got cured meat. Carrots. Potatoes. My mouth waters. There's a tiny and somewhat battered camp stove, and a small tank of kerosene that fits onto it. "You tried to bring a kitchen with you," Brig says.

"I didn't want to starve," Tam says.

Eira pulls a dented pot out of the bag next. She shakes her head. "It's amazing you didn't sink with all of this on your back."

"I sent it out through the stacker first," Tam says. "As a trial run."

There's more food, and a single knife, which I tell Eira to give to me. "You can put the rest of it back in the bag," I say to Tam.

He crouches down, moving stiffly as if his body is bruised, too, and gathers the food into his arms. "I'll cook some of it now, for dinner."

"You can't cook out here," I say. "They'll see or smell it."

"All right," Tam says. "Then give me back my knife and I'll cut up the food and season it for you. If we have to eat raw potatoes, they might as well have some flavor."

"Why would I trust you with a knife?" I say. "You were stealing gold."

Tam's composure slips a little. "I told you. That wasn't me. I don't know how it got in my room."

"And you expect me to believe that."

"I've had time to come up with a better story," he says. "But that's the truth."

"Maybe you're just too stupid to think of a better story."

Eira draws in her breath.

"Fine," Tam says, his voice bright. He's trying to be the cheerful, open-faced charmer he was on the dredge, but even he can't quite pull it off. We're out here in the woods trying to figure out a way to get our ship back, and we've got very little going for us. Again, that edge of panic creeps into my mind. I push it away.

"I'll cut the food." I hold up Tam's knife. Eira hands me a carrot, and I slice it into the pot, the blade sharp against my finger. I cut carrots and potatoes and strips of cured meat while the rest of them watch, all of us wary and hungry in the dusk.

I hand the pot to Tam and he begins to season the food.

"Tell us what the raiders are doing," I say. "What have you learned about them?"

"They're trying to get the ship going again," Tam says. "They know you're the one who shot out the control panel, and they know you made it off. Your name's a curse on the dredge now."

"They know my name?"

"Of course they know your name." Tam raises his eyebrows. "Not only are you the captain, you designed the armor, and you blew out the control panel. They're furious that you escaped."

"We haven't noticed anyone searching for us," I say.

"They aren't wasting time on it," Tam says. "They think you'll come back when you run out of food. And that you can't stay away from the ship. They want to get it going again as soon as they can. They have somewhere to be."

"How do you know all this?" Surely they wouldn't speak so freely in front of an enemy.

Tam shrugs. "People talk when they eat. And I was still cooking all the food."

"Who's their leader?" I ask. "Is he or she on the ship?"

"I don't know."

It's my turn to raise my eyebrows. With everything else he says he heard eavesdropping, how did he not discover *that*?

"Really," he says. "They didn't talk about it in front of me, and not all of the raiders came through the line for meals. Some of them took food to the others. I couldn't figure it out."

I shake my head. I don't know if I believe a word he says.

"This is going to get exhausting," Tam says, tossing the food around in the pot. "You have to decide if you trust me. And you'll have to do it soon. I'm making your supper. I could have poisoned it."

He holds the pot out to me.

"You first," I say.

Tam takes a few bites, using his hands to scoop out the food, and gives the pot to Naomi to eat. When she finishes, she passes it to Eira, who eats, then hands the food to Brig. When it comes to me, I hold it in my lap. Waiting to see if anyone suffers any ill effects.

"How many raiders did you count today when you were watching the village?" I ask Eira and Naomi. I'm not crazy about Tam hearing all of this, but it doesn't seem like we have much choice.

"Seventy-three," Naomi says. "Some left and came back. We tried not to count anyone twice."

"We saw thirty-four," Brig says, and I nod confirmation.

"There are about twenty-eight raiders on the dredge full-time, as near as I can tell from the amount of food I cooked," Tam says. "Plus the prisoners. There were nineteen of us."

"Do they have a leader in the village?" I ask Naomi and Eira.

"I think that their main leader is on the ship," says Eira.

Naomi nods. "There are several in the village who seem to have some authority, but I get the sense they're reporting to someone else."

"A few of them go back and forth from the dredge," Eira says.

"Brig and I have seen that, too," I say. "Can you tell what they're planning?"

"They're excited about the gold and the capture of the ship," says Naomi. "They talk about the victory and the amount of gold on board. Beyond that, we haven't figured out much."

"Why does everyone want gold so badly?" Eira asks.

"Gold can do a lot of things," Naomi says.

"Jewelry and money," Eira says. "What else?"

"It doesn't tarnish," says Brig.

I've asked myself the same question Eira posed just now. *What good is all this gold?*

What do I know about gold? Why would *I* want it?

To make things. "It's easy to work," I say. "And it's a conductor."

"A conductor?" Eira asks.

"For electricity." Saying the word makes a spark catch inside me, an idea run through the circuits in my brain.

What if the raiders want to *use* the gold, for its myriad of practical purposes? The ones we don't have to think about as hard in the Outpost, where we gathered in everything valuable, where we have more facilities and resources to make things?

We're plundering what they have, and they don't have much.

No wonder they're willing to kill us.

If using the gold to create things is why *I* would want it, and why the raiders might want it, could that also be why the *Admiral* wants it?

I haven't heard of him building anything. And I should. I'm one of his best machinists. He always says so. But is it true? Or has he decoyed me away on a job that's merely a scaffold to the real work he's doing?

I remind myself that the Admiral and I struck a bargain. I was the one who came to him with the idea for the armor. Killing the raiders was all I wanted.

I haven't thought much further than that.

"If they want gold so much," Brig asks, "why do you think they burned the last dredge instead of taking it?"

"They got the gold off before they set it on fire," I say. "They probably thought it was the only dredge we had. I think they thought that if they destroyed the ship we wouldn't come back. And that was worth it to them, even though they could have used the dredge."

"And they hated what it was doing to the river," Brig says.

"How do you know that?" I ask, suspicious.

"I heard things when I was in the militia," Brig says.

"But we didn't stay away," Eira says. "We came back with a new ship, one that killed them instead of just taking the gold."

Thanks to me. "What else do the raiders talk about?"

"They're all obsessed with the *Lily*," Tam says. "They love trying to figure out how she works."

"It's not a she."

"Of course it is," Tam says. "Lily's a girl's name."

"The *Gilded Lily* is a stupid name."

"The drifters don't think so," Tam says. "They think it's perfect."

My temper bristles at his mention of the raiders' other name. "They're not drifters to us," I say. "They're raiders. Call them that."

"Aye-aye," says Tam. "And we still call you Captain, I see."

"She *is* the captain," Brig says.

"You can all call me Poe," I say. "It's shorter. And if we get caught, it won't be so obvious who I am." But my tone warns them: *Don't take this as a sign of familiarity. You'll call me Poe because it's better right now. Not because we're friends.*

"What's it short for?" Tam asks.

"Posy," I say. Brig laughs out loud and then freezes, his face going still.

"I know," I say. "It doesn't suit." I stand up, brushing the crumbs from my hands. "Tam can stay with us for now. I'll take the first watch. The sun will be down soon."

I move away, hoping that they'll think I'm too far off to hear them, and then, softly, I step a few paces back. I want to know what they say when I'm not around.

At first, nothing. Perhaps they'll all fall asleep. I have both knives in my pocket. Tam's and Brig's. I'm safe. As long as I'm awake.

In the dark of the trees, I feel the chill in my fingers and smell the smoke from the raiders' camp. I'm still hungry. Tired of being cold and alone.

And then someone speaks. Tam. Of course.

"So," he says. "You knew Poe before."

He must be talking to Naomi, because she's the one who answers. "Yes."

"Could you tell back then she'd become the most successful killer in the history of the Outpost?" Tam asks.

"Even if you argue that she's responsible for all the raiders who died," Naomi says, "there are others who have killed far, far more than Poe."

"But she designed the most efficient weapon the Outpost has seen in years," Eira says. "That's why the Admiral loves her so much."

Why does Eira know this about me? Does everyone know?

I haven't thought about my kill ratio in those terms.

And the Admiral does not love me.

"*This* will mess up her percentages," Tam says. "I don't think she was supposed to lose the ship."

He tries to turn everything into a joke, but how much of his easy, cheerful insouciance is an act?

I understand. It can all be a joke or it can all be dead serious. Maybe I chose the wrong way the night Call died. Maybe it should have been funny, Call laid out there on the deck. Maybe I should have laughed at the way his eyes stared.

You don't always have time to choose in the moment you survive. Sometimes your body makes the decision for you. You laugh. You scream. You freeze.

I don't entirely blame them for talking about me. After all, I'm their leader and I'm not easy. I'd want to know more about me, too. But I hate it. It reminds me of when people whispered about me at school before we came to the scrap yard. *Not right. Something odd about her. She's awkward when she tries to talk to people. Sometimes it's like she can't even look at you.*

"Is it true," Eira asks, "that the boy she loved died on the dredge? That she made the armor because of him?"

Don't tell them, I think to Naomi. *They don't need to know.*

"Yes," Naomi says. Just the one word. She liked Call. Everyone did.

"Tell us what *he* was like," Tam says. "The person who started all of this."

Call *didn't start any of this,* I want to say. *The* raiders *started all of this.*

What if I marched back into the clearing and told them about Call?

How it felt to walk with him through the scrap yard? With metal glinting everywhere, sharp edges all around, but his hand on my shoulder, on my back, always gentle? His lips, his mouth. The sunset on his face as we walked home, our dirty, scarred hands touching. I'd glance at him across the yard and sometimes, not every time, he would turn and look in my direction, his hand shielding his eyes.

But I never blinded him.

I was never too much for him.

Even now, I don't think I would be. Even now, with what I've done.

I can't tell them about you, Call.

They would never understand. They would never get you right.

"He was strong like Poe," Naomi says. "One of the few people who could match her, I think. He was also very kind. He was easy to read. So was she."

I don't like this. I don't like other people hearing about him when they could never understand what and who he was. And yet I don't want Naomi to stop talking. It's a pleasure to hear someone else—someone who talked with him, knew him even the smallest bit—say his name and what they remember.

"You think she's *easy* to read?" Brig asks. He sounds like he's been surprised into speaking. "*Poe?*"

"Yes," Naomi says. "This whole time, she's been blazing with rage."

"Rage?" Eira asks. "She's so calm."

"Rage," Naomi confirms. "She was like that on the first voyage, too."

What? Not on the first voyage. I wasn't angry then.

I hear someone shifting, a crackle of leaves.

"But that time, it was love," Naomi says. "Some people always burn."

Chapter 17

AMONG THE TREES, keeping watch, I hold the knife in one hand. With the other, I open and close Call's ruler. I've perfected this move over many sleepless nights; fingers and palm flick open the ruler, work together to slide it closed.

Before the dredge and our plan to escape, Call hardly ever broke the rules. He was where he was supposed to be, doing what he was supposed to be doing. Steady. Strong.

But one night, soon after we'd moved into the machinists' dormitory, I saw him walking on the women's floor. The door to the bedroom I shared with five other girls was open. He didn't pause or look inside our room, but I knew his shape.

I climbed from my bed and slipped out to follow. Wandering at night was not allowed. Was something wrong?

I caught up to him. The dim safety lights on the stairs gave off a soft glow as we went down to the main floor. He didn't wait for me the way he usually did, so I walked behind him, watching his muscles shift under his shirt, looking at the back of his head, his dark hair cut short as always. I imagined what it would feel like if I ran my fingers through it—surprisingly soft. I reached out to touch his arm when we came to the main floor. He turned in my direction. In the low light, his eyes were gray. I would have thought he would be softer after sleep but his edges seemed even more defined.

"Did you have a dream?" I asked.

He had a look on his face I hadn't seen before.

"I want to steal something," he said.

"What?" I asked in surprise.

He didn't answer.

We crept down the hall to the kitchen. Worn industrial cabinets, wooden counters grooved deep with cuts over the passage of years. We'd both taken our turn in the kitchen, slopping trays and washing up, or helping make the meals. At night it seemed foreign, every surface taking in the light or reflecting it back in ways I couldn't predict.

Call opened one of the cabinets. He looked through the flour, the sugar, the crackers and bread. The fruit in the cold-storage bin—apples, pears. That was what I wanted to steal. I breathed in deep and smelled them, their fresh outside scents.

I took one, a pear that would be red in full light, and bit into it. Call turned at the sound.

"Want one?" I asked him, but he didn't answer.

"Someone's going to find us," I said. "If you'd tell me what you're trying to steal, this would go faster."

He looked at me and his eyes were puzzled. He knew who I was, but he wasn't quite with me.

That's when I finally realized he was walking in his sleep.

Talking in his sleep. It should have frightened or worried me, but it didn't. It made sense, somehow. I thought to myself, *Maybe that's why he never finishes a dream. He gets up to go looking for the end of it.*

Call sank down, sitting on the floor with his back against the cabinets.

I knelt in front of him.

"I'm tired of being lonely," he said. "Aren't you?"

"You mean hungry?" I asked, because why else were we in the kitchen?

"No," he said. "Lonely."

"Not really."

"Not really tired?" he asked.

"No," I said. "Not really lonely. You're here."

He pulled me close. He was warm, and his arms were strong, and then he kissed me, hard and sure. I was surprised, but I wasn't afraid. And then I was the one with my back up against the cabinets, and Call was against me, and we stood together, sliding up, his hands in my hair, and everything felt so good, it felt so good to be held, to have him right with me.

And then he broke away and looked at me.

And I knew he was awake.

"Poe," he said. We were both breathing hard. "I was dreaming. I was kissing you."

"And it was happening *to you?*" I asked to make sure, because he was usually watching, he was usually outside, in his dreams.

"Yes," he said.

"Good."

His face was full of wonder. "But it's *really* happening to me. Now. I'm awake. We're kissing."

"Well, not now," I said. "You stopped."

He laughed then, a low sound because we could still get caught. We could still get caught but I didn't care.

"And you don't mind," he said. "That we're kissing."

"No," I said. "I don't. I wish you'd start again."

He wasn't looking for anything anymore except me. Looking at me, kissing me, touching me, laughing again when he found the pear that I still held in my hand. We ate it before we left the kitchen, taking turns, destroying the evidence of where we'd been and what we'd done.

CHAPTER 18

THE MINUTE I WAKE IN THE MORNING-DARK, I know what's coming. I feel it low in my bones, stirring my soul, calling my blood. I bolt upright.

A crack of a twig. Brig. He had the last watch.

"*Captain?*" he says, soft, to keep the others sleeping.

"It's going to move," I say, and when he doesn't seem to understand, I say, "The *dredge*," and my voice is impatient because *of course it's the ship, the ship is the only thing.*

"Watch the others," I tell him. "Keep them here." Should I leave one of the knives with Brig, in case Tam gives him trouble? But then what if they use it against me? I can't decide. And then—

Churn. Clamor. Rumble.

Roar.

The sounds set my heart to racing.

River, rock, motor, gold.

My ship is running again.

Brig's eyes widen. "How did you know?" he asks, and the

wonder in his expression, the way he looks at me for that one second—I have surprised him, I have astonished him—reminds me of Call waking up and seeing me when we were kissing and a pinpoint of pain, specific and clear, pierces through the clamor in my body that the ship has sent humming.

I hand Brig one of the knives. "In case you need it," I say, "I'll be back," and I leave him there, standing with the blade in the forest.

I run as fast as I can, through branches that snatch at my arms, over rocks and dirt that catch at my feet. It doesn't matter how much noise I make.

My ship is covering my tracks for me with its grinding, terrible, wonderful sound.

The light is still dim when I reach the shore. And so across the river I go. Dark satin water laps over my legs, moss slides beneath my feet on stones underfoot. I stagger, swim, slip. Closer, closer, close as I can.

I'm coming.

The sound has awakened the raider village, too, and lights flicker. Some up in the trees near the shore, some moving lower, coming closer. Dawn is lightening the horizon by the time I reach the other bank.

The nearer I get, the stronger I feel it. It rolls more deep and powerful than a pulse, shakes my teeth, kneads my insides. And then. I hear something thin and near over the throb of the dredge.

Cheering. The raiders on board are cheering because they're on the move. They stand up on the top deck, silhouettes and shapes pumping fists and raising arms in the direction of their compatriots on the shore. I hiss in my breath. *Get down. Get off. This is* not *yours.*

Wait. They're on the deck.

Which means they haven't been able to get the armor running again.

They're steering the dredge to the other side of the bank, the western side. My ship makes its way across the river slowly, deliberately. And I'm right. The armor is completely still.

Using the ship to screen myself, I cross back again, keeping enough distance that the rocks can't churn up and hit me as the dredge remakes the riverbed.

Be careful, I mutter to the raiders between gritted teeth. *Don't run it aground, or you'll kill it beyond what I can fix out here.*

They turn the dredge in time, bringing it broadside near the western sandbar. I can't hear the raiders anymore, but I can see them well enough. Waving and signaling to one another, those on the dredge and those onshore.

How do we defeat so many of them?

We don't. We'll have to distract them. And we need to mitigate their numbers. I need an idea that can do both.

Lights still flicker up in the trees. Some of the raiders must have stayed behind in their houses while the others came down to see the ship on the move. I wonder again how they manage to have lamps without electricity, near so much wood.

And then, like a match to kindling, I have an idea of how I'll get my ship back. It might be that Naomi gave me the spark of the idea last night, when I overheard her talking about me.

Some people always burn.

I have torn them into bits. Now I will light them up like candles.

Chapter 19

ON MY WAY BACK TO OUR CAMP, I notice that someone has cut words and names into the trees. The words stand out, scarred-black against the white of the bark. The wounds are old; they have had time to heal over, to blur with lichen. Still, I can read them.

Names, mostly. A few dates.

Sometimes there are two names, with a heart in between them.

I shouldn't carve anything. It might give us away, if anyone else passed through here. They'd notice the newness of the cuts. But if I did, what word would I choose?

Revenge.

Brig appears around the side of one of the trees. I didn't realize I was so close to the clearing. He has his knife out, too. Neither of us makes any move to put ours away. His eyes are hollowed and alert.

Tendrils of hair have escaped my braid and fall into my

eyes; I push them back with the heel of my hand. "We're going to need to move."

"The ship's moving again, then?"

"It is," I say, "But the armor still isn't working." I hold out my hand for Brig to give me the knife. He returns it carefully, the blade pointing away from me. My fingers close over his on the handle. There's no way around it. Our eyes meet briefly, then he drops his hand and we head back to the clearing.

The others are awake, waiting for us. Naomi cradles her arm. Eira stands next to her. I notice she has her pen and pencil in her shirt pocket. I should have taken those away, too. You could stab someone with one, run the point of a pencil right into their eardrum, their eyes, while they were sleeping, awake.

I keep walking, toward Tam. He's sitting near one of the logs, his back braced against it.

"Good news, Tam," I say. "You brought us exactly what we need." I'm so close that the toes of my boots touch his. If he stands up, we'll be eye to eye. He leans back slightly, resting his elbows on the log behind him. A nonchalant gesture, but he's putting distance between us.

I do intimidate him, at least slightly. Good. I don't like needing people. But I do. For this.

"Food," Tam says, shrugging. "Everyone needs it. Not hard to figure out."

"Not just food," I say. "You brought more than that.

This, for example." I flick open Tam's knife. I think the handle is made of some kind of animal horn, thick and dappled dark brown and gold but almost translucent in places. I know the material because the Admiral has a knife like this, but bigger. Much bigger. He told me it came from a bison, an animal that went extinct long ago. I turn Tam's knife in the light sifting through the trees. Everyone else is silent. Do they think I'll strike? Tam keeps his eyes on my hands as he stands.

I sense Brig moving closer to me. Again, I wonder: to protect or attack? Are Brig and Tam working together? What combinations are in league against me in our leftover, skeleton crew? There are so many possibilities. Brig and Tam. Naomi and Tam. Eira and Tam. Brig and Naomi. Naomi and Eira. Eira and Brig.

Or four against one.

The five of us, a small circle, all of our eyes darting back and forth, asking one another: *Who are you?*

"Thanks to you," I say, "we can take back the ship."

I have Eira draft us a map of the raiders' village as it is now. We pack the dirt down wet and she uses her pencil to score lines in the mud. Her memory is precise and exceptional and her hand steady. Even in these less-than-ideal circumstances, she renders the village neat and clear. Brig kneels to get a closer look.

I point at the map Eira's drawn in the dirt. "We have to take them down before they figure out how to get the armor running. Otherwise our chances of getting back on are almost zero."

"Agreed," says Naomi. She's holding her arm very carefully. Does her voice sound weaker than it did yesterday?

"They outnumber us," I say. "And they have better weapons."

"We have two knives," Tam says drily. "And a pencil and pen. Also a cooking pot."

"What we need is a distraction to get them off the ship," I say. "Make them focus on something else."

"But why would they do that?" Naomi asks. "They're sitting pretty. They've got the ship and the gold, everything they care about."

"No," I say. "They care about their village. And the people onshore."

Eira catches her breath. Tam presses his lips together.

Can my crew handle this? Brig's been in the militia. Naomi's been on the dredge and seen violence. But Eira's a mapmaker, an artist. And Tam's a cook. Will he be able to kill?

As if he knows what I'm thinking, Tam meets my eyes. "I've seen blood," he says. "I've sawed through bone."

But were the animals alive or dead when you did it? I want to ask. Instead I reach around Tam for his bag. "With any luck," I say, "and thanks to you, we won't have to see too much blood or bone."

"What do you mean?"

"It's like I said earlier." I pull out the kerosene tank. It's small, but with kindling and flame and the right planning, it should be sufficient to get things started. And once fires get big enough, they're hard to stop. "You brought us exactly what we need."

Brig inhales deeply. "We're going to set their houses on fire."

"Right," I say. "We go upriver, close to their new village. We gather kindling." I tap Eira's drawing. "At night, when they're less likely to catch us, we sneak in and stack the kindling at the bottom of the trees. We douse as much as we can with Tam's kerosene and set it all on fire. Hopefully, the wood and canvas go up fast, and the fire's likely to spread to the trees and the houses. The other raiders will see it from the dredge." A flare of relief sparks in my heart. This is a real, workable plan for getting the ship back. We don't have much, but we have something.

It will be a perfect distraction. The raiders will have to leave the dredge to help. If we get enough of a blaze going, it might diminish their numbers. Permanently.

And after all, the raiders burned us first.

"It hasn't rained," Naomi says. "Everything's dry. The fire might leap where we don't expect it."

She's right. We might get caught in the fire ourselves. We'll have to run straight to the river, or a stream, if we can find one nearby.

And the raiders know some of us are out here. They'll have people keeping watch.

"If they catch us, they'll shoot us," Tam says.

"So we have to be careful," I say. "And quiet."

"How do we start the fires?" Eira asks. "We don't have matches."

"That's why Tam is so perfect," I say. "He didn't just bring the kerosene. He also brought the cookstove. We use the stove's lighting mechanism to start the fires."

"What if people die?" Eira's face is ashen.

"It's a terrible way to go," says Tam, his voice grim. "I've seen kitchen accidents. Even an injury from fire is awful."

Naomi bows her head.

Brig's jaw is clenched. "What other choice do we have?" he asks through gritted teeth.

Maybe it's good Naomi told them the story about Call. So they know what the raiders do.

"I wouldn't do this if they hadn't taken our ship," I say.

I wouldn't do this if they hadn't killed Call.

But.

They did.

"We could walk back to the Outpost," says Eira, after a moment's pause.

"Poe's not going to do that." Tam's watching me.

"I'm the captain of the ship," I say. "It's my job to get it home."

"What about us?" Eira asks. "Is it your job to get us home, too?"

"Of course," I say. "I want to bring back as many of the crew as possible."

Eira laughs. "*That* was convincing."

I'm taken aback. I meant it. Didn't I say it right?

"If we return without the ship and the gold, the Admiral will kill us," says Naomi, low. "He almost did last time. Poe's invention is what saved our first crew. Every one of us."

"If any of *you* want to run, you can." My voice drips with scorn. As if that's the most spineless, small, *stupid* idea I've ever heard.

The crew is quiet. The dredge is not. It reminds us that it's working again, moving inexorably away up the river.

Without us.

"Does anyone have a better idea?" I ask.

A pause. Eira is the first to speak. "I don't."

"Neither do I," Naomi says.

Brig shakes his head.

Tam sighs. "I can't think of anything else."

"Then let's take a vote," I say. "All in favor of striking against the raiders tonight, raise your hand."

Brig and Naomi raise their hands. After a second, Eira does the same. Tam is the last to lift his hand, the motion reluctant.

"Then it's settled." I level my gaze at them. "No one runs."

CHAPTER 20

"ALL RIGHT," I say. "We'll need to gather kindling later, but first we should split up again and take one more look at what the raiders are doing. Tam, you come with Brig and me to scout out where the dredge is now. Eira and Naomi—"

Eira exhales, visibly frustrated.

"Eira had to stay with me last time," says Naomi, with a flash in her eyes that disappears quickly. "I'm not as fast as the rest of you, not with this injury."

But I want us divided along these lines for several reasons. Brig and I are the strongest physically, so we should take Tam with us because he's the least-known factor. I still trust Naomi the most, so it makes sense for her to lead the other party.

"It's not that," says Eira, sounding contrite. "I'm just tired of watching the raiders' village."

"We need you there, Eira," I say. "I want you to notice any changes and draw us an updated version of the map when you get back. When the sun's in the middle of the sky, at noon, we'll meet here, go over the map, and gather kindling."

"I think the three of *you* should watch the village," Eira says. "Maybe you'll notice something we've missed." Her arms are folded, her eyes spark. "And you know how to draw blueprints and schematics. I'm sure you can help us update the map."

She's challenging me.

But she's right. I might see something she missed.

And vice versa. I wouldn't mind having Naomi's eyes on the dredge.

"Very well," I say. The dredge can run without me for a few hours.

Can't it?

Tam and I are up to our elbows in garbage, in the refuse of the raiders. It's smelly, squishy, disgusting, rank, and very, very interesting. Because I'm not as hungry, I can pay better attention to what the scraps reveal. Brig's keeping watch for us while we pilfer their garbage.

"Keep an eye on him," I say to Tam. "Let me know if you see him sneaking back to murder us." Tam laughs. I wasn't trying to be funny.

In the morning, the raiders cooked, cleaned up, and met together in smaller groups. To my frustration, we couldn't get close enough to hear what they were saying. They climbed up in the tree houses, and from the movements we were able to make out, it seemed that they were packing some of their things again. Which surprises me. I thought they'd stay a few days in that spot, since the dredge is so slow.

Not long ago, they all headed in the direction of the river.

What are they doing there? I wonder. It's good they left, so we can take a look at things in the village, but it unsettles me that they all went together. What do they have planned?

"Look at this." Tam holds up a scrap of bread. Flat, not light and fluffy like the kind he made on board the dredge, but still. *Bread.* The type that would require grain to bake, and ovens to cook.

"Where do you think they got it?" I ask.

Tam takes a tentative bite out of the edge of the bread. "It's wheat," he says, "but different from ours."

I take a piece of it from him and chew, thinking and counting. There are seventeen houses in the village, each with a group living inside. The groups seem to range from three to four people up to seven or eight. These houses are light and portable, but they're not heavy-duty. They wouldn't stand up to harsh winter snows—there's not enough insulation. They don't allow for ovens or for staying in one place for a long time, which would have to be necessary at some point, for wintering or illness or gathering food.

I was so struck with admiration at the beauty of their engineering, by the houses that fold into boats and out again, that I didn't think far and hard enough.

This isn't how the raiders usually live.

"Wheat isn't the kind of thing you grow on the run," Tam says. "They must have long-term crops somewhere."

"So there must be more than just this group," I say. "Somewhere, some of them are farming or cultivating."

"Or they trade with people who do."

All of this dovetails with what Brig noticed earlier: the lack of children. It makes sense now. Of course they wouldn't bring their kids on a raiding journey if they had a safe place they could leave them.

"And it's not the Outpost," I say. "They don't trade with us."

"It's kind of exciting," Tam says. The curve of his cheek makes it look like he's smiling, even when he isn't. He has a turned-up nose and freckles and his sandy hair is a tangled mess. He's too young and he shouldn't be out here.

"How do you figure?" I ask.

"You know. That there are probably more people out here. Not only the raiders."

"That's not exciting," I say. Other groups add variables to our mission. More and more, I'm certain that we have to do this *fast*. "It's problematic."

"But haven't you wondered?" Tam asks. "The world is big. I know a lot of people died during the Desertion when the Union withdrew from the Territory. But if the raiders found a way to live out here, maybe others did, too."

Flies buzz around the compost. My eyes meet Tam's across the scrap pile.

"The sooner we get done with this, the better," I say. "They're going to come back."

I glance in the direction where Brig is hiding. I told him to stay where I can see him and I didn't give him a knife. There he is, crouched low in the grass a dozen yards away. He's watching us. I jerk my head at him and he lifts his chin in acknowledgment before turning his attention back to the path the villagers used when they went toward the river.

"Do you know who your parents are?" Tam asks.

"That's a strange question," I say. I've found a bit of cloth, soaked through with some kind of grease. From meat? Cooking? It might be good for setting fires, and I don't think the raiders will miss it. I tuck it in my shirt pocket, where it sticks out like a filthy pocket square. At this point, I've been sleeping in dirt and digging through garbage. What does it matter?

"They're going to smell us before they see us," Tam says, and I snort—not quite in laughter at his joke, but more in acknowledgment of the fact.

"What kind of meat is this?" I pick up a piece of bone and gristle and hand it to Tam. "Is it an animal you can find around here, or do you think they packed it in?"

"Looks like chicken." Tam takes a small bite. "Tastes gamey," he says, making a face. "Some kind of bird. They probably could have caught it out here. Quail, maybe? I don't know."

We're almost at the bottom of the compost pile. With so many people to feed and support, the raiders don't waste much.

"So I guess you *don't* know who your parents are," Tam says.

"Actually, I do," I tell him, investigating a small carcass

that I am almost sure is a squirrel. "I remember my mother." I don't bother telling Tam that she's dead. He probably already guessed that. "What about you?"

Tam shakes vegetable peelings from his hands and takes a deep breath. "There's something I should tell you," he says.

"What?" I ask. *Not now,* I think. *All we need to worry about is getting the ship back.*

And then Brig is upon us. I didn't even see him coming. "The raiders are on their way," he says. "We have to go."

We beat Naomi and Eira back to the clearing, which makes sense as they had farther to go to get to the dredge and we came back earlier than planned. But, as the sun turns the bend at the top of the sky and begins to slope down, I start to worry. Is Naomi all right?

This is why I wanted them to stay near the village, I fume. *Why did Eira challenge me? Why did I let her?*

Tam and Brig and I spend the time gathering all the kindling we can find—dry brush and branches and leaves.

"How will we haul all of this to the raiders' village?" Tam asks, looking at the piles.

"We'll use your bag," I say. "And if we take off our shirts, we can use those to bundle some of it, too." Tam blinks, and I roll my eyes. We all have undershirts on beneath our button-ups and it's ridiculous to worry about propriety at a time like this.

"It's going to take a while and a lot of trips to get it all over there," I say. I didn't want to gather kindling much closer to the raiders' village—what if one of them saw or heard us, now that the dredge's noise is fading slightly as it churns farther up the river? "We'll need to start hauling as soon as Naomi and Eira are back."

We work in silence, dragging sticks into piles as if we're setting a multitude of campfires. Brig makes his way over closer to me. "That was a nice show of democracy earlier," he says, loading up his arms with fallen branches. "When you had us vote."

"It was, wasn't it," I say. "I'm sure it caught you by surprise."

"Not really." Brig's voice is deep, and when he keeps it low it's almost the pitch of the dredge. I have to lean closer to hear. He smells like apples and pine, clean, in spite of swimming through the river and sleeping on the ground.

"Why not?"

"Because you want everyone invested in the plan if we do it," he says. "You want us all to have ownership so we try to make it succeed."

"You're right," I say. "And, speaking of that, I have a question for you."

Brig shifts the load of wood in his arms. "Go ahead."

"How do you know Eira?"

"We worked together on an assignment," he says.

"For the Admiral?"

"Yes," Brig says, and now there is some emotion in his voice. Is it—*embarrassment*?

"What was the assignment?" I ask.

"It had to do with art." Brig's keen to be finished with the conversation; he looks over his shoulder at the other piles of sticks almost longingly. I think of Eira and the work she does, and suddenly I have it.

"The mural," I say. "Is that it?"

"Yes," he says. "I'm half of the men in the picture."

"What?" I'm not sure what he means. "The top half or the bottom half?"

Brig laughs, for real. "I mean that half of the men in that mural are modeled after me."

"Really?" I ask. I suppose it could be true. The bodies are only placeholders; Eira is copying the usual style of figures in murals. And when I think about Brig's body, he *is* that kind of tall, lithe, athletic figure that is one of the prototypes for perfection. Call had that body type. The Admiral has the other—thick, muscular, bullish, strong. I wonder if he is the other half of the mural, in addition to being the ruler of it, the one standing on top of the ship.

"Poe! Brig!" Tam calls out to us in a half whisper. "*Look.*"

Naomi's and Eira's figures slip through the trees in the late-afternoon sun. I stride through the brush as best I can to meet them.

"I'm sorry, Captain," Naomi says, when we can speak without calling out and alerting the raiders. "We were slow on the way back, thanks to me." Her face looks grayer than it did this morning.

"Let's check out that wound," I say.

"I don't think we're going to like what we see," says

Naomi. Tam reaches into his bag for an antiseptic solution he brought for cleaning his hands before cooking; we sterilized Naomi's wound with it last night. Eira rubs some on her hands, and then begins to unwrap the strip of cloth she tied around Naomi's arm when she dressed the wound.

"What's happening with the dredge?" I ask, as Eira's fingers gently pull at the material and Naomi braces herself against the pain.

"It's moving," Naomi says. "At about the same pace we had it going. The mining gear sounds fine. The armor's still not working." She draws in her breath as Eira peels away the fabric closest to the wound. It's not septic—I've seen a couple of injuries like that on the yard, when people wanted to keep working and didn't get the proper care—but it doesn't look good. The cut is ragged, and the edges ooze blood and pus.

"Dammit," says Naomi, looking down at it.

"I'll clean it this time," says Tam. "I've had to dress injuries before, in the kitchen."

Tam gets to work and Naomi looks up at me. "Captain," she says. "There's something you need to know." Eira nods. She looks drawn, too. And I remember—there was something Tam wanted to tell me as well. But he doesn't give any sign that he wants to bring it up again. He's focused on Naomi's injury.

"What's wrong?"

"The raiders killed one of the crew." Naomi winces as Tam swipes the antiseptic solution across her wound.

My stomach sinks. But I'm not surprised. It's what they

promised the first time, when they killed Call. *Tell your Admiral that we're done with you taking from us. Tell him this is the last time we leave anyone alive.*

I knew they were lying when they said they'd let us live if we surrendered.

"Could you tell who it was?" I ask.

"No," Naomi says. "A man. Brown hair. But his face was all battered." She keeps her gaze firmly averted from her arm as Tam cleans the wound. "The body was in bad shape."

"We found it when we were making our way along the shore," Eira says. "It was downriver from the dredge."

"It was tangled in the reeds along the river," Naomi says. "It looked like the raiders got rid of it through the tailings stacker." Tam is wrapping her arm up again and she nods to him in thanks.

"We couldn't tell if he'd been killed before he went through the stacker, or if he was crushed under the weight of the tailings," Eira says.

"Maybe he was trying to escape." Tam finishes tying up the wound. His face is grim. From the way Naomi's injury looks? Or because he's realizing how lucky he was that the raiders didn't get the ship started when he was slipping away through the stacker?

Or *was* that luck? Is anything he said about his escape true?

"Could you tell for certain that he was one of ours?" I think of the men on the ship who had brown hair. The chaplain, Corwin, who else . . .

"He was wearing our uniform," Naomi says, "but no boots."

That seems to argue against escape. Why would someone try to go out through the tailings stacker barefoot if they planned to make a run for it?

The raiders must have taken the boots before they disposed of the body. They're scavengers, after all.

I grab Tam's bag and start stuffing sticks into it, my fingers stiff with fury. "How long had he been dead?"

"Not long," Eira says. "There was no sign that animals had gotten to him." She winces at the way the words sound. "And he wasn't too waterlogged."

"What did you do with the body?"

"We left it," Naomi says. "We didn't want to draw attention. And we didn't have time to dig a proper grave."

That was the only decision, really, but I still hate the thought of one of my crew belly-up on the river. It reminds me of how we had to leave Call's body behind. Anger and tears rise in me and I push them both down, but not far. Tonight, we'll return.

Finish it for me.

I used to tell Call the ends of his dreams when he didn't know them.

I reach down to gather more kindling.

Finish this *for me, Call.*

If only he could.

Chapter 21

"THIS COULD BE OUR FINAL MEAL AS A GROUP," Tam says, in a deep, faux-ominous voice. He puts the last of the food into the pot.

We're fortifying ourselves before we have to lug everything over to the edge of the raiders' village in preparation for the fires. We won't sleep at all tonight.

"It's heartbreaking," agrees Eira, playing along. Tam grins at her.

"Are you saying we're not going to make it out of this alive?" Brig asks.

"Of course not," Tam says. "Soon we'll be back on the dredge eating with everyone else. That's all I was saying."

It must be the adrenaline, the thought of what is to come that is giving me an edge of hilarity, of hysteria. This is all ridiculous, impossible. I'm sitting in the woods, eating with a ragtag collection of people, planning to set a village on fire. And we're all pretending that we're going to make it back to the dredge, when so much could go wrong.

"So," Tam says. "We've got biscuits, cheese, and meat. Who wants to start?"

"The captain should eat first," Brig says.

"No," I say. "Naomi should. She's injured."

Naomi lifts her chin. It was the wrong thing to say. "Start with Eira."

Eira shakes her head. "Brig's slept the least. He should go first."

I almost laugh. How will we ever get the ship back working like this? We're starving, but we'd all rather go hungry than admit weakness.

Some crew.

"Fine." Tam plucks a biscuit from the pot and hands it to Eira, who is nearest him. "Everyone grab what you want and pass it along." He takes an enormous bite out of the biscuit. "You'd think you'd know by now that none of it is poisoned."

"Let's go over the plans again before it's too dark to see the map," I say after we've eaten. We crowd around Eira's precise drawing in the mud. "Brig, you start." I want to make sure everyone has the plans straight.

"First, we finish hauling our kindling over to the edge of the village," Brig says. "We wait until they're asleep and all their lights are out. Then, we slip in. We have two teams stacking kindling at the base of the trees—Poe and me, and Tam and Eira. Naomi will pour kerosene on each pile as soon as we're finished."

Naomi takes up the thread. "We start with the middle tree and work our way outward. That way, if they hear us and we can't get to every tree, we can start the fires on the centermost ones and hope it spreads." I nod at Eira to take over the narrative.

"When we're finished," she says, "we retreat into the woods, and make our way back here to the clearing to meet up, unless it's compromised and the raiders have tracked us."

"In which case, we go downstream to where the dredge was initially attacked," says Naomi.

"Because they'll expect us to flee deeper into the woods or head toward where the dredge is now," adds Eira.

"Once we're all gathered, we assess the damage and decide on our next step," I say. "If all goes well with the fires, the other raiders will come to shore to help the villagers. We'll steal one of their boats and what weapons we can, and head over to the dredge to take it back."

The forest's hush seems to surround us as I finish. When the plan is laid out like this, it's easy to see all the holes. It's not watertight, shipshape, the way I'd like it to be. There are so many uncertain factors. So many ways it could go wrong.

Naomi's weather-worn, pain-drawn face is almost unreadable. Tam's energy radiates off him as he crosses his arms and stares at the map. Eira tilts her head, thinking, her neat, agile mind on the move. Brig leans back and stares into the forest, considering something, his alert, capable strength present in every move.

I hope I can trust them.

I put my boot in the middle of Eira's map, covering some of the raiders' houses, printing the tread of my sole in the heart of their village.

"Let's get started."

CHAPTER 22

THE LANTERNS IN THE TREES FLICKER OUT.

Except for one.

The night slips on. And on, and the light remains.

It's in the tree house to the left of the centermost one, where we intended to begin. We've brought all our kindling near the village, and no one has noticed us yet. We crouch together over sticks and branches and twigs, our giant unlit bank of fire.

"Do you think they know we're coming?" Eira whispers.

I thought we might wear out and fade as the night wore away. Instead, I feel a kind of charge growing in the air between us. I don't know what it is. Purpose? Fear? I can't see the others' faces well in the dim wash of starlight and moonlight, but it's as if all of our veins have turned to gold, conducting electricity, sparking and slipping to and through one another.

As if, for now, we're all connected.

"If the light doesn't go out soon," I say, "we'll change the plan. We'll start with the trees nearest us, and work our way into the middle."

The sky is night-black. It will soon lighten to deepest blue. We are at the edge of morning. We are where the night turns.

"Should we try tomorrow?" Tam asks. His tone is fearful, hopeful.

"No," I say. The stars are not perfectly aligned for us, but they may never be. They could get the armor running again at any time. And some things *are* in our favor. There's no rain. We've managed to bring all the kindling here without being caught. We are close. So close.

And two years ago I made a promise.

"All right," I say, and I feel them all tense. "*Now.*"

Brig and Tam and Eira and I run low, racing to the tree house nearest us, carrying our shirts and Tam's bag full of kindling. Branches flex and snap against my bare shoulders as we push through.

"*Now,*" I whisper again, once we're at the base of the first looming tree, and we ease our kindling to the ground. Our hands scurry over the bits of wood, stacking as fast as we can. What seemed like so much now looks paltry against the solid mass of the tree trunk.

We'll have to change the plan again.

"Double up on the kindling for each tree," I whisper to the others. We are a breath away from one another, their eyes locked on mine. Before I can explain—*better that we get half of them burning well than spread it out too thin*—they make sounds of agreement.

They are with me.

"Tell Naomi she can start as soon as we finish the first pile," I say to Brig. Tam, Eira, and I sprint, soft-footed, back to the piles of kindling to gather more. Brig joins us moments later. We dart through the trees and lay the tinder at their feet.

We rubbed dirt into our undershirts to keep them from flashing too bright against the dark trees and night, but I still catch glimpses of the whites of the others' eyes, teeth, as we steal back and forth.

The scent of the kerosene that Naomi pours out surges through the air as the rest of us work. I breathe the fragrance in deep—that chemical, flammable, *familiar* tang.

It reminds me of my ship.

Can the raiders smell it? In their dreams, do they wonder what it is? Do they smell the first ship burning? Will they remember why they deserve this?

The five of us gather breathless in the forest. There is no kindling left, no kerosene except the small amount left in the cookstove, which I strapped to my back with my belt. I don't trust anyone else to set the fires.

"It's time," I say. The sky has lightened a degree or two while we've been working and now I can make out the sheen of dirt and sweat on my crew. Naomi's bandage. Eira's deft, delicate fingers. Tam's mouth, with the wry quirk at the corner that never entirely goes away. The cut on Brig's nose from jumping off the dredge. The scratches from the past days, and from this night. The forest scored our skin with lines from branches and trees. It etched and scribbled on us in a language we don't understand.

None of us are caught.

Yet.

"I'll help you," Brig says.

"No," I say. "I'll do it alone."

"We'll wait here for you until you're done," says Naomi. Tam turns away, as if he can't bear the sight of me because of what I'm about to do, and Eira puts her hand on his arm.

"No," I say. "This way you'll have a head start. *Go.* I'll catch up to you."

A hesitation. Then Tam moves into the brush, without a backward glance or a goodbye. I feel the current between all of us falter, fall. Naomi nods to me and follows him, and after a quick look at Brig, Eira is gone, too.

"Get out of here," I say to Brig. "Keep everyone with you if you can. We don't know what the fire will do. I'll find you all as soon as possible."

I don't wait to watch him go.

Quick-down, low to the ground. At the bottom of the tree, ready to warm my cold hands and weary heart with the lighting of this fire, I lean in. Flick the lighter on the stove. It flutters to life, a blue-orange flare, a moth, a heartbeat. I hold it near the kindling.

The flame catches.

No time to watch it go up. On to the next tree.

And the next.

Fires crackle as they drink in the kerosene and consume the kindling. My breathing sounds loud and feral to my ears as I run to the next tree. Don't the raiders hear me? Can't they feel, smell, taste me coming?

No one, nothing, stirs in the houses.

My heart sinks. What if they're empty? What if the raiders managed to disappear into thin air somehow? What if they abandoned their village?

I'm not careful enough setting the fifth fire and flames lick my fingers. I hiss in my breath and plunge my hand into the dirt next to me to put out the flame. *Not good.* I can tell.

Nothing to be done about it now. *Ignore the pain. Keep going.*

My burned hand shakes as I light the sixth flame. As it takes, it illuminates my blistered skin and my stomach turns. My skin is puckered and hot, the top layers peeling back raw. I shouldn't have put out the fire with dirt. Now tiny grains of it are working into the wound.

Tam was right. Burning would be a horrible way to die. I'm almost silly with pain, but there are more trees to go.

A shriek sings through the night.

"Fire!" someone calls out from up high in one of the trees. "*FIRE!*" A woman's voice, terrified. Someone else calls back.

They *are* here. In the houses, in the trees.

In the smoky dark, my hand still aching, lights beginning to bloom above me, I realize: *I don't want to be here for this.*

When they die and scream. I have never been there for it. Not when the dredge cut them.

I wasn't even there when Call died.

There are two more fires to start.

Can they see me in the dark? A demon crouched against the blue white orange of the blaze?

The fires take the trees like lovers. Lick, flicker, touch and taste, and then—

A roar of consummation.

I've reached the last tree. I hiss my breath in, steel myself against the pain.

In the moment before I touch the stove to the kindling, I make another mistake. A movement above me catches my eye, and I look up.

A silhouette against the lamplight. Someone lowering a ladder.

They're trying to escape, of course. I should set the tree on fire. But. Something about the shape of this shadow.

I set down the stove, put my good hand on the ladder.

Call?

The figure, outlined against the canvas walls. Coming closer.

It could be true.

What if he survived? What if I only thought he was dead? What if the raiders took him with them?

You know what you saw, Poe. You know you saw me dead.

Don't tell me you're dead, Call. Don't tell me what I saw.

The idea inside me is an enormous, beating bird, a huge, flopping fin-over-fin fish. It is not even part of me but it's living in me. How long has it been here? This thought? This open-mouthed, hungry hope?

Ever since the first night when I saw the raiders' houses, I've been drawn to them in spite of myself, like a moth to the flame. Maybe this is why.

I'm coming, Call.

Up the ladder, into the tree. I leave some of my skin on the rungs when I forget and use my injured hand. The ladder creaks slightly under my weight.

A figure darkens the doorway. Come to meet me. My lips open, my eyes close.

Call. I have missed you. More than I can say. Or breathe. Or live.

Do you know how it has been to exist without you?

I open my eyes.

CHAPTER 23

THE LAST THING I NOTICE before the figure takes my hand:

My crew. I glance over my shoulder and see their eyes reflected in the underbrush, like animals. Watching me.

They came back.

I told them not to but they did.

I'm sorry, I want to say. I looked for the traitor in all of them. Brig. Naomi. Eira. Tam.

I should have known it was me.

CHAPTER 24

HE REACHES FOR MY HAND.

When I see him up close, I know my mistake.

Not Call.

Tall, spare, dark eyes and hair, older than Call will ever be. It's the man who was in charge the night they took the first dredge. The man who gave me the message to take back to the Outpost: *This is the last time we leave anyone alive.*

I saw his shadow, and I turned him into Call. I thought of that night, of a ship burning bright, and I betrayed myself. I told myself Call might be alive when I knew he was dead.

The raider grabs my burned hand to pull me up into the tree house, and the pain of it, the nerves on fire and seeing the face of the person who killed Call . . .

Not Call.

The light goes out.

.   .   .

When I wake, the raider is sitting across from me. My hands and feet are tied. It takes me a moment to focus, to look around into the shadows and adjust my eyes, but when I realize where I am, I almost laugh.

The captain's cabin.

I'm back on the ship.

Even though there's a bed and a chair in the cabin, they've got me propped up against the wall, rivets and seams poking against the knobs of my spine.

Still, they haven't killed me outright. And someone has dressed my wound. My hand is wrapped in gauze and the skin around it is clean. The rest of me—what I can see, anyway—is filthy, still dressed in my undershirt and uniform trousers and boots.

"How many died?" I ask.

The raider has weather-beaten skin, dirt under his fingernails. He holds Brig's knife, and Tam's knife, in his hands.

I should have given one to Brig.

Did they capture him? And the others?

And then I notice that my shirt pocket is missing the familiar weight of Call's ruler. *No.* Did it fall out when I was setting the trees on fire? When I climbed the ladder?

Did it burn?

I want to ask the raider if he took it, but I can't, not without giving away how much it means to me. Instead, I repeat my earlier question, making it more specific.

"How many *raiders* died?" I shift my legs, bringing my knees up in front of me, trying not to panic at the loss of the ruler and the way they've trussed me up.

"We're not called raiders," he says. "We're drifters." He puts both knives in his shirt pocket. *Is the ruler in there, too?* Then he stands and stretches his arms up to touch the low ceiling. It's torture. I wish I could do the same.

"And you're the leader." It must be him. He's the one that led them the night Call died; he's the one occupying the captain's cabin—*my cabin*—now.

"Now I lead your crew, too," he says. "They've agreed to help us in exchange for their lives." He sits back down on the chair, tapping his fingers on his knee. "Poe Blythe. Former captain of this ship. The architect of its armor. You're going to help us repair it." He indicates my hand. "We bandaged your burn. It's bad, but you should still be able to work."

Does he expect me to be grateful? I study him closely. He has plenty of gray mixed in with the dark of his hair. He's clean-shaven. His eyes are inscrutable, and his mouth gives nothing away.

"I'm not going to help you fix the ship," I say. And then, I ask my question again. I won't stop until he answers. "*How many raiders died?*"

"My name is Porter," he says. "Don't you want to know how many of your crew are left before you ask how many of mine are dead?"

"I know you killed at least one," I say. "The body was in the river."

"He tried to escape through the tailings stacker." Porter hitches the chair closer to me. His eyes are unafraid, calm,

158

though one of his legs bounces up and down, burning nervous energy.

"Without his boots?"

Porter shrugs. "He wasn't as lucky as your friend Tam."

"Tam's not my friend," I say. I'll cover for the others as long as I can. It's better if Porter thinks I'm working alone.

But from the raise of his eyebrows, I don't think he's buying it. "Whether he is or not, we'll find him. We'll find all of them." Porter pushes back the chair and stands up again. The whole time I've been awake, he's been in perpetual motion. It's killing me that I'm not.

"None of them matter to me," I say. I sniff the close air in the cabin, trying to smell what Porter won't tell me. Do I smell charring, burning, death on his clothes?

There are familiar scents. Singed cloth, kerosene, something else I can't quite describe, though I recognize it. Something cold.

Porter flicks a glance to me and then one at the door. He reminds me of a bird, watching, eyes on everything and wings at the ready. "If you fix the armor, I'll know you're really Poe Blythe."

I almost laugh. What kind of game is this? He wants me to fix the armor to earn my own name? And why would anyone want to be me? "Everyone knows I'm Poe Blythe." I think of how I must look—knotted braids, filthy clothes, angry, dirty face. "You said it yourself. My crew told you."

"The whole crew knows the Admiral *said* you're Poe Blythe," he says. "They didn't know you before."

"Naomi did," I say. "The second mate. We were together on the other voyage."

Porter shrugs. "I can't ask her. We haven't found her yet."

Unease bubbles up in me. Is this a good sign? That they didn't capture her in the woods? Or is it bad? She was sick. I hope the others have stayed with her.

"*You* know," I say. "You saw me on the ship. Two years ago."

There. This is the first time I've said it. Admitted that we've seen each other before. That I know him and what he's capable of.

Porter doesn't blink. "Doesn't mean that you're the same person who built the armor." He takes hold of my upper arm, leans in. "For all I know, Poe Blythe is a myth."

The myth is true, I want to say. *Because of you. You killed Call.*

"The sooner you cooperate, the easier it will be," Porter says. "You won't eat or drink until you work." He lets go of my arm and opens the door. "I'll be back soon."

"How many?" I ask, as he leaves me behind. "How many died in the fire?"

He disappears without answering.

But I think I can make a rough estimate.

For him: too many. For me: not enough.

CHAPTER 25

THE NEXT PERSON TO COME IN is a young woman who looks a few years older than me, with long red hair and a rifle strapped to her back. As soon as she enters, I know she's angry.

She sits down in the chair and brings her face close to mine. As if to show she's not afraid. And she isn't—I can't find any trace of fear on her face or in her movements. But she hates me and wants me to know it.

She doesn't even wait for me to speak first.

"They're leaving your friends out there," she says.

Friends. Everyone keeps using that word.

I wonder if anyone would use it for me.

"They can either die or come back to the ship," she says. "But we won't waste any resources looking for them."

"You tried that earlier," I say. "And it didn't work. You realized you needed me to fix the armor."

"Maybe." She raises her eyebrows. "Or maybe you walked right into our trap when you tried to set your little fires." She makes me sound pathetic. I don't try to sit up straighter. That would be too obvious a sign that she's getting to me. But I level my gaze at her.

"Or it could be," she says, "that they turned you in. Maybe they betrayed you. They might be in the cafeteria right now, toasting your capture. You don't know if *anything* I'm telling you is true."

She has an accent I can't place; one that doesn't sound quite like the other raiders. When she leans back and crosses her feet at the ankles, I notice that her boots are different, too—the design is sleeker than any I've seen, and the leather is good quality. They're made for use, though—they are scuffed and worn. I'd like to try them on.

"The ship's taking on plenty of gold," she says. "Mining system's working fine."

The ship.

I try to stay expressionless, but something in my face seems to let her know that her thrust has struck home. She smiles at me, a smile that's less an expression of emotion than a calculated twist of her lips.

"What's *your* name?" I ask.

"I'm not going to answer that." She rolls up her sleeves, cuffing them neatly. Is she planning to hit me? Her forearms are scarred. She's been burned, too, but a while ago. Though the injuries have healed, the scars make some of her skin look mapped. I envy every easy movement, and the relative cleanliness of her blue button-down shirt, her shining hair. "I've heard all the rumors about you. The story is that we killed

someone you loved on a voyage two years ago, and you decided to hunt us down."

Don't you dare speak about Call.

I turn away but she moves so she can keep her face in
mine. "Settlers *always* take," she says. The rifle on her back
points up to the ceiling like a finger gesturing in accusation or
obscenity. "That's what you do."

"You hadn't even figured out how to mine the gold for
yourselves," I say. "It was fair game."

"You think all you've taken from us is gold?" She settles
back, but every muscle is tense now, all pretense of relaxation
gone. "I want you to fix this ship, *Poe*," she says.

Hearing my name in her mouth makes me want to cringe,
but I don't let myself. "Too bad it's not up to you, *Lily*," I say.

"That's not my name."

"You wouldn't tell me what it was," I say. "So I'm naming
you after my ship."

"It's ours now," Lily says. "And you *are* going to fix the
armor. And then I'm going to feed you to the dredge and let it
chew you up."

I push myself away from the wall so that I'm sitting up
straighter. "*That's* specific."

"I've been planning it for a while," Lily says. She reaches
for my hands. I try to snatch them away from her, but the sudden movement peels the bandage from my skin and I hiss without meaning to. So I don't pull away again when she begins
to untie them, her fingers confident and quick. "We're going
down to the mining deck so you can get to work on fixing that

panel," she says. "If you try to escape, I'll step on your burned hand. Kick you in the ribs. Whatever I have to do."

I don't doubt that she would. Because I think I know what happened. Why she hates me in such a precise way.

"My armor killed someone you loved." And then, because I've lived it too, I amend that last part. "Someone you *love*."

Lily's lips are a thin line. Her eyes blaze into me.

"So who was it?" I ask. "Father? Mother? Sister? Friend? Lover?"

In a swift motion, Lily closes in on me, narrowing the small distance between us so I see her eyes, her freckles, the twist of her mouth and the glint of her teeth. In spite of myself, I blink.

"Fix it," she says.

As tempting as it is, as recently as I myself made the mistake of hoping that the impossible might be true—when I thought I saw Call, there and alive and waiting for me—it's important to remember what things are.

The dead are the dead.

Our eyes meet.

"You know I can't," I say.

CHAPTER 26

DOWN WE GO, into the belly of the dredge.

As we descend the stairwell to the mining deck, Lily and I are so close that I can hear her breathing behind me. For a minute I think about stopping in my tracks, bringing my head back to knock into her chin, catching her off guard and taking her down. She reads my mind, and I feel her press the rifle into my spine. "Keep moving," she says.

We go through the open door at the bottom of the stairs, and I breathe in the motor and dirt smells of the mining deck. Two of my machinists and an electrician look up, and their faces go slack and shocked at the sight of me. They're working on the disemboweled control panel, the one I shot, and they're surrounded by wiring, capacitors, and solenoids. I wonder if they've used every single spare part we brought on board to try and fix the mess I made.

"Hello, Officer Wray, Officer Lopez, Officer Jones," I say, and Officer Jones raises his hand, the one that's not coiled in a fistful of red wire, to salute. Then he realizes what he's doing and drops his arm down to his side, darting a nervous glance at Porter, who's standing next to him. "Keep up the good work," I say as we pass by, as if I'm the captain and I never left and they're not working for Porter now. As if they're not undoing everything I've done.

They want to survive. I understand that. But it's going to make everything harder.

"Up here," Porter says. He motions for Lily and me to follow him up the metal stairs to the platform, the one where Brig and I stood before the raiders took the ship. I notice enormous canvas sacks and burlap bags and crew kit packs all stuffed and slumped against the railings, on top of the platform, and down on the floor of the mining deck. They're *everywhere*. Are they bodies? I nudge one with my foot. It's full of hard, lumpy, smaller shapes.

Gold. Have they really taken on so much in so short a time?

"It's exactly what you think it is," Porter says. At the top of the platform, he and Lily position me so I'm looking out over the main part of the deck instead of in the direction of the stacker. I have a bird's-eye view of the work they're doing and all the gold they've taken on. The storage bins are full. They've even taken the mining buckets off the elevator and filled them with gold. Sacks are everywhere. Several of the raiders' light little boats are down on the floor of the mining deck, and they're also filled with bags of gold.

As I watch, I notice that some of the crew is dumping gold

out of one of the mining buckets. It takes four men to do the job. The gold tumbles onto the floor. The men haul the bucket over to the opening where the buckets usually enter the ship and, to my shock, shove the empty container into the river.

They're jettisoning it.

"What the *hell* do you think you're doing?" I yell before I even realize it.

A flash of a face—someone on the floor looks up and spares me a glance, but not for long.

The workers tip over the second bucket.

"What are you *thinking*?" I ask Porter. Why would they dump the mining buckets overboard? That means they can't use them again. They've taken on about as much gold as they can carry, but wouldn't they want to keep the equipment intact for another voyage?

Think, Poe.

If they're throwing out the equipment, they're not planning on making *another voyage.*

This is it, for them. This dredge voyage will be their first and their last. They don't need the buckets anymore. They're full up with gold.

Why do *they* want gold? Is it for the reasons I thought of earlier, all the uses they might have for it? Or do they need it as currency? Do they owe someone something?

And why dump out the bins *now*? They could just store the gold in them until we get to wherever it is the raiders are going.

The answer comes to me quickly. Because the bins are heavy. *Very* heavy. They want to keep the gold, but lose some of the weight.

They have their precious cargo, but they need to speed things up. They're worried about something. Or someone.

"You want to go faster," I say. "And you're too heavy."

"The only people left on board are the ones we need to run the ship." Porter rests his elbows on the platform railing, but his gaze darts across the floor, back toward the tailings stacker. There are dark shadows under his eyes. "I've sent everyone else on ahead of us. When we arrive at our destination, we'll give the rest of your crew a choice about whether they want to stay with us, or die."

I laugh, hard and cold. "So now you give people a choice before you kill them?"

"It's more humane than what you've done," Porter says.

I take an involuntary step in his direction, ready to rush, but the handcuffs keep me locked. They slide back onto the hurt part of my hand, and I feel one of the blisters scrape and seep. "You shoot people in the back," I say. "We made the armor *after* you killed first."

"I'm not talking about what's happened on the river and the dredges," Porter says.

"That's too bad," I say, "because I *am*." Pain and anger literally make me see red in that moment. Blood and burning and everything the raiders have done.

"Listen for a minute." Porter's gone very still, and for the first time I can see straight into his eyes. They're brown like mine and just as angry. "You only know what the Admiral's told you," he says. "You don't know our side."

"I know *my* side," I say. "I didn't need the Admiral to tell me anything about you. I saw it for myself."

My whole body is burning. I'm ready to break. I want out of this skin. I want out of my own hot, blistering mind.

"He was about to sound the alarm," Porter says. "We had no choice."

"That's a *lie*," I say. "You could have shot him in the leg. Taken him down without killing him."

"What do you want us to do?" Lily asks. "*Fix* it?" She's echoing our conversation in the captain's quarters back to me. "You know we can't."

I was right then. She's right now.

There's no fixing this.

The dead are the dead.

"Don't you want to know what the settlers did?" Lily asks. "That's worse than shooting someone in the back?"

I don't. I look down at the crew working on the mining deck, the heavy bags of gold, anywhere but at these people who want to tell me that anything we've done is as bad as killing Call.

"Have you noticed that we don't have any children?" Porter asks.

Brig's face flashes in front of me, his careful, considering expression. He noticed.

"We hide them," Porter says. "Far away from here. Do you know why?"

Of course I don't. If I could move my hands I'd cover my ears. I have enough to bear without the raiders giving me more.

"Your Admiral took them," Lily says. "For years, *you* were raiding. You took our children and put them in your orphanages."

Orphanages. My body goes rigid. *My bed. The heavy doors. The other children. The loneliness.* So lonely, until Call.

"And you call *us* raiders." Porter's voice is soft and furious.

"That's not true," I say. "I grew up in an orphanage. And I remember my mother. I remember being raised in the Outpost before she died."

"Oh, *you're* Outpost through and through," Lily says, her voice poison. "But that doesn't mean everyone in those orphanages is." She points to a man down on the deck, who has a rifle trained on our machinists while they work. "That's Mac. The settlers took his daughter. She was four. She'd be eight now." Lily glares at me. "I *saw* it happen."

"The Admiral wanted more workers," Porter says. "He convinced his Quorum that it was a humanitarian effort. He pointed out that if the Outpost took our children, they'd have access to medicine and a trade education. They could be raised to supplement and support the society of the Outpost." Porter sighs, a long exhalation of anger and sadness. "He said it was a better life for the children than staying out here with us."

"That's when we started moving," Lily says, "but they kept finding us."

I take a step backward, stumbling over a sack of gold. Neither of them moves to catch me but I right myself before I fall. "I knew plenty of other kids in the orphanage where I lived," I say. "None of them ever said they'd been stolen."

"The settlers take them when they're very young," Porter says. "They give the children a medicine to confuse them, and they're told that their parents are dead. Later, memory will come back. Most children will remember their families. With time, they might even recollect the beginning of the raid. But they can't remember exactly how they got where they are now. They can't remember the end."

They can't remember the end.

No. This can't be true. Can it?

"Finish it for me," Call said.

Call. Is that why I see you everywhere out here?

Was this your beginning?

CHAPTER 27

I WOULD REALLY LIKE A DRINK.

Some food.

Medicine.

"It's right here," Lily says. "All of it."

We're back in the captain's quarters. My quarters. I suppose they're keeping me here because it's small and easy to secure. And if I'm locked up alone I can't persuade any of my remaining crew to help me. I don't think they would. But Porter doesn't know that.

My hand hurts so much that I keep forgetting to breathe, as if holding my breath could halt the pain. *In and out, Poe.*

In the circle of light from the lamp, I watch Lily. She's sitting on a chair. I'm on the floor again, back against the wall. On the desk is a glass of water and a piece of the dry flat bread we call tack, the kind that lasts well through a long trip. Next to the bread is the pack of medicine from my bag, the same pills we were all issued when we came on board. Antibiotics. Something for pain.

There's also a pencil on the desk and a copy of the schematics of the armor.

My armor.

My ship.

"You can eat whenever you're ready," Lily says. "You can have the medicine. All you have to do is fix your armor." She slides the schematics closer to me.

They'd have gotten these from the bridge. Who's up there steering the ship now?

And the motor. I can hear it. The ship is too heavy with all this gold. Off-loading the mining buckets didn't help enough. The motor doesn't sound as smooth as it should. There's a hint of something labored in the pitch; a weariness pervades the tune of the dredge.

My ship is struggling without me.

I swallow. My throat is dry. My stomach rumbles. My hand throbs. The infection is spreading. I can feel it in my body, sinewing its way from my hand to my limbs, my mind, my heart.

I don't want Lily to see me fall asleep, see me lose consciousness, but I'm barely hanging on.

I am a parched mouth, an empty belly, a seething, burning hand.

That's all.

"Water, food, medicine," Lily says. "Right here. All you have to do is help us fix your ship."

I don't know what I'm doing. I'm no leader.

I've tried and tried and it never ends.

I'm so tired, in the way I was right after the dredge came back from its first armored voyage, when the Admiral sent me word that it had worked perfectly. I went back to my apartment and slept for days.

I don't think I can do this anymore.

Call.

I don't.

I grind my back into the rivets on the wall in an attempt to stay awake. If I fall asleep . . . if I let myself go . . . Call will die too. Because I'm the one who remembers him best. I'm the one who loved him most.

Will I always be in love with him?

Am I doomed to live forever like this, always wanting, physically aching, for someone it is impossible to have?

Call's not here. I don't even have his ruler anymore. Every trace of him is gone.

I rest the back of my head against the wall.

I don't have love.

And there's a bigger problem.

In this moment, here in the ship I've lost, I don't even have hate.

"I know what you're trying to do," Lily says, her voice furious. For a minute I think she's going to spit on me, scream at me, and I welcome it.

"You're going to die to spite us," she says.

I shrug. It's one of the movements I can actually make.

Lily's lips come together in a line of anger. I smile. My eyes close.

On Call's last night, we were up on the deck looking for stars. But the first night on the dredge, we were down in its belly on duty, listening to the ship's grating, grinding sound.

"I don't mind having night shift," I told Call. My voice was already going hoarse with trying to speak over the noise. "I wouldn't have been able to sleep anyway."

"Me either." There was a streak of grease across his cheek. His blue eyes were the deepest, most vivid thing in the room.

My whole body vibrated with the pulse of the dredge. It reverberated through my feet; my hair was electric, crackling out of its braids. Call grinned at me and reached up his hand to touch the ends of it. We'd climbed up to the platform on the mining deck and stood looking at the scrawled codes for the bell rings and the messages that others had written there, long before the Outpost, when the dredge belonged to a different world.

TC is a damn fool, someone had written. *RJ + EL,* someone else had scratched.

"We're going to get kicked off the ship," I said in Call's ear, as his hands wrapped around me, his palms pressed into the small of my back. My heart pounded against his and I slid one finger under the neck of his shirt, across his collarbone. "And it's only the first night."

"That would be bad," he agreed, waiting, his lips a breath from mine. "Should we stop?"

The ship was so loud I could hardly hear him, but I knew the words he was saying. I saw them on his lips and in his eyes.

"No," I said.

No.

I wake up with that word in my mind, and my body on fire.

Fever. From the dream? From my injury? Or because I'm ready to do what I have to do?

I glance over at the desk. The food, water, and medicine are gone. The schematics are still there.

There they are. The sounds that woke me. Something on the other side of the door. Hints of movements made, of words softly spoken.

I get to my feet by propping myself against the wall and sliding up.

Who's coming in?

I crouch low, in the corner where the door will open. There's almost no room to move in here. I'll have to make it count.

The door opens, quiet. Someone doesn't want to wake me.

Rich, appetizing scents float in from the hallway.

I go weak in the knees. *Food.* It's something warm. Healthy. Fresh. Garlic. Meat. Sage?

And then, through the door.

Not Lily.

Not Porter.

Tam.

My thoughts go racing, flying.

He's in league with them.

They sent him to talk to me.

He brought me food.

We are inches apart. He has a rifle on his back and a tray full of food.

He's looking for me. He thinks I'll be on the bed or sitting against the wall.

In the split second it takes him to find me, I move, springing with all the strength I have.

In one motion, I bring my hands up, slamming my cuffs under the tray and sending everything flying. The food's hot, burning on me, burning on him, and he raises his hands to shield his eyes. I shove him against the bed, and he falls, and I pull the rifle from his back. It's not easy and I have to put one knee on him, use my weight to hold him down.

But then I've got it.

"*Poe,*" Tam says.

They wouldn't have sent him alone, so I turn for the door, where Lily is already pushing through, a rifle trained on me.

My aim is worthless with these handcuffs on. I don't even get her in the leg. But I hit the door near her and she jumps back.

A mistake. She hasn't lived in these close quarters as long as I have.

If she'd come in, I wouldn't have been able to get out. She could have blocked my exit.

But as it is, I'm through the door, her rifle pointed at me, and I'm facing her and moving backward down the corridor, shooting all along the way, a catastrophe of bad aim, a total waste of ammunition, and then—

I get lucky.

For once.

Tam comes out to help Lily and in that moment I shoot again and it hits. I can't tell who. Someone goes down, the other becomes tangled up with them and as for me—

I *run.*

There are only so many places you can hide on a ship.

But.

I was on another ship in another lifetime.

With Call.

And we knew all the secret places. Every one.

CHAPTER 28

IF I CAN GET UP THE STAIRS.

If I can get near the bridge.

If I can get to the closet next to the bridge.

If they've left the closet unlocked.

If. Over and over again.

Up the steps, the adrenaline rush carrying me fast, though I'm sweating way too much from one short skirmish and a couple of flights of stairs. The stairwell is empty. Didn't everyone hear the shots? Why didn't anyone come out of the other cabins in the hallway?

Too afraid?

No alarm sounds. Don't Lily and Tam know how to set it off? Do they not want to admit they've lost me?

I hear footsteps on the stairs behind. Just one person. Was my hit good enough to incapacitate one of them?

Even if it wasn't, they'll have had to divide. Lily or Tam coming up, the other one going down, trying to see if I've run to the top of the ship or down to the mining deck. They'll want to seal off the escape routes right away.

Last time I jumped from the deck. Not tonight. I leave the stairway a floor early and head for the captain's bridge.

There's a closet there, a deep, narrow one with a few odds and ends stored inside. Not everyone knows about it, because when the door to the bridge is open—which it often is, so whoever is steering can better hear how the ship is sounding below—the closet entrance is hard to see.

I slow down as I come to the bridge. The door *is* open. I catch one second, one quick glimpse of the bridge, all lit up, the night dark beyond its window, and a figure standing inside. Porter, at the helm. I think he's alone, but then a shadow moves near him, out of a corner.

Is that Brig?

Did they betray me, like Lily said? Are they all on board already?

Don't get distracted.

My breathing is loud and ragged, but I think my ship will cover the sound. I edge the bridge door back an inch. Like most of the others on the ship, it's a sliding door to save space. I push it another inch.

Do I hear someone coming down the hall?

There's the closet. If I can edge the bridge door a little farther . . .

Footsteps, closer.

I have to take the risk.

I slide the bridge door back, fast, grab hold of the handle to the closet door. It's unlocked. I almost sob with relief.

I slide it open just enough to slip inside.

Please don't see me.

Trapped. Entombed. Cocooned and cut down.

The closet is not empty, and I trip over something.

My hands fly up to shield my fall and catch on cloth, thick and clinging to my face, keeping me from pushing any farther inside. My knees hit hard, bulky bundles resting on the floor.

I reach back blind with my foot, kicking wildly, until I feel the door, and then I shove it shut. A metallic ricochet, a *clang* and a *click*. It's closed.

I'm inside.

I can't catch my breath. A pencil-thin rectangle of light seeps around the door frame. At last I pull my hands away from the cloth, push myself up from the thing on which I'm kneeling.

I put my burned hand to my chest in an attempt to calm my racing heart.

It's a trick I taught Call, one night after a bad dream.

"My heart won't stop pounding," he said.

"Remind it where it is," I said, and I put his hand over his heart. "Remind yourself who you are."

He left his hand there and I kept mine there too. I could feel the beat. *Call. Call. Call.* I said it for him.

Call. Call. Call.

I nudge the bundle on the floor with my foot. As soon as I do, relief and realization immerse me. *It's gold.* Of course. They've stored more bags here. But what about the cloth that seems to be hanging from the ceiling, floating, reaching out to enshroud me?

I touch the edges of it with my good hand. Feel along it, and up, up, up. It's attached to something, but part of it has come loose. My hand meets a smooth surface, but it's not metal. Not as cold.

A curve of wood.

A boat? And then I realize. The raiders have stored some of their gliders here.

A voice, close to the door. "Get up to the deck," someone calls out. The light around the doorway flickers as people hurry past.

They think I jumped again.

But I'm not going to make the same mistake twice.

This time, I'm not leaving my ship.

CHAPTER 29

MY MIND IS A MIX of galloping, haphazard thoughts, my body flush with fever and fear. *Focus.* What happens next? I have to stay ahead of the raiders, but I'm not sure of their strategy. Why didn't they set off the alarm when I escaped? Don't they want everyone to know I'm on the loose, to be out looking for me?

No. They don't.

The raiders have misplayed their hand by leaving so many settlers on board to run the ship and by keeping only enough of their own to make sure we stay in line. They can't have my crew search for me—what if they help me instead of turning me in? And, more elementary than that, the raiders need the crew to stay at their positions and keep the dredge going.

I hear it working, the motor still toiling on. Doesn't everyone hear what I do? The ship is in trouble.

Is it real—something they can't fix, like the armor—or contrived?

Is *this* how they intend to smoke me out?

. . .

I can't stay in one place for long or they'll find me. But my body aches for rest.

Where should I go next? The mining deck two levels below, the top deck, or somewhere else?

If I go down one level, to the ship's cafeteria and the cabins, there are a few possible places to hide. Would any of the crew conceal me in their cabin? I know where each person was assigned to sleep before, but the raiders have likely moved everyone around.

I have Tam's rifle. But I also have these handcuffs. If I can get to the kitchen, there's got to be a fork or *something* I can use to pry them open. And Tam said they had plenty of knives in the kitchen.

Tam.

What if I have to kill Tam?

Could I do it?

I hear a grind, a strange catch in the motor. It lasts only a moment. But I've never heard the ship speak that way before and it decides me.

I've got to get to the mining deck.

I slide open the closet door, so, so slow.

I peek out. No one in the hall. I slip through, slide the door shut, every movement gratingly, achingly deliberate so that the motions don't draw the attention of the people on the bridge. Who's in there now? Is Porter still steering my ship, or has he gone to look for me?

Through the doorway I hear the voice of someone I don't know. I freeze. "They think she jumped from the deck. But it's dark. We haven't been able to see her in the water."

"Someone told me she was injured." Another unfamiliar raider's voice.

"She hasn't had food or water since they brought her on board." The first voice.

"And she got burned when she set fire to the trees. She was in bad shape. If she jumped again, she might not have survived this time."

"Let's hope."

Good. You keep thinking that. You keep thinking I'm down in the dark river instead of up here, on board the dredge.

I was the ship's captain.

Now I'm its ghost.

Down, down, down, my boots as soft on the metal as I can make them. I clear the first level and am on my way to the mining deck when my vision brightens, flashes at the edges, goes dark in spots. I grip the banister. *No.*

Don't pass out here.

The stairwell is the most dangerous place for me. It would be easy to get caught coming or going. And I need to reach the mining deck and try to get an idea of what's happening with the motor.

This much closer, I can hear it better. I hadn't imagined the discord in its timbre, the hum of something wrong. I've got to figure out what it is. We can't lose the ship.

I slip on a step and fall hard, grabbing at the banister with my handcuffed, awkward hands. My head snaps back, hits a step with a dull thud. Through the pain, all I can think is, *How much noise did I make?* The rifle on my back is like an external backbone, painfully bruising against the knobs of my real spine.

I'm a wreck. I need to go eat something and get these handcuffs off before I try anything.

I crawl as fast as I can up the few stairs back to the landing and glance down the hallway.

Nothing. No one.

Go.

I stumble into the cafeteria, use the edges of a table near me to brace myself. I'm making too much noise, but the ship's agony still covers my own.

The raiders are gambling with the dredge. They're hazarding that it will hold up long enough to get them where they need to go. But they're greedy. This is too much gold and weight. They're running the dredge into the ground.

I edge into the galley kitchen, Tam's domain. A single lantern is lit—safety protocol. The raiders trust Tam, that's for sure. He's working for them: another certainty I can't ignore.

Has he been a traitor this entire time?

In the forest, he was helping me. Us. I thought. He voted to go along with setting the village on fire. But did he warn the raiders? And if he *is* in league with them, why didn't he turn us in as soon as he found us in the forest?

Think about that later.

I open each cupboard and peer inside. There are enormous containers of water stored at one end of the kitchen. I don't remember where the cups are and I'm too thirsty and hurried to look carefully, but the stove has pots and pans stored underneath. I pull one out and fill it from a spigot on the nearest container. When I've finished, I wipe off the pot with the edge of my shirt and put it back.

A cabinet with flour, sugar, spices. Another with tack and other staples inside. The cold-storage bins are picked over, with an apple or two rattling around inside.

They're running out of food. We had enough to last us for the return, but the raiders never planned to journey back to the Outpost, so they've been using it up. And, of course, there are more people on the ship now.

I take a piece of tack and chew it carefully, trying not to leave any crumbs.

Once my hunger pains are appeased, I pull at the kitchen drawers until I find a fork. Jimmying the handcuffs requires thought and precise movements, neither of which is my strong suit right now. I accidentally bump my burned hand, and the pain sends a shrill scream ringing through every nerve in my arm. I bite down so hard on my lip that I taste blood. My heart races, judders.

Get control.

I put my good hand on my chest. *Remind your heart where it is. Inside, safe. Remind yourself who you are.*

Poe. Poe. Poe.

Bearing down against the pain, barely breathing, I focus on putting the tines of the fork into the keyhole of the hand-cuff. My wrists and fingers twist awkwardly, agonizingly. *You can do this.* I press, and the cuffs spring open.

Tears of relief and pain leap to my eyes. I pull off the cuffs and stuff them underneath the refuse in the compost bin.

What about medicine? There should be a first-aid kit here, because of the risks in cooking—getting cut or burned. I should know where to find it. Once I became captain, I stud-ied everything about this ship. Where the fire extinguishers are. Where the spare parts are stowed. *Think.*

In the cabinet next to the stove, on the left.

There it is, screwed in just below the top shelf. I take down the kit and open it up. There are bandages, gauze, and, yes, several bottles of pills. Will they notice what I take? I double-dose myself with antibiotics and pain medication, shaking tablets into my pockets for later.

Though it's dangerous to stay in one place for long, I pause for a few moments, hoping the pain medication will kick in fast. I use my teeth to pull at the gauze and unwrap my wound. Raw-red and angry; yellow, seeping, infected. I pull out ointment and rub it on, then apply new gauze.

As I wrap a fresh bandage around my hand, I remember my mother doing this. After I fell. And scraped my knee on the uneven sidewalk near the shop where we had gone to buy tea—the woodsy, scrappy kind made from a plant common in the Outpost. The shop was on the second floor of an old brick building that had a mural on the side. I had tipped my head back to look up, up, up at the giant rendering of the Admiral, who was wearing his gold watch and holding his hat in his hand, looking down, down, down, smiling and showing his perfect teeth, his swept-back hair. So hale, so hearty.

If my mother was there to bind up my injured knee, then she was in the Outpost with me, too. Which means I wasn't stolen. I was not torn from my family. I am an orphan, plain and simple.

But. Call.

What else did he tell me about his mother? His family? His life before the orphanage?

He mostly told me dreams.

I saw a boy running, running.

There was a man standing by a tree late at night, holding a lantern.

My mother was walking in a field and stopped to pick three flowers.

I tell myself those dreams don't mean anything. A boy could be running anywhere. We have some trees in the Outpost. There aren't many fields there, it's true, but once Call picked a purple flower from a weed growing in the scrap yard and gave it to me.

My heart beats a panicked dance against my chest. *What other dreams did you have, Call?*

He's gone. And even if I ever get used to that, how do I get over *this*? The fact that I will never, *ever* know his whole story? I know the middle and the ending, but I can't know his beginning.

Unless.

What if Call *was* a raider? What if he *was* stolen as a child?

Could they tell me more about him?

The raiders killed him. I saw his body with my own eyes. But what if I can find out more about Call from the raiders, before I bring them down? Is that a reason to work with them? To play along for a while?

I hear the hidden anguish in the motor, the roughness and strain in the way the ship moves that's new, but fast becoming chronic. And I don't think the raiders have done this on purpose to get me to come out. The sounds are subtle, intimating trouble in ways that only a machinist would notice. For someone who knows the ship as well as I do, it's a call for help.

"*I'm coming,*" I whisper.

Light slivers through the doorway. Someone has entered the cafeteria. They might be on their way here to the kitchen.

There's no other way out.

I slide open the cold-storage bin, the one with the apples. It has no latch, so I should be able to get out when the time comes. I scramble inside and curl myself in the bin, reaching up to push the bin back into alignment with the underside of the shelving above me.

Footsteps. Boots. A single person.

Surely whoever it is came in for something other than that last apple. Maybe they'll leave the bin alone.

Noise. Clanging. Pots and pans.

Tam, making breakfast? But I don't think it's time. I think it's still night.

Someone's searching.

I don't know how long I can stay curled up like this, my body contorted, every muscle weary and taut.

As long as I have to.

Which doesn't turn out to be long at all.

Someone walks over and tugs at the bin. When they find out how heavy it is, they grunt in surprise and I feel them dragging it out, across the floor. I don't have time to run or shoot or fight; I don't even have time to unfold myself. So I do the one thing I can think of that might throw off the person who's found me. I smile up at them, though with the pain I'm in and the anger I feel, it might look like a scowl, a scrawl across my face.

"Tam," I say. "It's good to see you."

CHAPTER 30

MY TONE THROWS HIM OFF. I almost laugh. I attacked him and ran away and now he's found me tucked in a bin in his kitchen. I'm filthy, I smell like a forest fire, and I'm acting like everything is fine.

Well, Tam, I want to say. Nothing *really makes sense anymore. Would you like to tell me who you really are?*

He misses a beat before he responds. "It's good to see you, too."

"This is not your river," I say. "This is not your gold."

He doesn't pretend not to know what I'm talking about, not to recognize the words from the notes left in my cabin. *Good.* His face is harder than I remembered. He's tired. We're all tired and lit up, all at the same time, and fissures run through each of us, everyone on this ship. We are going to wind up and break down; fracture into new pieces and go under.

"You wrote the notes," I say.

"Yes."

"Help me out of here." I stretch out my good hand. "It's ridiculous to talk like this."

His eyes flicker over my face as he pulls me up. He can't quite hide his shock as he takes in my appearance. I must look even worse than the last time he saw me. I'm struck by how clean he is. His hair has been washed; his skin almost glows. He doesn't seem to be the one injured by my shot in the hallway near the captain's cabin. So was it Lily who went down?

"You left the notes in my room," I say. "It's been you all along." I move away from him so he can't try to take the rifle from my back. "But how did you shut off the mining system? You were with me when it went down. We were searching the rooms."

Tam's lips tighten, as if he's thinking about what he'll say and how to say it.

"And where did you get a copy of the key to my cabin?" I ask. "Who gave you the maps to write on? Eira?" I lean against the kitchen counter in an attempt to hide my fatigue. I don't think I'm fooling Tam. "Is she the other traitor?"

"Eira didn't give me anything," Tam says, his voice low. He looks so wholesome, so honorable. So believable. But he's an enemy, not a friend, no matter how familiar he seems to me after days spent on the ship and in the woods. Right now I think I have the advantage—I have a gun and he doesn't—but we're in his kitchen, and he knows where to get a knife. "I had it all before we left the Outpost."

"Then who gave it to you?" I ask.

"Someone who was on one of the earlier voyages."

"Naomi?"

"It wasn't Naomi," he says. "That's all I'm going to say."
An expression close to fury briefly crosses his face.

"And Brig?" I keep my voice conversational, while Tam's
brow is furrowed, his voice tight. We've changed roles. Now
he's the one ablaze, and I'm keeping cool, easy, light. "Was *he*
in league with you?"

"No," Tam says. "None of them were. When the drifters
caught you, we decided to come back to the ship."

Drifters. He doesn't bother using the Outpost's term. I
suspected him for so long; do I feel any betrayal with the confirmation that it's true?

"Are the others following the raiders' orders?" I ask.

"Naomi's trying to fix the armor."

Naomi? I try not to show my surprise. I thought she'd
hold out longer. "Brig?"

"He won't cooperate, so they've got him locked up for
now. He's the Admiral's boy, through and through." Tam's
mouth twists into an almost sneer. It looks wrong on him.

The Admiral's boy, through and through. I've wondered
that all along, too. But hearing Tam say it makes my heart
sink. Did Brig jump ship not because he trusted me as a leader,
but because the Admiral had ordered him to watch me? "And
Eira?"

"The drifters promised that if she joined with them, she
could work on something new," Tam says. "She was sick of

drawing the Admiral's maps and murals. She didn't like being his pawn."

"No one does," I say.

"You don't seem to mind." Tam's quiet now, his voice honest and sad.

"You're a fool if you think that's what I am." My façade slips, an edge of anger singes my voice. "The Admiral is my means to kill the raiders."

"Don't you want anything more?" Tam asks. And just like that, we're back to who we were before, me piqued and Tam earnest, trying to convince me.

"Don't *you* want anything more than to be the raiders' puppet?" I counter.

"That's not what I am." Tam wants me to understand. He wants us to fix this, to come out on the same side. Why?

"What kind of deal have you made?" I ask. "You gave the ship and the crew to the raiders. So you could have . . . what? More gold?"

"The drifters aren't going to kill anyone as long as we agree to join with them," Tam says.

I laugh, a rusty sound as wrong as the dredge. "You forget. I was on the voyage where they said they'd kill us all."

"They changed their minds."

"*Did* they?" I ask. "So none of our crew has died since the raiders took over the ship?"

Tam's face falls. That's the difference between us. He is good. He regrets when his enemies die. "We lost three," he says. "That body Eira and Naomi saw, and two more. They tried to escape. That's the reason they were shot."

"Why did you come with us at all?" I ask. "Why jump off the ship? Why help us set the fires?"

"Because the drifters wanted you," he says. "I offered to be the one to go out and bring you back in."

"So you didn't really go out through the tailings stacker," I say. "Those bruises. The battered equipment. Did you have a raider rough you up? I'm sure they were happy to oblige."

Tam exhales, a touch of chagrin on his face. "It had to look believable."

"You didn't make very short work of bringing us in," I say. "You fed us and followed us around. What was *that* about?"

"I wanted to gain your trust." Tam leans forward, his voice earnest. "I was trying to find out who you really are. To see if you might turn. That's why I left the notes in your cabin. I was hoping they'd make you think." His mouth twists. "I even tried to tell you about the stolen drifter kids. Remember? Back when we were going through the village compost pile? But then Brig came back."

I remember that. We were talking about whether or not I knew my parents. Tam was pretending to be learning things about the raiders as we picked through their garbage. "Why would you tell me about the children?"

"I thought knowing about them might change your mind."

I'm running out of energy, and time. I push myself away

from the counter, praying my feet hold steady, and ready my hands to make a grab at the rifle on my back. I don't want to shoot him. But there's no way I'm letting him catch me again.

"You warned the raiders that we were going to burn them."

"I never had the chance," he says. "You watched me too closely. Besides, I knew the drifters were on the move. That most of them had been told to vacate that camp."

"I didn't," I say. "I thought there were people inside those tree houses, and I still burned them."

Silence.

"So what did *that* teach you about me?" I ask. "What did you learn that you could tell the drifters?"

"Nothing," Tam says. I can't quite make out the sound in his voice. Hurt? Grief? His eyes meet mine. "The drifters already knew you were merciless. I was hoping to learn something new."

We are at an impasse. Neither of us is willing to give. The weight of the rifle on my back feels heavy.

"Tell me," I say. "Who shut down the mining equipment?" My question comes out more like a plea than I'd intended and I try to right my voice, make it firm. "It's my ship. I deserve to know."

"It was Owen Fales," Tam says.

I recognize the name, from the voyage and from the manifest. Of course I do. I thought I knew them all. "One of the miners."

Tam nods. "He was one of my bunkmates. I got to know him pretty well from sharing a room, and from when I was helping down on the mining deck. I could tell he was someone who might break. I talked to him one night, offered him freedom with the raiders if he'd help me shut down the mining system when we got to a certain spot on the river."

"That was a risk," I say, trying to keep my tone light. "He could have told someone else. He could have come to me."

"But he didn't," Tam says. "I'm good at reading people."

And I'm not. I know. How many more times will this point be driven home?

"So he decided to join the raiders."

"No," Tam says. "It turns out he wanted gold of his own instead. So I helped him steal some. I didn't realize he'd hidden it in my part of the room." His face twists in a wry smile. "Smart. I guess I didn't read him as well as I thought."

"So you stole from me, you betrayed me, and you shut my ship down." This is when I should snatch the rifle from my back, point it at him, make him sorry he ever turned traitor. "Is there anything else you need to confess?"

"No," Tam says. "I think that covers it."

We stand there, alone in the kitchen, the ship dying beneath us. Did I think Tam was my friend? Had I made that mistake without realizing it? I didn't let myself trust him. I suspected him all along. And yet there is a hollow in my stomach, a heaviness in my heart that I thought I had steeled myself against.

Tam swallows. When he speaks, he sounds hollow, too.

"Look. Help us fix the armor and get the motor running right. We're going to move the gold upriver, take it to where it needs to be. Once that's done, you can go wherever you want. You don't have to stay with the drifters."

"I'm not abandoning my crew," I say. "They have families back home."

"The crew has already abandoned you," Tam says.

The words smack me straight on. I try not to flinch; not to show that I care; that I dared to think differently.

"They know they can't return to the Outpost," Tam says, his words soft as if to ease the blow. "They're outnumbered. And even if by some miracle they *did* get the ship back, the Admiral would punish them for allowing the drifters to capture it." Tam lifts his hand, like he's about to touch mine and then he thinks better of it. "The Admiral knew what he was doing when he picked this crew. No one on our voyage has a family. Not one they care about, anyway, or who have been good to them."

"Brig does," I say.

"That's what he told us," Tam says. "But we can't be sure if it's true." His eyes narrow. "As far as the Admiral is concerned, we know too much."

"All we know about is the gold," I say.

"Exactly."

This damn gold.

"The raiders act high and mighty about the way we ruin the rivers to mine the gold," I say. "But they want it, too."

"They're not like the Admiral," Tam says. "They *need* the gold."

"For what?"

"You said it yourself in the woods," Tam says. "It has plenty of uses. As a conductor and an alloy. It doesn't tarnish. All of those reasons."

I shake my head. "Maybe that's some of it, but I don't think so." I frown. "There aren't *that* many raiders. They could make a little gold last a long time." I'm guessing, but something about Tam's face, his stance, makes me think I'm coming near the mark. "So they must be planning to give it to someone else." But who? And for what?

"You'd better worry about what the Admiral plans to do with it."

"You think *you* know?" I say. "I'm as close to him as anyone outside of the Quorum and he hasn't told me."

But Tam doesn't miss a beat. He has an answer at the ready. "Palingenesis," he says. "Do you know what that is?"

It's a big word. I didn't go to school long enough to learn anything so fancy. But I'm not stupid. I know *genesis* means "beginning."

"It means rebirth," says Tam. "Creating again." He takes a step closer, and I hold up my burned hand. *Back off.*

I want him where he is. I need space to think about this. *What does the Admiral want to re-create?*

"Himself," Tam says, as if I've asked the question out loud. "People used to believe that you could use gold to re-generate things that died. They thought that if something had been turned to ashes, you could use gold as a catalyst to bring it back. They called it alchemy."

Back from the ashes. If you could do that, you could bring back a ship that was burned. A person who was killed.

"That's ridiculous," I say. "You can't bring anything back from the dead." *But what if,* a little bird of hope says inside me. *What if you could.*

"There's rumors that the Admiral has already done it once," says Tam. "Some of the drifters say he's lived longer than any human."

"I don't believe it."

"You don't have to believe it's possible to believe the Admiral wants to use the gold to try it," Tam points out.

"The Admiral isn't crazy," I say. "He's practical." But a little nagging thought nudges at my mind. It's true that he's been consumed with mining these rivers.

"A drifter spy saw the papers on the Admiral's desk," Tam says. "The file was marked 'Palingenesis,' and the details for this voyage were inside, along with stories and legends about people who came back from the dead."

I know the Admiral. This kind of thing—mystical, magical—isn't like him. He's got his feet on the ground and his eyes on the prize, which is the here and now. He knows better than to dream of the impossible.

I know better than that.

"*Poe.*" Tam's voice is warm again. I narrow my eyes and he corrects himself. "I'm sorry. Captain Blythe. I want to ask you about your friend who died."

I'm in his face, my good hand gripping his collar and hauling him closer. "*Do not,*" I hiss, "*talk about him.*"

Tam holds his hands up. "It's just—"

"Do. Not." My nose is almost touching his. I smell his clean, soap-and-apple-and-bread scent.

"I'm sorry," Tam says, low. "I'm *sorry*."

I let go, try to get my composure back. I throw everything I can think of at him, trying to deflect from any questions or talk of Call. "Why, Tam?" I ask. "Why all of this? Why betray the Outpost? You're so young. What could you know about the raiders? You've never even been on a voyage before." The moment the words are out of my mouth, I catch my breath. *Of course*. It's so obvious. "You were one of the stolen children, weren't you?"

Tam shakes his head. "I'm not," he says. "But I want to help them. And our crew. I want us *all* to get away."

"And that includes me?" I don't understand. Why is he trying to help me? Why hasn't he sounded the alarm? Why bother trying to change my mind?

"Yes."

"Why?"

For a moment, he doesn't answer. Then he meets my gaze and something new is in his eyes. Or not new, but free. Made plain.

"Because I want you to come with us." He swallows. "I admire you."

He's looking at me in a way that reminds me of Call. But Tam can't mean what I think he means. Call and I knew each other for years. Tam's known me for weeks.

Tam laughs. The softness from moments ago is gone, and his voice is unyielding. "You're not the only one who's seen things you didn't ask to see," he says. "Things you wish you could forget. I'm not any younger than you."

I look in his eyes and I know he's right.

CHAPTER 31

"WHAT IS IT YOU'VE SEEN?" I ask. I can tell Tam doesn't mean the things we've witnessed together—the raiders taking the ship, the fire in the trees. It's something deeper. Something older.

And then it happens.

The motor *screams*.

I don't think.

That someone could catch me.

That Tam might try to stop me.

That this is foolish and stupid and reveals who and where I am.

I just run.

For the mining deck.

I can't save Call. I don't know how to save a single person in this world.

But my ship.

My ship, I can save.

I slam open the door to the mining deck. "You're going to ruin the motor," I say. "Shut it down *now*."

Naomi looks up at me, her eyes wide in shock. I have no time for her. She should know better. Than to help the raiders. Than to ruin the motor like this.

Than to think I'd give up on my ship.

"*Stop the motor!*" I call out, and Tam's at my elbow, and there are guns trained on me from every direction. I look up: Lily's standing on the platform. "Lily!" I shout. "I'll help you. But you have to stop the motor."

Lily hates me. You can see it even now, as she stares down, her hands gripping the railing. And then I see it: a bandage wrapped around her shoulder, where my bullet must have grazed her. But she's standing. She's fine.

"Where's Porter?" someone calls out.

"You don't have time to get him," I say. The ship decides to prove my point, listing heavily, inevitably. One of the propellers must have stopped working. I swear internally.

"You'll *burn out the motor*." Right as I say it the motor begins to smoke, to curl its anger—at being made to run everything for everyone, all the time—out into the air in searing, burning wisps. The smell of ozone is thick. "You will *burn it out*, and we'll sink."

"Do it," Lily orders the crew. "Stop the motor."

Naomi hesitates. The raider with her nudges her with a rifle.

"*Now*." Lily is halfway down the platform stairs, her rifle at the ready.

Naomi reaches her hand into the main control panel, which still has loose wires spiraling out from the jerry-rigged repairs. She pulls a lever. The motor spins a last, screaming round and falls still. The dredge is no longer propelled forward. We've stopped.

"Take me to Porter," I say. "I'll do it. I'll help you fix the dredge."

Lily strides across the floor, her boots loud on the metal in the silence of the weary ship. "I'll take her." She points at the rifle on my back, which I'd forgotten about in these last few moments. "Put your hands in the air. Mac, take her rifle."

I hold up my hands, and one of the raiders pulls the rifle from my back.

"Let's go." Lily trains her own gun on me.

"Where?" I ask.

"Up top," Lily says.

Of course. I should have known. Where all the ghosts are. I've been through this before. I thought I couldn't do it again.

This isn't your river, the notes said. *This isn't your gold.*

Maybe not.

But this *is* my ship.

CHAPTER 32

A SLIP OF CRESCENT MOON ducks in and out of heavy clouds; the wind is strong, sailing and sending them across a silver-dark sky with snips of stars. The smells of rain and night and ship fill my lungs. I swallow the air, draw the deepest breath I can to take in more. I was right. It's still night.

The snarls and swirls of my armor have depth and shades in this light. They look almost ornamental.

Porter turns to face us. He's holding a lantern. Was he looking out over the edge, trying to figure out where we are, why we might have stopped?

I wonder whether I'm supposed to say something. Should I grovel? Put my hands up in the air? I'm not sure how to surrender.

So I don't.

"The motor started to burn," Lily says. "We shut it down."

"All right." Porter's voice is weary and I am surprised that he lets it show in front of me.

"And we found Poe," Lily says.

"I see," Porter says drily. "Where was she?"

"She came to the mining deck," Lily says. "Told us to stop the motor or we'd burn it out. She says she knows how to fix the dredge."

"Thank you," Porter says to Lily. "You can go back down." He looks at me. "Will this take long?"

"No," I say. "Neither of us has the time."

"I'm not sure this is a good idea," Lily says. "If I leave, you're the only two up here."

"I don't have a gun," I point out. Does she think I'd kill him with my one good hand?

Could I?

"It's all right." Porter nods to Lily. "They need you on the mining deck. I'll be there soon."

Lily turns on her heel to leave. *Some people always burn.*

"This is where we killed him," Porter says after she's gone. Waiting.

"No." I take a step in Porter's direction. "He didn't die on *this* ship."

Porter holds up the lantern so that the light glances at and off our faces. The play of shadows makes him look older. I wonder whether the light is doing that to me, too. I *am* older, a hundred years older, than I was the night Call died.

"Why did you destroy the other dredge?"

"We took off the gold first," Porter says. "There was no point wasting it. The river was already torn up. But we burned the ship so the settlers wouldn't be able to use it again. We didn't know you had a second dredge."

"You should have known the Admiral wouldn't give up," I say. "He's relentless."

"So are you," Porter says.

The Admiral. Our driving, red-blooded, obdurate leader, larger-than-life and yet so painstakingly human. His ruddy face, his blue eyes, his workaday clothes. I can almost hear him in my ear, telling us that he has the Outpost's best interests in his mind and heart, that we are all his children. The Union abandoned us, and the first Admiral gathered us in, and he is doing the same. That's what the Admirals always do—they gather.

My Admiral has been in power as long as I remember and yet he hardly seems to age. *Has* he managed some kind of magic? I imagine him sitting reborn in a pile of ashes, his teeth dripping with blood, enameled in gold. He smiles, wipes his mouth on his sleeve, stands up, offers a hand to clasp in brotherhood and love.

"He's coming." Porter's voice drops into the darkness. It's a low rumble like thunder, a cooling on the air, and I shiver.

The Admiral rarely leaves the Outpost. Why now? Did he hear about the raiders taking the ship? How? We haven't had contact with the Outpost since before the braid on the river.

Unless I've been lied to about the communication systems and how far they reach.

"Does he know I lost the ship?"

"I don't believe so." Porter shifts the lantern to his other hand. "I think that he's always planned to come meet the dredge near the end of its voyage, though he didn't tell that to you or any of the crew."

"I don't understand," I say. "Why would he meet us? The plan was to bring the gold back to him in the Outpost."

"We think he's going the same place we're going," Porter says.

I remember what Tam told me. That the Admiral chose our crew carefully, that it was made up of people who wouldn't be missed. What does he have in mind?

"Our scout reports that the Admiral is traveling with plenty of guards and guns," Porter says. "We think it's to guard the gold and escort the dredge along the river. But he won't hesitate to use them on us when he finds out we've taken the ship."

Is Porter telling the truth? How can I know for sure?

I don't even know what I want the outcome to be. I want my ship back. I want the Admiral to help us fight the raiders. But I don't want him to take the ship from me. Or to punish the crew.

"You're out of time," Porter says. Behind him, the clouds move and the light changes. There is a sun somewhere low beyond the horizon, waiting to come up. "We didn't hunt you down when you jumped. We've kept you alive so far. But you've become a liability."

"So I fix the armor, or you kill me," I say. "Like you're going to kill us all."

"I'm not going to kill anyone unless they don't cooperate," Porter says.

I spit out the words. "'This is the last time we leave anyone alive.'"

Silence on the ship. Porter's face, drawn in the lamplight. I think I hear him sigh. "Do you remember what I said before that?"

"'Tell your Admiral that we're done with him taking from us,'" I say.

"He took Call from us."

"*No.*" I'm livid at the lie. "He didn't. *You* shot Call."

"The Admiral's guards took Call from us when he was a child," Porter says. "We didn't realize who we'd killed until you'd all gone and we got a closer look at the body." He swallows. "Even then, we weren't sure. He'd changed over the years. But his mother knew when we brought him home."

Sun-black hair. She walked in a field and picked three flowers.

"Where is she now?" I ask. My hands are trembling. *Maybe I could see her. Maybe we could talk.*

"She's gone," Porter says. "She died a few months after we brought back the body."

"What about Call's father?" There has to be someone left. Someone who knew him. *Please.*

"He died before Call was born." Porter shifts his weight. This is the longest I've ever seen him stay in one spot. "It's not an easy life out here."

"Brothers or sisters?"

"He didn't have any."

"Wait," I say, realizing something I should have noticed sooner, the minute Porter spoke of Call. "How do you know his name?" I never told anyone out here. Naomi didn't say it in the woods, when she spoke to the others. But did she tell Porter?

"It was the one his mother gave him," Porter says. "The settlers let him keep that, at least."

The settlers stole Call. The raiders shot him.

I want to push Porter over the deck, swing the lantern against his head, rake my nails across his face. Call was one of their own, and they *killed* him. And Call's family is gone. Even the possibility of meeting them is stolen from me. I thought I hadn't let myself take hold of it, but the tearing in my heart tells me that I did. I dared to hope again, a bit. Not that I could get Call back. But his family. Others who loved him.

That's not for you either, the stars seem to say.

Am I ever going to heal?

"Are you going to help us?" Porter asks.

My mind races, running over the ship, the armor, the Outpost in the unseeable distance, the houses in the trees, a boy's body on another boat, wagons on their way.

Can I believe Porter about the Admiral? About Call? About any of it?

Who *can* I trust?

My ship. Myself?

"That depends," I say.

"On what?"

"On how greedy you are," I say.

"I'm not as greedy as a settler," Porter says.

I laugh. The sound rings out in the night and I fold my arms. "If that's true, then we'll get away fine. The solution is simple."

"What is it?"

"If you outrun the Admiral," I say, "you'll never have to fight him. All those guards and guns won't matter. Get to where you're going and hide."

"We can't outrun him."

"Leave the gold," I say. "Leave the ship, too. Get in your little boats. And *run*."

A pause. "We can't do that," Porter says. "We need all of the gold, and the ship is the only way we have to carry this much."

I let his words and what they mean hang in the air. *You are just as greedy as we are.*

"I see," I say, finally. "Then you're dead."

"Fix the armor," Porter says. "If you do that, we have a better chance of fighting them off."

"It'll take too long. He'll catch us before we can repair it."

"So you're not going to help us," he says. There's a rifle on his back. He could finish me now.

"I am," I say. "There's one more option. One last thing you can do to make a run for it on the ship, and keep the gold."

"And that is?"

"What else can you dump that's heavy?" I ask, goading Porter, gilding my words with the urgency, the certitude in my tone.

"I already told you," he says. "We're not going to kill everyone. Most of the settlers have been cooperating."

"That's not what I'm suggesting," I say. And he's a fool if he thinks that dumping bodies would make a difference. Human bodies are nothing compared with the weight of gold. "Do I need to spell it out for you?"

"Please," says Porter.

"The armor." I point to the gears glimmering in the moonlight, the metal teeth hungry for more. This thing I made. "Get rid of it."

Chapter 33

"YOU'RE LETTING HER DO *WHAT*?" Lily asks, outraged.

Porter hands me a torch for cutting metal. I resist the urge to light it now, to let it blaze and blind them.

"Mac's going to watch her," Porter says. "He has orders to shoot if necessary."

"*I* could cover her," Lily says. "Or I could do it myself. There's no reason to give her a weapon."

Porter ignores that. "She knows the way the armor is put together better than anyone," he says. "She'll be able to dismantle it faster." He hands a torch to Naomi as well. We know how to work them best, but I'm sure Lily isn't the only one uneasy about this. The assembled raiders and crew Porter called up to the deck to help with the demolition all look wary. Porter's trying to mix oil and water by having us work together.

"Taking off the armor leaves us too vulnerable." Lily balls up her fists in fury. "I *know* she can fix it."

"You're right," I say. "But with the Admiral on his way, we're out of time." I smile at Lily. "And it turns out that you aren't willing to give up the gold. So this is our last option."

Naomi's expression as she watches me is wary, weighing. As if she can't believe what I'm doing. The way I'm betraying my own creation.

"Let's get it off," I say to her. "As fast and neat as we can." We have three cutting torches on board. They were intended to aid in repairs, not demolition. But they'll work for this.

"We have no reason to trust her," Lily fumes.

"Enough," says Porter. "We're wasting time."

"This is our best chance." I've washed my hair in the bath and sluiced off all the dirt from the forest, and I'm wearing the change of clothing left in my room. I ate real food for breakfast and took medicine and slept for an hour.

I feel . . . not happy. Not that.

Ever since I told Porter about the armor, I've been full of a reckless *something*. Something wild and free, terrifying and exhilarating and angry.

The Admiral wants me to kill the raiders and get him gold. Porter wants me to fix the armor and double-cross the Admiral.

These leaders. *These men*. They push and push and they back me into a corner, they follow me there and block my escape and ask the impossible. But I'm going to slip away through their grasping hands and leave them with nothing.

Both of them had a part in killing Call, so they can *both* pay.

Lily makes one last appeal to Porter. "She deliberately delayed fixing the armor. How do you know this wasn't her plan all along? Maybe she wasn't *really* surprised when you told her the Admiral was coming. She could have been buying time for him to catch up to us. Maybe that's what she's doing now."

The door to the deck opens.

There he is.

The one I asked for.

Two guards haul Brig out on the deck. He has to duck through the doorway like I do, like Call did. The raiders are none too gentle, shoving him toward Porter, but Brig doesn't stumble. His eyes, when they meet mine, are clear but weary. The cut across his nose is a neat red line. They haven't let him shave, so he is shadowed, his hair more unkempt than I've ever seen it. His cheeks look hollow, as if the time without food has already set in to wasting him. And yet the word that comes to mind when I see him isn't *beaten* or *weary* or *broken*. It's *contained*. Not by the raiders. Within himself. *"He's the Admiral's boy, through and through,"* Tam said.

Is that really what Brig is?

"Is it true?" Brig asks, his voice low and familiar. "You're helping the raiders tear apart the ship?"

"We're getting rid of the armor." I hold up my torch. "The raiders don't have any experience with these. Do you know how to use one?" Brig didn't work on the scrap yard like I did. And he's still the most likely of us to be the Admiral's watchdog. But I want to see what he'll do. What he'll say.

Will he join me?

I swear I see a flicker of a smile on his lips, a lick of fire in his eyes.

"Yes," he says.

Minutes later, Brig and Naomi and I hang on ropes down the side of the ship. Mac and two other raiders cover us with their rifles. Another raider belays Brig, Lily's got Naomi, and Porter is lowering me. I guess he thought anyone else might decide to drop me right into the churn of the river below.

Maybe the three of them *will* drop the three of us. They could. It would be a neat way to get rid of the former captain and first and second mates in one fell swoop. With one hand still bandaged and wrapped up, I'm not as fast or agile as I'd like. They could take me out easy.

Brig and Naomi have the torches. They run on acetylene and oxygen gas in the small tanks, and when the flames are lit, they spit fiery sparks. I have a grease pencil in hand, which I'm using to mark the best places for them to make the cuts. Once I finish marking, I'll use a torch, too. All over the dredge, the rest of my crew dangles from ropes, sawing, hammering, bludgeoning my armor to death the fastest way they can, using whatever they can find. Crowbars. Wrenches. They unscrew and unhinge; they worry at the puzzle I created years ago in the safety of the Outpost.

But my armor is sound. Solid. It doesn't give up easily.

I hear grumbles of frustration and muttered epithets, and I shove the grease pencil into my breast pocket.

"Brig," I say. "Give me your torch for a minute."

His sleeves are rolled up and I see singes from the torch on his arms as he makes his way across to me, pressing his boots against the side of the ship as he walks. "What are you doing?" Mac calls down.

"I want to give it a try," I say, pulling the leather gloves out of my pack to protect my hands. Brig hands over the tank and the torch, carefully.

I bring the flame to the mark on the metal. Sweat trickles down my back as I bear down on the cut, bracing my boots against the prickly, serrated side of my ship. The torch hisses and spurts; people batter the dredge all around me, all of us locked in battle by and with the choices we and others have made.

And then. A give. A groan?

I push away just in time.

The armor drops. The motion feels slow; it feels like I sink with it, the heavy, inevitable fall pulling something within me. I tighten my grip. *Don't follow it down.*

Below, the piece of armor hits the water like an oversize stone thrown by a child.

Am I helping the raiders run faster? Or am I giving the

Admiral a chance to assist me in finishing them? Maybe I can ruin them both, Porter and the Admiral, the men who killed Call. I'll bring them together, let them kill each other off, and I'll slip away through the cracks.

Will it work? Will I finally run?

I'm not completely sure why anyone on the dredge is doing what they're doing. Including myself.

Am I going to get what I want out of this?

Or destroy the one thing I have left?

CHAPTER 34

MY ARMS SHAKE, my shoulders ache, and my face is dirty and hot. Small burns cover my forearms where sparks singed through the sleeves of my shirt. My injured hand throbs, though I've tried to go easy on it. We've been de-armoring the ship all day, dawn to dusk. I feel the heat of a sunburn prickling my nose and the back of my neck.

Others will work through the night while Brig and Naomi and I steal a few hours' rest. The beating and uncoupling of the armor still takes place all over the ship, a dissonant song of destruction and severance.

Tam and the kitchen crew carry soup and bread up to the deck for supper. I linger near the railing, wanting Brig and the others to have food first, but Tam brings me my portion himself. He peers over the side of the ship and whistles. The dredge looks like one of the feral dogs that run through the back streets of the Outpost, mangy and mottled, pieces of their coats torn away or dangling. "Why did you decide to do this?" he asks. "You love the ship. You hate the drifters."

"Why did *you* decide to do this?" I ask, sending the question back to him. "Why turn on your own people?"

He levels his gaze at me, his expression unusually earnest. "Didn't you ever get sick of the same old story?"

"What story?"

"The Outpost story." He's still holding the tray, but he seems to have forgotten all about it; the tray tips, a bowl slides. I reach out and take the tray from him, balancing it with my good hand as I listen. Tam's voice is full of feeling. "How the rest of the world abandoned us, so the first Admiral gathered us in, and now we all scrap and scrape to survive at the edge of the Territory?"

Yes. I am. I'm *so* tired of that story—of the Union deserting us, of the Admirals protecting us ever since—that I could scream. It's why Call and I wanted to *run*. It's why we were going to leave, together. It was time for something new and unwritten. My throat knots and tears sting my eyes. "Of course I'm tired of it," I say. "But there's no other story to tell."

"I started to wonder if it was even true," Tam says. "What if the people living outside of the Outpost never *wanted* to come back in? What if they'd left for a reason?"

The ship shifts. Somewhere below, we've lost armor, and the motion tilts the tray, sends the dishes sliding into one another. Tam and I reach out to catch them; he grabs at the soup bowl, my fingers close on the bread. The water tips, spills out onto the deck, is lost.

"When I found out what we'd done, taking the raider kids, I knew I had to do something," Tam says. "Can you imagine what it would be like to have been torn away from everyone you know? From where you *belong*?"

"I know what it's like to lose your family," I say. "The place where you belonged. I was raised in one of the orphanages."

Tam looks taken aback. He must have forgotten that about me.

And the truth is, I *can* imagine what it would be like. Too well. The dark of night, someone coming and taking you away. Bringing you to another night with terrible false stars and lights and so many buildings and people, and someone saying, *This is your home*, and you know that isn't right, and you cry out for help.

But no one comes. You never get to leave. You don't go home.

And when you try, they can't see your face in the dark, they don't know the shape of you anymore, and that is how someone else finishes your story.

Chapter 35

BY THE END OF THE NEXT DAY, it's clear we've made headway. Sparks dance near Brig's hands and face as he cuts through the metal. Another piece of armor splashes into the water below and the ship seems to sigh in relief. I tell Porter that we can try the motor soon, since we've lost so much mass.

It's hard to look at the gears and mechanisms that I designed fall into the river, to watch the ship stripped of its defenses. The armor is everything I've done. The one thing I've ever created.

I steel myself against the unsettled feeling of loss that turns at the back of my mind. This was my idea. I made something. Everyone else wants to take it. Everyone else gets to use it.

And I have decided, *Not anymore.*

I made this.

It's not yours.

If I can't have it, then I'll unmake it.

• • •

Without warning, the rope to which I'm tethered jerks sharply. I shoot a glance up at Mac, who's belaying again.

Is he going to let me go?

But he's hauling me *up*, hand over hand, shouting, "Hurry!" I use my boots against the wall of the ship to help him, gripping the rope with my gloves, the torch slung into its strap across my back. Brig and Naomi climb next to me, Brig fast, Naomi not far behind, even with her injury. Once I'm over the railing, I ask Mac, breathless, "What's happened?"

"Someone's coming," he says, "on the shore." All around me, crew and raiders who were cutting and sawing and clubbing at my armor clamber over the railing and onto the ship.

"Duck down," someone says. "They might have a gun."

"Is it the settlers?" I ask, dropping to a crouch next to Mac.

"Just one." He points through the bottom rung of the railing. A rider moves fast along the edge of the river, where the grass and sand are smooth enough for a single horse. A plume of dust follows.

"They've sent someone to bargain," Brig says.

"The Admiral doesn't bargain," I say. If you deal with the Admiral, you will pay and pay and pay.

The group Porter gathers in the cafeteria is largely the dredge's original crew, plus a handful of his women and men, who are armed. He left a few of the raiders on the deck to keep watch. He has me stand next to him, on his left. I'm at the Devil's hand. Again.

As I look out over my crew, I say their names in my head. Eira Clyde, cartographer, and one of the only people who jumped with me. Ophelia Hill, navigator. Laura Seng, medic. Corwin Revis, chief machinist. Owen Fales, miner and traitor. But the chaplain is gone, and so are two others, and maybe more.

Do they think I betrayed them? Failed them? I told them to jump off the ship and run with me. They didn't follow. Then I came back and shut down the motor, had them start hacking away at the armor.

"The Admiral sent an emissary," Porter tells us. "I went out to meet him. He's on the shore awaiting our response."

I watch Porter, trying to decide what kind of leader he is. A good one? He didn't let the emissary on the ship. He went out and took the danger upon himself. Those seem like brave choices. But are they stupid ones, as well?

"Kill the emissary," Lily says. "Right now. While we can. That's a message the Admiral will understand."

"The emissary offered a deal from the Admiral," Porter says. The raiders in the room mutter, and crew members shift warily in their seats. Does the Admiral want us back?

"He says that if we give up the gold and Captain Blythe, he won't hunt us down."

What?

Eyes in the room, all on me. Why does the Admiral want me? When the emissary goes back, he'll tell the Admiral what he's seen. And what will he do when he hears what I've done to the ship?

"Kill the emissary," Lily says again. I can tell her mind is threading the same needle as mine. "He's going to tell the Admiral that we're taking apart the ship. That we don't have any armor anymore. They'll get to us as fast as they can. We'll be sitting ducks."

Porter's eyes meet mine. "You should," I say. "That's what the settlers would do. They take gold and they kill." I don't say the rest. *We're all the same.* But it hangs there in the air anyway.

"Killing him won't buy much more time," Porter says. "If he doesn't return to their camp soon, they'll come for us nevertheless."

"We can give the Admiral half of what he wants," says Mac. "Send the captain back with the emissary and see what happens."

Why has the Admiral asked for this?

I can think of only one reason. Somehow, he knows I've failed. He's going to punish me.

"That's all the Admiral wanted?" Tam asks.

"*All* he wanted?" Lily says, her voice cool. "You think taking the gold is *reasonable?*"

Porter holds up his hand and everyone falls silent.

"This is the point of no return," Porter says. "If you are a member of the ship's original crew, and you don't fight with us when the Admiral attacks, I've given my men and women permission to shoot you."

"How do you know your raiders won't just gun us down anyway the first chance they get?" Brig asks.

"We need the numbers," Porter says bluntly. "If you fight with us, we won't kill you."

"What about the rest of you?" asks Naomi. "There are plenty more raiders out there who aren't on the ship now."

"They won't be fighting," Porter says.

"Why not?" Brig asks.

"You'll make us die for you, but you're not all going to fight for *yourselves*?" Even as the words leave my mouth, the image of the raiders in their boats comes to mind. And then I know. They're not going to help us fight because they're not here. Not on the dredge. Not waiting on the shore or hidden in the forest.

"They've gone on already," I say. "In the boats." That's why the relocated village was almost empty when we came to set fire to it; why there were so few houses left in the trees. Even if Porter and his crew are killed and the gold gets taken by the Admiral, the rest of the villagers have a fighting chance and a running start. He could have used those boats to carry some of the gold, but that was never the plan. The plan was always to keep as many people as safe as possible, while this small crew took the enormous gamble of taking the dredge and its treasure.

"The people on the ship are all we have now," Porter says. "And everyone here will fight. Hard."

"What about this one?" Lily asks, jutting her elbow in my direction. "Let's send her back with the emissary, like Mac said. Maybe filling half the bargain will buy us some time."

Porter studies me. What does he see? A tall girl with braided hair and grease under her fingernails? Someone who tried to set his village on fire? Does it matter that I once loved and was loved by one of their own?

"It's up to you," he says. "You can go with the emissary or stay on the ship."

Lily draws in her breath but holds her tongue when Porter gives her a fierce glance.

Everyone's watching. Tam's expression is conflicted—his eyes burning into mine, his lips twisted in a frown. He's on the side of the raiders, but I don't think he relishes the thought of sending me back to face the Admiral's wrath.

Most of my crew look as if they'd like me to go ahead and volunteer. *Why not?* I can see them thinking. *It* might *buy us time, and she's never been much of a captain. I wouldn't miss her if she were gone.*

Brig shakes his head, an almost imperceptible motion. He doesn't want me to go. Why? If he really were in the Admiral's pocket, wouldn't he want me to return to the Admiral to tell him what I know about the raiders' plans, so he could better take them down?

I don't know why, in this moment, I trust Brig the most. Because he was the first to follow me off the ship? Because he never turned on me in the forest, not once?

He could have been pretending then. He could be pretending now.

It may be that I'm a fool.

"We're out of time," Porter says. He folds his arms and fixes me with his eyes, brown and deep. Eyes that saw Call when he was young, that saw the Admiral take him away.

I want to stay with my ship.

I'm not going to walk into the Admiral's arms to buy time for people I don't know. But I can fix the dredge. "I'll stay," I say. "You need me to get the motor running."

It's not your ship anymore, my mind needles at me. *You had them tear off the armor you made.*

So why am I hanging on to it?

The dredge took on gold. Killed people. Ruined the river.

The ship deserves to die. It should be stopped.

It's me.

And I can't leave it.

Chapter 36

"IT'S NOT WORKING," Lily says.

"I can see that," I say, irritated. I rub my dirty hands on my pants and lift my chin to Porter, who's come down to the mining deck to check on our progress. "I *swear* what I've done should get it going again."

I've removed the metal shielding around the motor so I can get at it better. The motor's not in good shape. They pushed it too hard. But we don't need to go far. We don't have to get back down the river. We just have to get to the raiders' rendezvous point as fast as possible.

I'm not just trying to fix the motor. I'm also disengaging any of the power take-off systems we don't need so that I can increase torque. That will make us go faster than we ever have before. Faster than the ship was designed to go.

I am keeping this fact from the others.

"How long do we have?" Lily asks. She's trying to calculate how soon the settlers will reach us. Porter sent the emissary back with the news that there would be no bargain.

"The Admiral doesn't travel often," I say. "When he does, he uses wagons and riders. The riders are fast, but the wagons aren't."

"How fast *can* they go?" Lily asks.

"I'm not sure," I say. "I never worked on them." The wagons are made of metal. They're old trucks from before the Desertion with the tops sawed off to let in air. Some of them still have motors that work, but they use gasoline, which is a precious commodity in the Outpost. Others are pulled by horses that heave and strain.

It's not easy to get up the river, by motor or by horse.

You have to feed them both.

Why didn't the Admiral adapt the solar technology from the dredge for the wagons? I wonder. *Surely someone could have figured out how to re-create it.*

Well. He never asked me to do it, and it's not my problem now.

"I'd think we have a couple of days," I say. "It's a lot easier for an emissary to ride ahead on the river. There's no road for the wagons near the banks. They're going to have to clear the way."

I *hope* we have a couple of days. I'm guessing based on what I know of the wagons and what Eira and Porter and I have deduced from a combination of the settlers' and raiders' maps.

I gesture for Porter to go up with me to the smaller deck so we can talk without anyone else trying to listen in.

Lily follows us, of course. We climb the metal stairs and, though it's only a couple of flights, I'm dizzy when we reach the top. I'm not getting enough rest, and the infection from my burn lingers. I lean against the wall in feigned nonchalance to hide the fatigue, my palm next to the written signals: three short rings for an emergency. The metal is cool and grainy under my hand.

"I think someone's undermining what I'm trying to do," I say.

Lily mimics my stance, propping one arm against the wall in a mocking way. She's been following me around on the mining deck ever since Porter gave me permission to try to fix the motor. "So it's someone else's fault you can't do your job?"

I ignore Lily and address Porter, whose fingers drum against his leg. His face never shows panic, or fear, even as time slides away from us faster and faster. "I want everyone to leave the mining deck," I say. "I need quiet. I need to think. I can't do it with people watching."

Porter shakes his head. "I can't allow that."

"I'm making no progress." I grit my teeth. "And I *know* I could. *You* could stay. That would be fine." But he can't spare the time. He has so much else to do.

"I have to leave someone down here with you," Porter says.

"Then have Lily stay," I say.

"Who?" Porter asks.

Lily can't hide her surprise. "*What?*"

"If anything happens to me when the Admiral catches us, you're going to need someone to know what I've done," I say. "And I don't think it can be one of my crew." It pains me to tell them this. But I don't think it's a raider who's trying to keep me from fixing the ship. What reason would any of them have to do that? I point at Lily. "But she can stay. As long as she doesn't get in my way."

"All right," Porter says. "I'll have the others leave. But I can't give you long."

"This means you're going to have to watch what I'm doing," I tell Lily, "and you're going to have to *listen* to me."

Lily rolls her eyes.

Porter's lips twitch in what might be a smile.

"Where did you come from?" I ask Lily as I work. I can tell—from her accent, her boots, the way she acts sometimes—that she is neither raider nor settler. What intrigues me is that she's still herself, still different, but she's found a place to belong. Porter respects her. The raiders see her as part of their group.

"Why do you need to know?"

I want to know how you do it. Instead, I say, "I want to know what else is out there." I flip the switch to power up the motor, and it hums to life. *Beautiful.* I put my hands behind my head and stretch in satisfaction, letting myself hum along.

Lily's face lights up. "You did it!" For a few minutes we

stand there, both of us listening, the motor running, sounding better and better until—

I kill it.

"What are you *doing*?"

I make a motion for her to be quiet and I listen to the way the motor sounds when it's stopping. I reach inside carefully. There's not much room.

"What are you doing?" Lily asks again. This time, there's a note of curiosity in her voice.

I wipe my hand on a dirty rag and gesture for Lily to listen closely. "Pay attention. This is something you might need to remember. I removed the check on the motor that keeps the propellers from spinning at maximum speed."

"What does that mean?" Lily asks.

"The check is meant to keep the motor from burning out," I say. "The propellers were designed to never spin at a one-to-one ratio from the main motor." Lily's hands are on her hips, her brow furrowed, listening closely. I try to make it as simple as I can. "I've removed the check, and I've cannibalized some parts from the mining system so that we can run at a full one-to-one ratio now." When I say this, her blue eyes flash up to mine and I see that she understands. I'm going to burn out the motor. I'm sacrificing all its power to the propellers for speed.

"We don't need it to last forever," I say. "Just long *enough*. And we need to move more quickly than we have been."

"You really think you can get us going fast enough to out-run the settlers?" Lily asks.

"That's the hope." I study the motor. I didn't feel anything wrong. It sounds good enough, but we aren't going any faster. Which should be happening now, with my modifications. So what's holding it back?

"Hang on to this for me," I say, giving Lily a kit full of tools. I slide underneath the motor, my back pressing uncomfortably against the metal floor of the ship.

"The place I came from," Lily says, after a few moments. "It was good and bad. Both."

"Will you ever go back?"

"No," she says.

"Why not?" You can't expect anywhere to be *all* good. One that's both good and bad seems like a reasonable place to stay.

"I like the drifters," she says. "It takes everything they have to get food and shelter. But somehow it hasn't made them mean."

I raise my eyebrows as I keep working. She must know what I'm thinking even though she can't see me because she says, "It's true. They can be merciless when they have to. But they're not cruel."

There it is. Someone had added a rheostat to the motor, to reduce the power the motor is *supposed* to be retrieving from the solar-battery reserves.

"I need the crowfoot wrench," I say to Lily.

Lily hands it to me. "Porter and I work well together," she says. "He respects me."

"He does." I've seen it. Been jealous of it. I want someone to treat me like an equal. Not lesser. Not greater.

"He knows I understand," she says. "That I accept that there will always be danger in keeping the others safe."

She doesn't say it like she's bragging, but like she's proud. I wish I were that kind of person. I want to be that kind of person. To know I am trusted and respected, to say it out loud.

"What made you that way?"

"I've already died," she says.

I wrinkle my nose at the absurdity of this statement. "You're not going to tell me that you believe in palingenesis, too, like the Admiral."

"No," Lily says. Her voice has gone sober. "I crashed. I almost burned. I could have lost everything. I'd rather not come that close again. But I will if I have to."

Her face appears under the motor, her hair hanging into her eyes. She pushes it away. "Am I supposed to be learning how to do something here?"

"Watch me," I say. "And don't worry. You don't have to know *how* to do it all. As long as you know *what* to do and can tell it to one of the machinists later, you'll be all right."

"So we should try to keep at least one machinist alive," Lily says drily.

"And you'd better pray that it isn't one of them who's trying to compromise the ship."

"Do you think it is?" she asks.

"It seems the most likely," I admit.

I've finished removing the rheostat. I slide out from under the motor and engage the propeller's power take-off system.

I glance at Lily, my face dirty and sweaty, and then grin so wide I can feel my eyes crinkle. The ship sings with new momentum.

I'm letting it loose.

Faster. Faster. We are on the move and alive at last. "You feel that?" I ask Lily.

She does.

Over the next day and a half, the motor holds up, but no one lets down their guard. A crew batters and torches the remaining armor on the top of the deck, stripping it down the way we did the sides.

We're making good time, but we're still running *out* of time.

I stay on mining deck duty in order to guard the motor. Either Lily or Porter or Mac takes turns with me. I sleep for a few hours at night; Tam brings down my meals when he has a chance. I miss seeing Brig.

"People don't hate you as much," Tam says.

"Thanks a lot."

"No, really," he says. "A lot of them think you made the right call. And someone brought up that the armor wouldn't have been much good against the settlers anyway."

"My armor worked *perfectly*." I'm offended.

"They mean that even if we hunkered down and kept

going with the armor running, the settlers would eventually catch up," Tam says. "They wouldn't even need to attempt boarding the ship. Just wait until we ran out of food and had to come out."

Porter comes down a few moments later and stands near the motor, listening. "It's working hard," he says.

"But running smooth."

"Not much farther." His eyes meet mine. I nod to him, pick up the scattered tools I got out to make a few adjustments. As I wrap them in oilcloth and put them back in their case, I hear Porter say, "We might make it."

He sounds surprised.

I want some air after all the heat and noise on the mining deck. I wonder about what Porter said as I climb the stairs to the top of the dredge. Did he think all along that what they were trying to do was impossible?

I understand why he'd attempt it anyway. The one thing worse than struggling for the improbable is doing nothing at all. Demons catch up with you that way. *You* catch up with you that way.

Brig is among those keeping watch. He smiles at me and I cross the top of the deck, which is pitted and scraped with scars from where the armor used to be.

"It's a whole different ship," he says. "No armor. And we're *moving*." He reaches out to touch a strand that has escaped my braid. "Look," he says, because my hair is practically streaming behind me. We've never been moving fast enough for that to happen before.

The dredge is burnished by the light, orange and pink and gold, and it still cannot hold a candle to the sky, to the trees, to what the water can do with all this light and color.

"It's hideous out here," I say, and Brig laughs.

Clouds race in the distance, and the trees onshore dance in the sunset. Even with the breeze, the air is heavy and hot. Relief will come later, after the clouds burst and the rain comes through. I want to be up here so I can feel it, the cooling breath after the heat, the release.

"Why did you all give up?" I ask. "Why did you come back to the boat after the raiders caught me? You could have stayed out there. You could have run." I want to know. *What are* you, *through and through?*

"Naomi needed medicine," Brig says. "And Tam said we could help you better if we came back on board. Eira agreed with him." He shakes his head. "Of course, that was before we knew Tam was in league with the raiders."

"And you?" I ask. "What about you?"

"I decided to come back with them." Brig's eyes hold mine. "He loved you." Brig swallows. "The one Naomi told us about. The one you burned for." Brig knows I'm thinking of Call. It's impossible not to when I'm up on the deck like this.

"Yes," I say. "He did."

"I wish," Brig says.

What does he wish?

But that's all he gets out. I hear the ache in his throat. I see want in his eyes and in the press of his lips. His hair ruffles in the breeze; the air has not yet cooled.

I understand how it feels to love someone you can't have. Someone you know you will *never* have. You will never touch their face, lay your fingers along their cheek; they will never put their hands on you.

Never.

And I understand something more.

I think Brig knows how much I wish he were Call.

Brig and I do not speak or touch. We stand side by side as the sun vanishes behind the trees. My ache is as vast as the universe, as specific as each individual star.

CHAPTER 37

DEEP DOWN IN MY DREAM, I know something is wrong. My mind begins the swim to the top, to the real world. Away from Call and where he has met me in the dark, in the last place I can find him, low and secret, when I'm suspended in sleep.

The ship has stopped.

I sit straight up and reach for my boots. *Why isn't it running? What happened?*

"*Poe!*" Lily's voice outside my door. "*Hurry!* The settlers have caught up to us!"

I pull on my boots, yank open the door. "Why didn't you sound the main alarm?" I ask, taking the rifle and spare clip she hands me. We head down the hallway toward the stairwells.

"It's not working," Lily says, her voice grim. "Someone disabled it."

"Who's on the mining deck now?" I ask. It was supposed to be Lily down there for the night shift. "*Why is the ship stopped?*" My heart races. Have I made another mistake? Did the motor burn out because I worked it too hard? I thought we'd have longer than this.

"Porter ordered it stopped when he saw the settlers closing in," Lily says.

"Why would he do that?" I ask in disbelief.

"Come *on*," Lily says, ignoring, impatient. "We need everyone up on the upper deck who knows how to shoot. The settlers are on both sides of the river."

I stop. I won't go up until she tells me. "*Why* did he order it stopped?"

Lily growls in frustration. "He doesn't want to lead the settlers to the rest of our group."

I swear. He's going to get us all killed to save them.

"Who's with the motor right now?" I ask.

"You're not going to start it," Lily says. "It's against Porter's orders."

She's not getting it. Yes, I'd like to start the ship running and prevent anyone from tampering with the motor again, but there's another problem. "Who's watching the tailings stacker?"

"Dammit," Lily says. "I didn't think of that."

"You didn't *think of that*?" I ask. "It's how *you* got in!"

"We had gliders."

"Maybe the settlers invented something, too."

We've reached the stairs. "I'll go down there," she says. "You get up top. Porter asked for you."

.   .   .

I shove the door open and crawl out onto the deck, toward a spot on the west side of the boat near the others. My knee scrapes against a rough piece of metal where my armor used to be and I feel the slice against my skin. The raiders and my crew crouch along the railings. When I catch a glimpse of the shore, I see the settlers in their metal wagons, riding their horses, coming for us. They range along the shore, the sandbars.

They're gaining on us.

"Keep down," Porter calls out. "We wait for them to fire the first shot."

I check my rifle to make sure it's ready. As I do, I hear a familiar voice to my right.

"We almost made it," Tam says.

"We still can." Desperation edges my voice. I try to tamp it down, to mirror Porter's even cool. "We take them out, one by one, until they're gone."

"Have you been in a fight like this before?" Tam asks. "On your first voyage?" He sounds determined and afraid. His hazel eyes are flint-focused on the riverbank.

Before I can answer, the settlers open fire.

The first shots hit the side of the ship below the railing, and my heart knocks against my chest so hard I put a hand over it. *Poe. Poe. Poe.* In this moment, I know what I want. I know whose side I'm on.

"When you can get a good read on them," Porter calls out, "fire at will."

I can't get Lily's words out of my mind. Someone destroyed the main alarm. Someone is *still* sabotaging us. Are they up here on the deck? Will someone shoot me in the back, the way they did Call?

A shot from our ship. I can't see who fired it.

And then a volley. Ours and theirs, ricochets and noise and bullets driving home.

Someone on the south side of the ship goes down.

Mouth, dry. Hands, cold. *Do it. Hurry.*

I take aim, narrowing my eyes. There. A settler, crouched near a bush, gun in hand. I fire. Did they fall? I can't tell.

Again.

Crack. Tick. Echo.

The sound of a rifle. Of my rifle.

Crack. Tick. Echo.

Over and over, everyone around me, all over the deck.

Cracktickcracktickcracktickecho.

There are so many more settlers. The drifters overcame our crew because of sheer numbers. They no longer have that advantage, since most of them have gone upriver to safety, to their meeting place. The settlers have more people and more guns. And they have snipers, climbing up in trees and on top of wagons. I don't look over to the east side of the river to see what's happening there. We have our hands full.

Crack. Tick. Echo.

One of our people falls over the railing into the river.

It's surprising how intimate it is. How, even though the

river is wide and the ship is big, I can see the settlers' faces, upturned toward us, their rifles, their arms raising to kill.

I liked it better when I didn't have to see them die.

Tam takes out a sniper, who falls slack from a tree and hits the ground hard.

"When did you learn to shoot like that?" I ask Tam.

"I grew up near the militia training grounds," he says. He's lightning quick about reloading his gun and I'm not far behind. Every moment counts, every *crack* is a bullet headed our way. "We've got to bring those snipers down if we want to give the drifters a chance."

When Tam speaks of the drifters, he never says *we*. It's not as if he wants to hold himself apart—he's eager when he speaks about them. Rather, it's as if he's not certain he belongs.

"You weren't stolen from the drifters," I say. "But you still helped them. Why?"

"Because they know a bigger world than we do," Tam lifts the gun to his shoulder. "You care about them, too."

"You're right," I say. Tam smiles at me, a smile with nothing of humor but with a certain understanding. We bring our rifles up between the rails, get our sight lines on a sniper riding toward us.

"One," Tam says, "two," but then the shot is perfect, and he takes it without waiting for three, me firing a second after, and the rider goes down, swinging-slinging in his saddle, rifle dropping out of his hands. That's Tam's shot. Mine goes wide, missing the mark and sending a spray of leaves in the tree near the rider.

"What a *shot*," I say to Tam, and out of the corner of my eye I see the twist of his grin, and then

and then

a spray of blood,

on his chest,

and he falls.

"No, no, *no*," I say, pressing my hand against the wound, trying to stop it. Blood and flesh on my fingers, Tam's skin still warm. "He's hit!" I cry out to the medic, Laura, who crawls across the deck as fast as she can while staying low.

But it's no good.

Tam's gone, too.

This time I saw it happen.

CHAPTER 38

TAM'S BLOOD ALL OVER MY HANDS. His body on the deck next to me.

Again.

I can't think of what to do.

I can think of one thing.

I crouch-run toward the steps down from the deck. Amid the *cracktickecho* all around, someone shouts at me—the word *coward* I think—but I have no time. I have thought of this one thing and I will do it.

Too fast. I fall halfway down the stairs, but it's fine, I'm back on my feet in a second. Race down the hallway, open the door to my room, find what I want sitting on my desk.

My captain's hat.

Will the settlers be able to see it from where they are?

Will it matter?

I tear the case off my pillow and start for the stairs up to the deck. Partway there, I crash into Eira from behind. Her arms are full of ammunition from the weapons closet.

As we right ourselves, I see her taking in my hat, the pillowcase. "What are you doing?"

"Tam's dead," I say, and she ricochets back, as if she'd fired a rifle and the kickback from it has rocked her, and from above we hear cries and the muffled cracks of guns.

I shove my way past Eira and head up the steps.

Please let me be doing the right thing.

Please let this make a difference any difference at all.

Someone has dragged Tam's body aside, out of the way, and piled it with several others. We have lost seven all told. Already. We can't afford any more.

I don't want to look at Tam, dead, but I can't help myself.

I'm sorry I'm sorry I'm sorry

There are his eyes, his mouth, that horrible gaping wound in his chest where the bullet came out—

Wait.

The bullet came out the front? But we were facing the settlers. It should have *entered* his chest from the front, not exited that way.

Someone on our ship shot him.

My entire body vibrates with fury. *Steady.* I crouch down and dart my eyes all over the deck. And *there.* A movement, strange and precise, amid the turmoil. Someone turns, careful. Someone waits until the *cracktickechoes* are so fast and wild that no one notices, and then they fire, right across the ship, into our own people. A drifter falls.

Someone small and gray-haired and collected, cool, relent-less.

It's *Naomi*.

How could she why would she? my mind asks, and my heart sinks. I don't want to believe this, but I saw enough to know. She shot. One of our people fell.

Where is Brig?

There he is. On the west railing, a few people down from where Tam and I were. I sprint across the deck—my eyes and my gun on Naomi—and shove in next to him.

"Brig," I say, "Naomi's shooting *at* us."

He keeps his eyes on the settlers, and I keep mine on Naomi.

"Are you sure?" he asks, and right then—

She turns and looks at me and something shifts in her face, locks into place, an expression of *satisfaction*.

As if she'd been looking for me this whole time.

She's going to shoot *me*.

Why now? I wonder. *Why not kill me sooner?*

But then Naomi lowers her rifle slightly. She's going to take me down but not kill me.

Why?

Something about my silence alerts Brig. I feel him turn and before Naomi fires, she's down, grabbing her arm, and Brig is on the move, heading across the deck. "Tell Porter," he says. "I'll lock her up below."

. . .

"Naomi was killing people on the deck," I say to Porter. "Brig shot her."

He nods, lifting his rifle, not taking his eyes off the settlers on the shore.

"She's not dead," I say. "Just hurt."

"We'll fix that," he says, and I feel sick rise in my throat.

"Tam's dead too," I say, because it matters, I feel like people should know, and this time Porter's face changes, some muscle twitches in response or sorrow. But we have no time for it.

"Why did you stop the ship?" I ask. "We might have made it."

"I'm not leading the settlers to the rest of my group."

"You protect your people at the cost of mine," I say.

"It's not only my people," Porter says. "There are others there, too." He calls out, "They're shifting north!" and then, to me, "Get back to your post."

"We're not going to die for gold," I say to him. "Not anymore."

Back in position, where Tam's death has left a hole in the lineup and a slick of blood on the railing, I stand up. I pull my braids in front of my shoulders and shove the captain's hat on my head. If the settlers are looking through field glasses, they'll know it's me. I lift up the white pillowcase, wave it like a flag.

Will I feel it? How bad will it hurt?

Please not in the back, like Call.

Like Tam.

Hit me where I can see it. Where I can watch the blood bloom as I die and know, for a moment at least, that *I was here, I am leaving.*

Chapter 39

HANDS PULL AT ME, try to drag me down. "What are you doing?!"

"What the *hell*?"

I grip the rail with one hand, wave my makeshift flag with the other.

A shot hits the railing.

"Poe!"

It's Brig.

Someone else falls on the deck a few feet away. On the shore, the settlers look invincible. There are bodies on the ground, yes, but most are standing.

There are so many more of them. And there. Behind the others, almost in the shadows, out of the range of fire.

The Admiral.

I want to drop the flag. Lift my rifle and try to hit him, no matter how far away he is. No matter that he's been certain to place himself out of reach.

"Don't shoot Captain Blythe!" I hear Porter call. How many drifters and crew had guns aimed at my back? I don't turn around to find out. "Hold your fire!"

"You're saving as many of your people as you can," I call out to him, in the new almost stillness that hovers in the smoke from our shots, in the pause that cannot last. "I have to do the same for mine."

"*Poe!*" Brig calls out, his voice desperate. "What are you doing?"

"Surrendering," I say.

Chapter 40

THE SETTLERS LOCK US UP in the cafeteria.

I was hoping for the mining deck.

Some of my own crew look daggers at me. The drifters spit and swear in my direction. Lily's eyes are full of anger, which I'm used to from her, and betrayal. That's new. She never expected anything from me before, so I couldn't disappoint her.

I'm sorry, Lily.

But Porter's the one who shut off the motor when the settlers first caught up to us. He's the one who told them all to stand down when I raised the flag. He's the one they listened to. Not me.

Porter's not here with the rest of us. I don't know where he is or what the settlers are doing to him.

I still have Tam's blood on me. I still have his look in my eyes. He hasn't been gone long.

He's been gone forever. He'll never be back.

"Quiet down," says a voice I recognize. It's one of the

Quorum. Sister Haring. She's wearing boots and a militia uniform and her blond hair is rolled up, pinned back. Her hands are nice and clean, the nails polished and smooth. I notice them because her hands are on her hips, her fingertips splayed out like claws, gripping tight.

When it was clear the settlers had seen our surrender, Porter went out to negotiate the terms. It didn't take long. I can't imagine that the settlers agreed to anything except to stop killing us, for now. When Porter gave the signal from the shore, we opened the gangway and the settlers came on. They took our weapons and herded us down from the deck and into the cafeteria.

There are so many settlers. Even though they've left most on the shore, it feels like they take up every inch of the ship.

I think it's clear to us all that the Admiral isn't just here to escort the gold back to the Outpost. There's something else happening.

"I'll deal with all of you in time," Sister Haring says. "Right now, I need Captain Blythe and her first and second mates. Come forward."

Are we going to be executed immediately? On full display?

Some part of my mind registers: *She hasn't asked for Eira. That's good.*

And another part tells me: *She won't kill us now. The Admiral isn't here to watch.*

I step forward. Brig does too. In the shuffle and confusion when the settlers herded us down, he ended up near the front of the cafeteria. He looks back for me, and our eyes meet across the room. He is dirty. His shoulder is bloody. Naomi is nowhere in sight. And then I remember, *Naomi turned on us. Brig locked her up.*

"Where's Second Mate Naomi Moran?" Sister Haring asks.

Naomi. Lifting her rifle and shooting Tam. Planning to shoot me. Fury darkens my vision, skips beats in my heart. *I'm not going to say where she is. Let her rot away, alone in a cabin without windows.*

They'll find her, though. They'll search every inch of the ship.

All along, I knew the Admiral would have sent someone to watch me, to watch all of us. I wonder whether Naomi had orders to kill anyone who betrayed him. That would explain her shooting Tam. Turning the rifle on me. We had decided to fight on the side of the drifters. We were traitors.

What did the Admiral promise her?

Is *she* the one who attached the rheostat? Who tried to keep us from running?

It must be.

"Where is Second Mate Naomi Moran?" Sister Haring asks again. I don't answer. Neither does Brig.

"We'll find out what happened to her," Sister Haring says, her eyes boring into mine. She continues her roll call, down the list of names. And then she comes to his.

"Where is Tam Wallace?" she asks.

Brig lowers his head. I raise my chin, stare into Sister Haring's eyes.

Silence.

People liked Tam. Drifters and settlers alike. They responded to his smile, his way of wanting to know you, how he cooked and took care.

How many of them know he's gone? And do they know who took him down?

"Where is Tam Wallace?" she asks again.

No one answers.

She walks over to me, gestures for a guard to cuff my hands. "Captain Blythe," she says. "Tell me where Tam Wallace is."

I open my mouth to spit out the words. *He's dead.*

But.

I can't.

They throw Brig and me into one of the small crew rooms together.

"I'm sorry," I say.

"It's not over yet," he says.

I lean my head against the wall behind me. "It's over for Tam." There are tears behind my eyes and I can't have that. I won't have the Admiral know I've been crying. I blink, looking up at the ceiling, and then I bring my chin level, rest my hands on my knees.

"I didn't have to see them die before," I say.

"It makes it worse," Brig says.

"I think we should have to see them, and they should have

to see us." My voice breaks. "We should have to look right into each other's eyes."

The drifters killed Call in the dark.

If they'd seen him, they would have known him.

But Tam was killed in broad daylight. Naomi knew what she was doing. She knew Tam, and she killed him anyway.

"Porter wouldn't have let you surrender if he didn't agree with it," Brig says. "We were getting slaughtered out there."

"We're going to get slaughtered in here." Why couldn't I think of anything else to do? I didn't think it through. I saw Tam die, and I wanted it to stop.

"There's got to be a reason they haven't killed us yet," Brig says. He lifts his hands, cuffed together, and rubs at his face—his cheekbones, his forehead. A spray of blood dots the chest and collar of his shirt, but I don't think it's his.

"Did Naomi say why she shot Tam?"

"No," Brig says. "And I didn't ask. I wanted to get back up to the deck as fast as I could."

"But you locked her up," I say. "Even though you didn't see her kill him."

He nods. "You were sure of it."

"Why do you trust me?" I ask.

Brig leans his head back against the wall, but he keeps his eyes on me. I see the pulse in his throat, the hollow at the base of his neck. "You do good things," he says at last.

If I could laugh, I would. "Like building armor that tears people up? Like trying to set a village on fire?"

"You did your best to get the crew off the ship safely when the drifters attacked," he says. "You kept track of all of us in the forest."

"That was just being practical," I say. "I wanted you all near me so I could keep an eye on you. And so you could help me take back the ship."

"You know how to change," he says. "You shift course."

I have never seen myself that way. He can't be right. I've always been driven, like an arrow, headed for one fixed purpose, one destination at a time. *To run with Call. To kill the raiders.*

"You've been trying to help the drifters escape," he says. "You fought alongside them."

"You think I'm better than I really am," I tell Brig.

"Poe." Brig scoots closer, the handcuffs sliding against his wrist bones. His fingers are dirty and tan, and up close I can see his eyelashes, the stubble shading his cheekbones, the curve of his top lip. "I don't—"

The door opens. Sister Haring. "Poe Blythe," she says, her voice cool, a cut. "The Admiral wants to see you."

CHAPTER 41

THE ADMIRAL HAS THEM BRING ME TO HIS ROOM.

Which is, of course, my room. The captain's room. He's taken it over.

The lantern glows on the desk. My bag is still on top of the dresser. The Admiral is sitting on my bunk and he leans back, arms folded, boots crossed at the ankle. I see the glimmer of his teeth.

I'm surprised. It's faded and far away under fear, under knowing Tam is gone, but it's there. *The Admiral really does want me for something. He doesn't just want me dead.*

So, what is it?

"Well," the Admiral says. "*Captain* Blythe. Would you like to tell me what happened?"

"I changed sides," I say.

"Of course you did," he says. "You thought it was to your best advantage." He smiles at me, lifts up the lantern, and sets it on the bed next to him. Now all of the light is on his side of the room. "Naomi told me everything."

"Did she," I say. "What does she get in return?"

"She gets to live."

"Do I?"

"That depends," he says. "On how useful you might prove to be."

"You want me to fix the ship."

He waves his hand dismissively. "Naomi can fix the motor. She's working on it now. But not everyone can design weapons the way you do." He rocks forward, sets his hands on his knees, the hairs on his arms glinting amber in the light. "Even so, I have to say that I'm not pleased you ruined the armor. Naomi tells me that was your idea." He tilts his head, looks right into my eyes, lowers his voice. "Why would you do that?"

"I made it," I say. "So it was mine to ruin."

"No," he says. "You designed it, but you didn't pay for it. That's all right, though. You will."

A grumble, low and deep. A roll of mechanical thunder. My ship. It's coming alive again. I feel the hum through the soles of my feet, in the beats of my heart.

"Well." The Admiral is pleased. "It sounds like Naomi has the motor going. We're going to go as far as we can as fast as we can. Run the ship into the ground. And then, we'll use the wagons to go the rest of the way." He gives a long, satisfied sigh. "Everything is working out fine."

He rises to his feet, filling the room, his shoulders squared and his voice warm, an invitation to fall into line. "We have the gold again. In the end, nothing is lost."

Nothing. Only Tam. And some of the others. "You're a fool," I say.

The Admiral's jaw tightens.

"Do you really think you can bring yourself back from the dead?" I ask him. "No one can do that." I am sure of this, and I know he hears it in my voice. I have seen the dead, just hours ago. I have seen the way their eyes look.

Something goes when you go.

That is the magic, the alchemy: the primitive, deep-seated element that is in you—that *is* you—while you live, and which leaves the moment you die. You can't get it back. Nothing can buy it. No amount of tears will ever call it home.

"What are you talking about?" the Admiral says. "I'm not dead."

"The palingenesis project," I say. "Tam told me about it."

"Ah," the Admiral says. "Tam."

Does he know that Tam is dead? He must, by now.

"Tam made a mistake." The Admiral shakes his head. "He chose the wrong side in the fight against the raiders. And I don't want to live forever." He laughs. The convivial, rich sound seems to constrict the room, to steal the air from the space above bed, table, chair, between us. "Captain Blythe. You know me better than that. I'm a practical man."

In some ways, he is. In some ways, he's not.

"The palingenesis project may have a whimsical name," he says, "but it's an extremely rational venture."

We've come down to it. Tam was right. This project is why

the Admiral wants the gold. So what *is* it? "What are you try-ing to do?" I ask. "What do you want?"

"Glory," he says.

He answered me. A single word, frank and brief. I believe him.

Will he answer my other questions with the same honesty?

"What happens now?" I ask. "Do you kill us all right away, or wait until we've helped you with the gold? Or do you torture the drifters to find out what they had planned?"

"Oh, we know where they're going," he says. "The raid-ers should have been more careful about who they bargained with. Those same people made a deal with us, too." He smiles. "Whoever gets them the gold first, wins."

"Wins what?"

"I can't tell you *everything*, Captain Blythe." The way he uses my title is mocking, as if he's pointing out the fiasco my leadership has been, start to finish. "Now. Tell *me* something. I know from Naomi that you were shooting at us from the dredge. But you had the raiders remove the armor. And you rigged your ship to go too fast. *Did* you want the raiders to succeed, or were you trying to help *us*?"

I could lie.

I should.

"I don't know," I say.

He hits me so fast I only see it coming in the last second, the backhand across my face that feels like it knocks my bones and my teeth clear through my flesh, my brain. I stagger back against the desk, stretch my cuffed hands out in front in a futile attempt to gain balance, but the impact of the desk sends me forward. My knees hit the floor hard.

I'm kneeling in front of him.

"I had to leave a mark that would show," he says. "Do you know why?"

I don't answer. My mouth is full of blood, and I think I'll be sick if I swallow it because it makes me think of Tam's blood and Call's blood and everyone's blood.

"Some of the Quorum think I'm too easy on you," he says. "They wonder if I have a tie to you. If you're some kind of family, maybe. I can't rightly see why. We don't look alike. Do we *act* alike? Is that it?"

I turn my head and spit the blood out, spray it across his pillow, his bed, his blanket, the things that used to be mine.

The Admiral makes a sound of disgust. "Like a dog marking its territory," he says. "Well then. You can lie in it."

He walks out of the room and shuts the door behind him. I hear him speaking to the guard outside but I can't make out the words.

There's something small and hard in the bed when I lie down on it. And a hole at the back of my mouth. He knocked out one of my teeth.

I don't think he'll spare me the gold for a new one.

CHAPTER 42

IN THE MORNING, they take me to the Quorum.

Two guards drag me from my room to the cafeteria. The Quorum looks up from their seats. I can tell from their expressions that the bruise on my face is doing the work the Admiral wanted. It's making them wonder.

"Sit here," says one of the guards. The chair is as far away from the Admiral as possible. He watches from the head of the table.

I've gone from being at the Devil's hand to sitting at his feet.

I take my position and look at the Quorum. They're all here. Not one has been left behind in the Outpost to govern in the Admiral's absence.

Why?

Sister Haring isn't smiling with her mouth, but her eyes have a satisfied look to them as she takes in my bruise, my cuffed hands, the dried blood on my shirt and in my hair. Bishop Weaver, who has never liked me much, twists his mouth sadly at the sight of my injury and I see new sympathy in his eyes.

Too late. If you have to see me broken and beat-up to care about me, I will never *care about you. If you only like me when I'm cast down, I will get back up and wipe the kindness right off your face.*

Wishful thinking. I'm in handcuffs on a locked-down ship.

"We have one spot left," the Admiral says. "We need to choose who will take it."

One spot for what?

"Are you certain we should have the candidates here when we decide?" asks Sister Haring.

"I think we might find it revealing," says the Admiral.

"I still argue for Brig Tanner," says General Dale.

As if he's summoned Brig by saying his name, the door opens, and two guards escort Brig in. He's been hit, too—his nose is swollen, the cut reopened, and his lip is split. His eyes meet mine as the guards walk him down to sit next to me. I wish I could reach out and touch his hand. I wish I could say, *I'm all right. Are you?*

"Of the dredge crew, we're taking Corwin Revis, Joseph Andrade, and Ophelia Hill," says General Foster. "They're the most useful for engineering and navigating."

"The last spot goes to Naomi Moran," says Bishop Weaver. "We agreed on that earlier. It was promised to her."

"I think the case for Captain Blythe is more compelling," says General Foster.

"We'll hear all arguments," says the Admiral. "You may each take a turn."

The door opens and guards bring Naomi in. She isn't handcuffed the way Brig and I are, but she still has to sit with us. I want to kill her for killing Tam. And I never want to kill again. I want both things at the same time.

I look away from her and at Brig. I don't know him as well as I wish I did, and I've been betrayed before, but I think I know something about Brig. I think he is my friend.

I may be wrong.

"Excellent," the Admiral says. "Now we can begin."

"What's going on?" asks Naomi. Her face is clean, uninjured. She doesn't look afraid, exactly, but she's wary.

"I know we told you we'd likely be able to bring you with us," says the Admiral, "but General Dale prefers First Mate Tanner, and it turns out that General Foster wants to give the spot to Captain Blythe." He gives a cheerful grimace, as if saying, *As you can see, my hands are tied.*

"*What?*" Naomi glances at Brig, at me. "After everything that happened? *Why?*"

"First Mate Tanner has many skills," says General Dale. "And he's loyal to his commanding officer. Almost to a fault."

"He didn't do what I did." Naomi's voice is steady, assured. The Naomi I know, the one who taught me about the ship on my first voyage. "I did everything you asked. Why would you take *her?*"

"Captain Blythe has proven inventive for death," says the Admiral. He is perfectly polite, hands on the table, nothing to hide. Is that blood from my lip on his turquoise ring? Or were those dark specks always there against the stone?

"We may have need of such a skill." General Foster shuffles the papers in front of him, and I realize what they are: the schematics for my armor. "Who knows what weapons we might need in the future. Having someone who can design them could be very useful."

"I don't design weapons," I say.

"Oh, but you do," says the Admiral. "And if we bring you to Palingenesis, that *will* be your job."

If they bring me to Palingenesis? It's a *place*?

Whatever Palingenesis is, I want no part of it.

"Wherever it is you're going," I say, "I don't want to come."

"I'm afraid it's not up to you." The Admiral pulls out the small, leather-bound notebook he carries in his shirt pocket. "We're wasting time. I'll keep a tally. Who would like to go first?"

"I withhold my vote," says Sister Haring. "They're all compromised. The space would be better given to someone else." She presses her mouth into a thin line. Will the Admiral indulge her in her slight defiance? He makes a mark in his notebook and moves on.

"Those in favor of bringing Brig Tanner." One vote. From General Dale.

"Those in favor of bringing Naomi Moran." One vote. Bishop Weaver.

"Those in favor of Poe Blythe." One vote. General Foster.

"I see it's up to me to break the tie," the Admiral says.

"We all know which way you'll go." Naomi's voice is bitter. "She ruined the ship and betrayed us all, but you don't seem to care."

The room goes still. My throat knots. I have no love left for Naomi after what she did to Tam, but I don't want to see her die. *Why* is she challenging the Admiral like this? No one moves or stirs. All eyes are on the Admiral, on his weatherbeaten, commanding face. Not a flicker of emotion crosses it.

And then, he smiles. Right at Naomi. "My vote is for Captain Blythe."

The air goes out of my lungs. *No.*

I know the Admiral might notice my frantic, desperate glance at Brig, deep into his eyes, but I can't help myself.

"I need someone with an innovative mind more than I need a boy who's good at following, or an old woman," says the Admiral. Brig doesn't flinch, but Naomi draws in her breath sharp.

"You *promised me*," she says to the Admiral.

"You'll still live," he says. "That's all I promised. And you're lucky to have that. You can make your way back to the Outpost."

"But then I'll never see it," she says. "*Palingenesis.*" For the first time, this voyage or last, I hear tears in her voice. She wants to see that place, whatever it is, as much as Call and I wanted to see stars. *"Didn't you ever get sick of the same old story?"* Tam asked me, and I remember the book of fairy tales we found in her room.

No. Naomi will *not* undo me. She was right. I did trust her. She betrayed that trust. I harden my heart against her.

Two guards yank me to my feet and haul me toward the door. I don't make it easy for them; I imagine I'm a dead bag of gold, dragging my weight.

"You *shot* Tam," I say to Naomi as they shove me past her.

Sister Haring flinches and Bishop Weaver presses his hands together as if in prayer. Didn't they know that Tam died? Who killed him? Has anyone in the Quorum bothered to look at the bodies?

"Tam betrayed us," Naomi says.

I'm livid. She's trying to rationalize that cold-blooded murder, that point-blank shot that took Tam down. "Tam *fed* you," I spit at Naomi. "He looked out for you. We all did. I trusted you more than I trusted anyone else."

"Of course you did," Naomi says. "I was with you on the other voyage. With Call." She meets my gaze. "At least *I* didn't forget who killed him."

CHAPTER 43

THE GUARDS HANDCUFF ME TO THE RAIL at the back
of the ship. I'm not sure why they lock me up on the deck and
not in one of the rooms. Is the Admiral hoping that exposure
to the elements will wear me down even more? Maybe voting
for me showed a weakness he now has to offset.

A single settler guard stays with me.

The deck is a scarred landscape, mangled from where we
tore up the armor and stained with blood from the battle. The
Admiral doesn't visit me, and the guard doesn't speak to me
or answer any of my questions.

The sun rises and crosses the sky. The ship churns on.

At noon a guard brings me medicine and food—tack
and water—and I try to find out more. "*Porter?*" I whisper.
"*Lily?*" Though that's not her real name, I remember too late.
I can't ask her now. "Brig? Eira? What's happened to them?"

The guard looks right through me as if I were a ghost.

The handcuffs chafe against the burn on my skin, which

isn't healing quite right. There's no infection anymore, but the skin is coming together in a puckered, uneven way.

Doesn't matter, I tell myself. *I've got the use of it. I'm alive.*

Who else is alive on the ship?

When I look down over the railing, I see that the wagons seem to be on the east shore now, keeping pace with us. How did they get them all across the river?

There are no signs of any of the other drifters, the ones who went on before.

The sun beats down. I duck my head to try to keep my face from getting too burned. I can feel the heat on the part in my scalp, on my shoulders. My lips are chapped and peeling, the end of my nose is bright red. How much longer will the Admiral leave me up here? Does he want me to see all of this—the inexorability of the settlers' wagons and numbers? Does he think that will make me go with him, wherever this Palingenesis place is?

The Admiral comes to the deck at the end of the day, at dusk.

Two guards follow him through the hatch to the deck, dragging a drifter along with them. *Porter.* He looks awful. Battered and beaten, black eyes, split lip, knuckles bleeding. He doesn't recognize me at first. Then, something clicks in behind his eyes and he smiles.

At *me.* After everything.

"Isn't this wonderful, Captain Blythe?" the Admiral says. "We're doing exactly what you wanted. Destroying the raiders."

I shut my eyes. I can't watch whatever is about to happen. I feel the thrum of my ship, the way its pitch is changing. *How much longer?* it seems to ask. But it's not pleading, yet. I smell river water, sweat, metal.

I *have* to watch. I can't abandon Porter.

I open my eyes and look at him. "I'm sorry," I say. "I didn't know."

"What didn't you know?" the Admiral asks.

"Anything," I say to Porter, and there are tears dripping off my cheeks, my jaw, though I'm not sure when I started crying. "I didn't know anything."

There are tears in Porter's eyes too.

"What do you know now?" the Admiral asks. He unties the silk handkerchief knotted casually around his neck and wipes his forehead, tucks the silk square into his pocket.

My tongue finds the hole in the back of my mouth where my tooth used to be. "That you stole the drifters' children."

"We gave them good lives," the Admiral says. "They live longer with us than they would have out here."

"You don't know that," I say.

"I think I do." The Admiral turns so it's his profile I see, his face burnished by the setting sun. "Look how quickly Call died when he went out on the river." He stretches his arms high overhead, a show of ease, of power. "Or was Naomi right? Have you forgotten who shot him?"

Of course not. I will *never* forget. "They didn't know who he was."

"But you did," says the Admiral. "And so you set about killing them. You did an excellent job of it, and your designs kept our gold safe. It's too bad you lost the ship, but you can make that right. You can make it *all* right, now."

He motions for the guards to bring Porter closer, and I taste bile rising in my throat. What is the Admiral going to make me do?

I think I know and my knees are trembling. My handcuffs rattle against the rail. I try to still them.

The Admiral nods to the guard nearest me, and the guard presses a gun into my locked-together hands. It's a revolver, an old, heavy gun that I think might be the Admiral's own. It has a heft and quality to it. I've never fired one before.

"Don't drop it," the Admiral warns. "It's loaded, and you don't want it to go off. In fact, it'd be best if you didn't move at all for the moment." Two of the guards have rifles trained on me.

I try to hold the gun steady. I'd have a single chance to shoot the Admiral. One quick movement.

"I'd like you to take care of Porter," the Admiral says. "It won't take long. Are you a good shot?"

I am, from far away. Up close I have the colors of Porter's eyes, the texture of his skin, the sorrow in every line on his face.

"If you try to shoot me instead," the Admiral says, his voice patronizing, "or one of the other guards, we'll take you down before you can kill anyone else. And we'll kill First Mate Tanner and Eira Clyde. Naomi tells me you care about both of them." The Admiral smiles. "In fact, if you *don't* shoot Porter, then we'll go ahead and eliminate Brig and Eira. You might be more effective in your task knowing that."

"It's all right," Porter says. "Better this way than another." He takes a long, ragged breath. "Think of it as being for Call."

"It would never be for Call," I say. "He would never want this." My hands are shaking and shaking and shaking.

The tears slide down Porter's dirty, beaten face. The Admiral would never let anyone see him cry, I think. But Porter doesn't lead like the Admiral.

"I shot Call," Porter says. "I couldn't see his face. But he was unarmed. Whether he was ours or not, I shouldn't have done it."

My heart catches. He's said the words. And so, I *know*. I'm looking into Porter's haunted, living eyes.

This is the man who killed Call, who made him nothing. Deep inside, something dark in me wants to take the shot.

"I need the guards to move away," I say. "I don't want to shoot them by accident."

"You may have a point," the Admiral says. "All right," he tells the guards. "Take a step away. I don't think Porter is in any condition to run."

They lean him up against the railing. Porter was always in motion. Never still. But now, he looks straight into my eyes. We are face-to-face. I know who he is. What he's done.

I will shoot to kill.

Before I can take my shot, before I can fire at the Admiral and feel the guards' bullets in me, Porter turns. He seems to lift off the ground in a single motion, a kind of stunning arc of flight, but it's really just a leap, a final movement, one last, decisive act.

He goes over the edge of the ship.

"Porter!" I'm straining at my handcuffs, sliding them as far as I can along the rail. *Please don't let Porter have gotten caught on the jagged remains of my armor. It would be a terrible, tearing way to go. Please. Please. Please.*

Who am I talking to?

The ship?

Please.

There he is. In the river below. Then gone. The wake of the ship is strong enough to push someone under, turn them until they can't rise to the surface, force their lungs full of water, batter them against the unforgiving rocks of the riverbed.

He doesn't come up.

CHAPTER 44

THEY LEAVE ME UP ON THE DECK all night. As punishment for not killing Porter? Because there's no other place to put me?

The night guard takes pity on me and clips my cuffs to the bottom of the railing so I can at least lie down as I shiver in the cold, my knees tucked up against my chest, not sleeping, thinking of Porter's jump into the water below. Did he know I wouldn't shoot him? What did he see in my eyes? There is no way to know. There is *never* a way to be sure what happens in those final moments.

As the sun rises, the guard has me stand, clips my handcuffs to the top railing again.

Just in time. I hear boots on the steps. The Admiral strides onto the deck. "How was your final night on the ship?"

"Long," I say, and he throws back his head and laughs.

"There's something I need to show you." He motions for the guard to unlock my cuffs. The bliss at being able to move and stretch is counteracted by cold and hunger and anger and loss.

What can you show me? I want to scream. *What more can there possibly be?* Is he going to bring everyone up to die, one by one? Make me kill them?

"No," he says, as if he can read my mind. "This is something beautiful." The Admiral leans his elbows on the eastern railing in an almost comradely, companionable way. "Amazing what this boat has done to the river. We noticed it the entire time we traveled upstream to find you. The ruin. The rocks." He turns to look at me but I keep my eyes on the water below us. "But this ship is nothing compared to what you're about to see."

He wants me to ask what it is. I won't.

"Watch the sky," he says. "Near us, to the northeast."

I swear I won't look, but then there's a sharp shimmer in the sky, a light so bright and sudden that I can't help myself. From beyond the woods, something huge and glimmering is rising, golden in the morning light.

What is it?

The Admiral was right.

Beautiful.

"What is it?" I ask the question aloud. I have never seen anything like this. It's the size of a dredge, but so much more streamlined, so elegant. It's in the *air*. And it *moves*. It's enormous, but lithe. Fast.

It soars over us and I find myself reaching up, trying to

touch it, snatch it out of the sky, my fingers tracing the arc of its passage. When it disappears beyond the western horizon I feel the loss deep in my stomach, in my heart. *Make it come back*, I want to tell the Admiral. I need to see it again.

"That's *Palingenesis*," says the Admiral. "Magnificent, isn't it?"

It *is*.

A ship. A golden ship in the sky.

"Where did it go?" I ask around the lump in my throat.

The Admiral laughs. "This is what I like about you, Captain Blythe," he says. "You're practical. One minute, you're sick with guilt over the death of someone you cared about, the next, you see something shiny and you want to play with it."

I should bend my head in embarrassment. I should tear my eyes from the sky. But I can't. "Will it come back?"

"Yes," the Admiral says. "This is a test flight. When it leaves the next time, we'll be inside of it."

"*We'll be inside of it.*" My heart soars. I'll be on that ship, in the sky? *That's* what the Admiral has planned for me?

"Where are we going?" I ask.

"To start a new Outpost," the Admiral says. "In a place far away, one that's been unoccupied for generations. It's a long flight. To the other side of the world. And we won't be coming back."

He laughs again at the expression on my face. The warm, booming sound that has so charmed his people for as long as I can remember. My whole life long, he's told us the story of the

Outpost, how we were abandoned and gathered in. And now the Admiral's *leaving*?

"All this time, you thought you were working on the most important ship," he says. "But the dredge was a means to an end. *This* is the end. This is what it's all been for."

He's right. The dredge is nothing compared to what I've just seen.

"Is it made of gold?"

The Admiral leans closer. He smells like soap and menthol, clean. I want to pull away, to put more distance between us, but I have to know everything there is to know about the flying *Palingenesis*. "No," he says. "That was the sun, reflecting off the ship's surface. But gold has been very useful in building some of the components of the ship. It's also paid our passage. *And* we'll bring some with us." He smiles. "It's a currency that has proven valuable across many cultures. And through time."

"You're deserting the Outpost," I say.

"The Outpost," the Admiral says, his expression turning to disgust. "All our broken-down buildings, the *scraps* we have to use to build anything. Where everyone's tired and dull and *dirty*." He pushes away from the railing, stands with his arms braced against it. "It's time to start over."

"You're doing the opposite of what the other Admirals have done."

"No." He folds his arms. "I'm doing exactly what they've always done, but on a grander scale. I gathered in the raider children. And when I learned about this ship, I gathered up the best of the Outpost to take with me."

And then I understand. He wants to build something he can take credit for. He can be immortal as the founder of something new and glorious instead of the protector of something old and broken-down.

"Who made the *Palingenesis*?" I ask. "Why would they let us on it?"

If the ship were mine, I wouldn't let anyone on it. I'd fly so far so fast.

"A group from a society beyond our maps," the Admiral says. "We paid to help them repair it. We paid for our passage. And we're giving them some of the gold from this voyage."

"They could leave us behind." I look at the sky. "Maybe they've left you already. Maybe it's not coming back." Again, that pang in my heart. That strange feeling of loss.

What is wrong with me? It's a ship, not a person.

"They won't," he says. "It's not only the gold they need from us. It's more than that."

"What?"

"Ourselves," he says. "The things we know. It's been a long time since they've had to live the way we have." He smiles. "And we've got new genes to mix with theirs. That can't hurt."

"They're not going to let you rule," I say. "They'll have their own leader."

"That remains to be seen." The Admiral shields his eyes against the sun. "We're taking the best of the best with us.

Our finest machinists, soldiers, physicians, builders. And the Quorum, of course."

Are they still taking me? Even though I didn't kill Porter?

"Go ahead," the Admiral says. "Ask."

He's going to make me do it. I swallow my pride, my fear, my anger, my loss. My throat is raw. "Am I going?"

"Yes."

The speed of his response is a shock, as is the fact that he doesn't toy with me. Just tells me straight. "Why?"

"It's like I said earlier," the Admiral says. "You've proven inventive for death. You've managed it on the largest scale in recent history. That counts for something."

That's what I've done. *That's* my immortality. My soaring heart begins to sink. I did not see their faces. But they died anyway. I did it. For Call.

No.

For me. Because the idea of revenge kept me alive.

What kind of person am I? The Admiral thinks he knows. What he's said is fact. I can't deny or refute it.

"Who do you need to kill?" I ask. "You said the place where you're going is abandoned."

"For now it is," he says, "but people will want to come and take it from us." A gold tooth glints in the back of his mouth. I think of my missing tooth, of the way he hit me in the captain's quarters.

I remember how I fought Tam there.

Tam.

Tam was brave. He wanted to know about everyone. He learned all our names. He made food that nourished people. He came into the woods with us. He fought on the deck. *This* deck.

I saw him go.

"I need a weapon. One that isn't broken." The Admiral's gaze flickers to me. "Are you broken?"

I stare past the river, to the horizon where the golden ship vanished. Everything here is wrong and ruined. There is something light and beautiful that can take us to another world. Two choices, a flip of a coin, stamped in gold and blood.

And there is something in the distance, low on the horizon. Something the Admiral may have missed.

"No," I say. I point up to the sky, where the ship, the golden *Palingenesis*, is coming back. "I'm reborn."

CHAPTER 45

"IT'S TIME TO SAY GOODBYE TO THE *LILY*," the Admiral says. "She has served us well."

He's called everyone together, drifter and settler alike, and has climbed up on the platform of the mining deck to address us.

Time has run out. We have come to the end of our voyage. The motor is silent for now, shut down by the machinists at the Admiral's order. It lasted long enough. I want to pat the casing surrounding the motor, whisper *Good job.* Even though of course it's not alive. Even though it's brought us to a place from which there may be no return. The ship did what we asked it to do.

Everyone knows about the other ship, the *Palingenesis*, now. But only the Admiral knows for certain who will be on board when it leaves for good.

Who will die? Who will live? Who will be chosen to leave and start again?

"It's time to run the dredge ashore," says the Admiral.

"Once that's done, we'll unload gold onto the wagons through the tailings stacker."

"Running the ship aground will ruin it." The moment the words are out of my mouth I curse myself. I'm supposed to be trying to *please* the Admiral, not lose my spot on the *Palingenesis*.

"It's the fastest and easiest way to load the wagons." The Admiral props his foot up on a bag of gold, leans on his knee. "And we have no need for the *Lily* anymore. She's fulfilled her purpose."

"It's going to be dangerous for whoever's left on board to steer the ship," Corwin says. "The force of impact will be tremendous." I fix my gaze on my chief machinist, who's dared to speak up on behalf of whoever might be given the unenviable and dangerous task of ruining the *Lily*. The Quorum has chosen him to go with them. Does he know? If so, is he glad? His face is inscrutable.

"It is," agrees the Admiral. "But we have someone who knows the ship inside and out and who is up to the challenge."

A stone settles in my stomach. The Admiral stands up straight again and makes a broad, sweeping gesture in my direction. I am standing with the rest of the group. I am no longer at his left hand.

"Captain Blythe will handle it." The Admiral smiles at me, his eyes and teeth bright across the whole length of the room. "She knows the dredge. She'll bring it to land. The rest of us will wait for her on the shore."

Of course. He's not really going to let me on the *Palingenesis* until I've proven myself. I failed the test with Porter, so I've been given another. The Admiral wants me to do this first.

To survive the wreck of my ship.

The Admiral takes me up to the bridge. To my surprise and the guards', he dismisses them at the door and tells them they can wait outside. Once they're gone, the Admiral removes a handgun from his pocket and places it inside the small metal safe set into the wall. He locks it and hands me the key.

"For you," he says.

"Why?"

"You'll see." The Admiral surveys me. He's wearing a clean shirt and vest this morning, not a work shirt. It's an occasion. "I hope you survive the crash," he says. "I think you will. And when you've finished doing what you have to do on this ship, you can come with us on the next."

He needs someone who knows how to run the dredge aground. Whom he can spare if they die. That's me.

It's always me and I'm sick of it.

One more time.

I'll do whatever it takes, one more time, to get what I want.

Once we've finished talking, the Admiral and his guards will use the drifters' little light boats to get clear of the ship. As soon as the Admiral's safe, I'm supposed to start the motor and gun it for the shore in reverse, toward a long sandbar that edges out into the river. I'll beach the dredge there, so that the stacker hangs over land instead of water. Then the settlers will board and send the gold out through the stacker directly into the wagons.

"All you have to do is get the ship up onshore and make sure the stacker isn't ruined," the Admiral says. "Any other damage doesn't matter."

"I understand." And I do. If I survive, I'll be useful to him. If not, I'll still have completed this task he needed me to do.

"Good." The Admiral rolls up his sleeves, folding each cuff neatly over his forearms once, twice. "I'll see you onshore." He slides open the bridge door and glances back at me. "Try not to kill yourself. I'd like to see you on the other ship."

He doesn't close the door behind him. I listen to his footsteps as he walks down the hallway to the stairwell, as he's joined by the guards, as they take the steps down to the boats that will bear them safely away. Once I can no longer hear them, I look out through the window on the bridge. Bits of the metal teeth that once surrounded it remain, ready to shred anyone who tries to climb in or out, but most of the armor is gone. The mining buckets and mechanism are somewhere back on the river. We left a trail they could probably see from the new ship in the sky.

We're scarred, battered, bruised. Almost finished.

A settler on the shore fires two rifle shots into the air. That's the signal: The Admiral has arrived.

Time for me to do my job. I leave the bridge and take the stairs to the mining deck. I run my hand along the rail, note the rivets in the floor. I swear I hear the echo of my crew's voices down among the machinery. Their joy at finding gold. For a few days, we were a real crew. I swallow.

The door to the mining deck is open. The voices in my mind grow louder, and I shake my head to clear them, frustrated at my own imagination.

And then. I'm standing inside the doorway, next to the main control panel, staring up.

At faces. People handcuffed to the rails of the platform on the mining deck.

Lily. Brig.

And three drifters.

No one else was supposed to be on the ship.

"What are you doing here?" I ask.

"What do you think?" Lily snaps. "The Admiral left us like this. He said you killed Porter." Her voice is beyond hate, beyond contempt. "And now you're going to do the same to us."

Of course. So *this* is why the Admiral left the gun for me upstairs. Why he said those words: *You'll see.* The test wasn't only to discover whether or not I could finish my ship and survive the wreck. He also wants to see if I can kill my friends and the drifters. Face-to-face. I have to perform these tasks before he'll let me aboard that beautiful golden ship.

I am so sick of his games. Of his using me.

These men. Who play a game of glory and gold and don't care who it ruins as long as they can take, take, take. Who see other people as their right, their pawns.

If they see them at all.

When that ship soared across the sky, and I looked at the horizon near the river, I knew what I had to do. Nothing is going to stop me.

Nothing.

And no one.

"Porter jumped," I say.

Lily laughs. "You expect me to believe that?"

"Where are the keys to the handcuffs?" I ask.

Brig answers, his eyes gentle and his voice steady. "The Admiral took them with him."

Of course he did. I stride over to one of the cabinets on the wall. *Please, let the settlers have left some of the equipment behind.*

They did.

I yank out one of the toolboxes and remove some of the smaller, intricate tools. A tiny screwdriver, a scalpel-like blade with a narrowed end. "Pull as far away from the rail as you can," I say to Lily and the others. "We have to hurry. The Admiral will know something's wrong if I don't get the ship moving soon."

I pick the lock on Lily's cuffs, then Brig's. Lily steps away, as if she can't bear to be near me. Brig stands right at my side, his shoulders squared.

"Me next," says one of the drifters. "Then I can strangle you." He flexes his fingers.

"She's *helping* us," says Brig.

"I have to start the motor," I say. "I'm supposed to run the ship aground. They're waiting." The next drifter is free. Two more left. I'm leaving the one who threatened me for last.

"They'll kill us as soon as we get to shore," says Lily. "You didn't buy us much time."

"You're not coming with me," I say. Another drifter, free. I crouch down near the last one, avoiding his eyes.

"What do you mean?" Lily's face goes pale. Does she really think I'd shoot her? After all this?

"I have a plan," I say. "But first, go and get the gliders. Some of them are in the storage room up by the mining bridge."

Lily's on the move almost before I've finished the sentence. "Come *on,*" she says over her shoulder to the other drifters. They follow her out.

Brig stays behind.

"Where's Eira?" I ask.

"She's with the settlers," Brig says. "She wants to go on the flying ship." His smile fades but doesn't vanish altogether. "Why wouldn't she? It's a whole new world to map. And see."

"It changes everything," I say.

Brig nods and leans against the wall near us, his back up against the signal marks. I wish he'd put his hands on me. The thought is a surprise. But it's been so long since anyone has touched me the way Call did. Two years. Two years without anything real.

I hear. The quiet of being with Brig. Quiet like Call.

I imagine. Brig's lips on my neck.

I don't need someone to hold me. I need someone to meet

me, the way Call did, to match need with need, strength with strength. I think Brig could do it.

I still don't know how to love someone else.

But I'm remembering how to want.

Feet pound on the metal stairs. Lily and the others race inside. My heart lifts at the sight of the gliders on their shoulders. Lily carries two.

"There's more upstairs," she says. "But we can't decide if we trust you enough to come with us." There's a warning in her voice, a firmness.

"Don't worry," I say. "I'm not coming with you."

"Poe," Brig says.

"I still don't see how it's going to work." A note of doubt wars with the hope in Lily's voice.

"You'll jump from the deck of the ship. At the front."

"They'll shoot us down."

"Not if you go right when I run it aground," I say. "They'll be watching the back because that's the end they want me to crash into the eastern bank of the river. That's why you can't go through the tailings stacker. You'll fall right into their hands." I pause. "But I think someone else is waiting for you."

"What are you talking about?" Lily's expression is wary.

"I saw some of your boats," I say.

That was the moment of my rebirth. I saw the golden ship in the sky, and it dazzled me, and it dazzled the Admiral. For a moment we had eyes for nothing else, but then I noticed something, earth- and-water-bound instead of sky. Boats, tiny, at the very edge of the shore in the distance, far below that beautiful bright ship.

People do come back for the ones they love.

"They were upriver, along the western shore. I think the rest of the drifters came back for you. I think they realized something was wrong."

"Are you sure?" one asks.

"No," I say. It could have been a trick of the light, a way of the sun glinting off the water, rocks along the shore instead of boats. It could be many things. But I know what it looked like to me.

"They'll kill you if you let us go," Lily says.

"I know," I say. "Go up to the deck. Stay low. When you feel us starting to run aground, *jump*."

Lily's face softens as she looks at me and it's so unexpected that my heart hitches. Does it mean she doesn't hate me? Even after everything?

"Everyone thought I was dead for sure, once," Lily says. "But I wasn't." For a moment, her voice sounds far away. Then she squares her shoulders. "You might make it," she tells me, shoving a glider at Brig.

He doesn't take it from her. "I'm not going," he says. "I'm going to run the ship to shore. Poe can go." There's a look in his eyes and a turn of his lips that I haven't seen before; not a snarl but a declaration, a holding ground.

But I will not move. "No," I say. "I won't."

"*Why not?*" His voice is wild with frustration, and time

is ticking, running away with every second. How long before the Admiral sends a boat back to the dredge to see what's happened? To find out why I haven't killed the people down on the mining deck and started the motor?

"Someone has to bring the ship to shore so the rest of you can get away," I say. "This is mine to finish."

"It's not your fault Call died," Brig says. "It was the Admiral's fault for taking him and the drifters' fault for shooting him. And Naomi killed Tam. Not you."

"I killed all those drifters with my armor," I say. "I can save a few others today."

His hand, on my shoulder, gentle and firm. His jaw clenched and his voice tight. I can feel the warmth of his fingers through my shirt.

"Brig," I say. "Go."

"You don't have to try to be the hero." His voice is rough and low.

"I'm not trying," I say. "I am."

CHAPTER 46

TIME TO BREAK MY SHIP FOR GOOD.

The motor hums. I grip the helm, sparing one backward glance at the safe with the gun locked inside.

Brig thinks I'm better than I am.

The Admiral thinks I'm worse.

Call saw *me*.

That's something to have had, at least once.

My life hasn't been nothing. It's been everything to me.

Are the drifters ready, up on the deck? Is Brig standing next to Lily? Will anyone come to save them when they jump?

I let the throttle go.

What if I was wrong about the boats? I've been wrong so many times before.

But I want to believe it's true. I want to believe that people come back for one another.

Almost there. I hold the helm steady. "*I'm sorry*, Lily," I whisper to the ship. The motor turns and deep inside I hear a scrape, a long, keening groan.

As the dredge and earth tear into each other, as the world ends, I close my eyes.

What would it be like to have someone come back for you?

Call couldn't. It's not his fault he never did.

And.

It's not my fault he never did.

CHAPTER 47

I SIT UP. My unburned hand dangles awkwardly, but I don't think it's broken, only twisted and bruised, because my fingers work. It's my head that hurts, on the temple and at the back of my skull.

I'm alive.

The ship groans and settles. There are shouts outside the bridge, and the sound of the tailings stacker running. The settlers are already on board, sending out the gold.

The Admiral stands in the doorway of the bridge.

His face is sunburned and sun-browned, his hat pushed back on his head. He doesn't look so tidy anymore. His tie is askew, his vest has a streak of dirt on it.

"I did it," I say. "I ran the ship ashore. Just like you asked."

Blood trickles down into my eye. I wonder how badly I'm cut.

"The raiders are gone," he says. "Where?"

I want to laugh.

The Admiral, sending me on this voyage, telling me to kill Porter, leaving the gun here on the bridge. He thinks I have to pass his tests to prove myself.

Even the drifters wanted me to do certain things.

The tasks and tests mean nothing. They are not mine.

I am who I say I am.

I am Poe Blythe.

"Nothing will ever be enough for you," I tell the Admiral. I understand this about him. Because nothing will ever be enough for me. I could kill and kill and kill and it would never be enough to get Call back.

Or I could stop.

I could just stop.

"Get off my ship," I say to the Admiral.

"*What?*" And here it is, at last and at once. The fury. The anger. The man inside. The real Admiral. His teeth bare; his eyes go hard. He points his rifle at me.

"I gave you every chance," he says. "But you're an animal. So you can starve like one. Cut yourself to shreds trying to climb through the window. Beat your head against the wall until your brains come out. You can die on this ship. We'll fly away, and you'll never see anything outside of this room."

"I'm not an animal," I say. "And I'm not your weapon. I'm not your *anything*."

The Admiral shifts his rifle. With his free hand, he reaches into his pocket and takes out a key.

"You're right," he says. "You're not anything." He shuts the door to the bridge and locks it behind him.

CHAPTER 48

CALL AND I SHOULD HAVE RUN when we had the chance. We should have slipped away in the starry dark. Holding hands, laughing, afraid and alive.

But we waited too long.

I should have run when I had the chance. When I was in the woods with Brig and Tam and the others, I could have slipped away and never looked back.

But I couldn't let go. Of what the drifters had done to Call. Of the ship.

The things I used to keep me moving, keep me alive, are now what tie me down. What will kill me.

I don't know why I'm crying. Because the Admiral was the closest thing I had to a father, even though I didn't want him for one? Because if he hadn't done that terrible thing, hadn't taken the drifters' children, I never would have known Call at all?

Because the Admiral rejected me? Because that kind of person is the only kind who has ever come back for me?

I'm hungry and thirsty and every bit of me aches. Through the window, I see the day turn into night and day again. The settlers have loaded up their wagons, and most of them are gone. I strain at the window, trying to see how many are left.

I scratch and scrabble at the door, exactly like the Admiral said I would. I try to pick the lock with anything I can find. I manage to tear the safe from the wall and use it to smash through the window, and the breeze and the smell of the river come in to meet me.

More and more, I wonder how much it would hurt to go through the window. Maybe it wouldn't tear me apart completely and I could drop into the water and swim for shore.

I remember when Call died, when I looked at his dead gone eyes and his beautiful face, his hands so still.

I thought *I will never be able to love anyone again.*

I thought *I will kill the people who did this to you.*

And I thought *I will do whatever it takes to stay alive.*

I turned away from his dead body and decided that no matter what, I was going to live.

I don't want to die.

I won't.

If I try to climb through the window, at least I'll die *trying*. I get to my feet and look through, careful not to touch the metal edges.

I can see the river if I bend my head down, and the sky if I tip my head up.

Oh.

A flash of gold, passing across the window. Without thinking, I press closer. The metal bites the edge of my hand and I bring it to my mouth. The taste of my blood is sharp.

The ship.

It's leaving.

As it passes near the sun in the sky, something flares white-hot, incandescent. I move my hand from my mouth to shield my eyes. Blood drips into my lashes.

Is the *Palingenesis* burning?

Or is it merely a trick of the sun?

Either way, the ship

is gone.

CHAPTER 49

I WON'T EVER SET FOOT on that golden ship. I won't ever see what's inside, or watch the world drop away beneath me.

I sink to my knees and rest my cheek against the cool metal of the door. It smells the way my blood tastes. "It's just you and me, *Lily*," I say to the dredge.

"That's not my name," she says.

Wait. Is the ship speaking? To me? After I broke her on the bank of the river?

No. It's a voice on the other side of the door.

"Poe?" someone else says. "We've got a welding torch. Get away from the door."

I know *that* voice. It's Brig.

And the other one—was Lily? The real Lily, not the ship?

I scramble away clumsily, back up against the wall. My heart pounding. I put my hand to my injured head. I'm not imagining this. *I'm not.* My head hurts, there's dark dried blood on my hands and face, and there *is* someone on the other side of the door.

And then it comes free from its hinges with a smell of fire and metal.

Lily. And Brig. Standing there before me, cutting torch in his hands, a rifle in hers.

They came back.

"*Poe.*" Brig goes down on his knees on one side of me and Lily does the same on the other. They each take hold of one of my arms; they lift me up.

"We've got you," Lily says.

"Brig," I say. "Lily." Then I remember. *Lily* is the ship. "That's not your real name. What is it?"

"Indie," she says.

Chapter 50

"HURRY," Indie says. "We're not the only ones who came back for you."

"What do you mean?"

"The settlers." She shifts her weight so she can better support me. "Some of them are outside. The ones the Admiral didn't choose to go on the *Palingenesis*."

I'm cold and bloody and tired. I need to think. The pressure of Brig's and Indie's arms against mine reminds me where I am in my body, grounds me to the ship that's here and not the one that left without me.

"I think they know we're here," Indie says. "I think they're waiting for us to come out with you."

We make it three steps, almost to the door, before Indie's proven correct.

"Captain Blythe." A voice, magnified through a bullhorn, drifts through the broken window. "Please come out. It's safe. We won't harm you."

"You shouldn't have come back." I straighten up, put more weight on my legs. They hold.

"I agree," Lily says. *Indie.* I have to remember that she has another name. "But we did."

"You can bring your friends with you," says the voice. It's not the Admiral. It's someone younger, and for a moment my mind skips and I think, *Tam?* before my heart sinks.

Tam.

He was ours, and I won't forget him. That smile. The way he handed us food in a clearing in the woods. His profile, as he brought the gun up to shoot, sure and fast.

He thought I was the kind of person who might change their mind. Who might be interested in other stories. *You read me right, Tam.* Tears sting my eyes, and I swallow hard.

"We can put a white flag up on the deck and wait for them to come to us," I say. "Let them board the ship if they want to talk."

Neither Brig nor Indie says anything. I know the deck is where Tam died. I know it's where Call died, on another ship. I know there is blood up there. But I want to be out in the open on the dredge when I surrender. I don't want to be on their ground. I'd like to be on mine.

"We'll decide together," I say. "I don't get to choose."

"You're the captain," says Brig.

"This is your ship," says Indie.

We get a sheet from one of the rooms, climb up to the deck, tie it to the railing, and wait. Out on the shore, several wagons are drawn up near the tailings stacker. The settlers who came all the way up the river with the Admiral and then got left behind when he didn't need them anymore.

I wonder how they felt when the ship flew away.

The white flag whips in the wind. Brig and Indie are pressed on either side of me, in case I fall. I can't touch the railings to hold on; both my hands are hurt, but I will not sit down. "Why did Porter let me surrender us to the settlers?" I ask.

"He trusted you." Indie pushes a strand of wind-whipped hair out of her eyes. Though we aren't moving, the wind is playing across the ship, as if it wants to help us pretend that we are. "He realized that you were the person most likely to know what the Admiral was thinking. What the Admiral might *do*. He thought we should take our cues from you."

"Because I'm like the Admiral." The words are sick-sour on my tongue.

"*No.*" Brig's voice is forceful, and I feel him looking at me, even though I keep my eyes on the shore. "Knowing someone well doesn't mean you're like them."

"Why did the drifters really want the gold?" I ask Indie. "Were you going to try to go on the *Palingenesis*, too?"

"No," Indie says. "We knew the Admiral wanted the gold. We knew what he had in mind for it. So we wanted to take it from him, get to his rendezvous point. If *we* had the gold he needed, and the protection of the others who lived out here, we could bargain with him. We could try to get our children back."

"Is that why the drifters wanted the gold from our first voyage?" I ask.

She nods. "We need it for a few things," she says. "And it's how we bribed people to get the information about the Admiral and his plans." She takes a deep breath. "But we didn't yet have enough to bring everyone home."

The Admiral wanted the gold to start a new world, to fly to glory and power and away from the disarray, the debris of the Outpost. The drifters wanted it to build, and to bargain for their own children.

"Will you still try to find them, even without the gold?"

"I haven't decided yet." Indie folds her arms across her chest.

"And what about you?" I ask Brig, still not looking at him. "You said you have family back in the Outpost."

"I don't know yet either," he says.

"To be honest, this is as far as we've gotten," Indie says. "Helping you escape. Which we haven't actually done yet."

"What about them?" I ask Brig and Indie, pointing at the settlers on the shore. They're talking to one another, pointing at the flag and at us on the deck. "The ones the Admiral left behind. What do *they* want?"

Brig isn't touching me anymore, but his shoulder is inches away from mine. "I think they want you."

CHAPTER 51

FIFTEEN SETTLERS, the three of us. We stand on the deck facing one another. I can almost see ghosts in the warming and cooling of evening, the changing of air and light.

Call, up here keeping watch. Tam, aiming at the sniper on the shore.

"We're not here to hurt you," says a settler with long black hair. She seems to be the spokesperson for the group and looks to be in her twenties. Now that she's closer, I recognize her—she was the medic on our voyage. Laura Seng. "We're going back to the Outpost, Captain Blythe. We want you to lead us."

They can't mean it. I look from one settler to another, waiting for them to laugh. But all I see are serious faces watching. Waiting.

"*Why?*" I rake my hand through my hair, which is sticky with dried blood and sweat. Bewilderment and anger run over me like I'm a rock in the river. "Didn't you notice how well things went the last time I was in charge?" I gesture to the ruined ship where we're standing.

One of the settlers frowns.

But Laura sticks to her plan. "We'll make it work," she says, turning halfway so that she can see both me and the settlers standing behind her. "We'll say the raiders killed the Admiral and the Quorum and everyone else who isn't coming back. We tell the other settlers that, when the Admiral was dying, he said Captain Blythe should be in charge of the Outpost. And then they'll want her." She nods to me. "We'll back you. All of us. We'll tell the same story."

Indie huffs and folds her arms. "So you'll blame us for everything."

"You deserve it," bristles one of the men behind Laura. "You raiders stole the ship. You killed some of our men and women."

"Oh *yes*," Indie says, her voice a cool clean knife. "Let's talk about what we all deserve. Let's list the wrongs from both sides. I'd like to see who comes out ahead."

"Wait." I hold up my bruised hand. "How many settlers did the Admiral leave behind?"

"There are twenty-three of us left," Laura says. "The others are back on the shore, waiting."

Brig draws in his breath next to me, and I catch his eye. He noticed the number, too. That's how many were on the *Lily* when we first started out.

But it doesn't mean anything. It's not an omen or a sign.

"Naomi?" I ask.

Laura's lips tighten. "She's staying out in the fields where they launched the *Palingenesis*. She thinks they'll return someday."

Naomi killed for that ship. Now she'll die waiting for it.

"The rest of us are either dead from the fight with the raiders or gone with the Admiral." Laura folds her arms. "We need someone to hold us together, or the Outpost will fall into chaos. The leaders of the old structure are gone. The Admiral took the entire Quorum with him."

The *Lily* groans, as if in protest or pain. I wonder how stable she is, beached on the bank like this. Is the river trying to take us back?

How can they ask this of me? To take the Admiral's place?

I was finally ready to run.

I close my eyes to listen. To the wind, the water, the ship.

What will people think of the dredge if they come upon it years and generations after this? They'll see it stripped of armor, run ashore, picked apart and savaged of everything useful. They will see what it destroyed along the river. The way it ruined.

But. If enough time has passed, perhaps the river will have healed a bit. Maybe the ship will be covered in moss and birds' nests and filled with what the wind brought through the widening cracks and rifts.

I open my eyes.

"No," I say. "We're not blaming the drifters. We tell the truth."

Will the settlers want to do it this way? Will anyone in the Outpost listen to me?

"Poe." Brig's mouth is hard on the word, his hand gentle on my arm. His eyes are worried, the stubble grown during days of fighting and coming back for me shadowing his skin. "You don't owe them anything."

"Why are you even considering this?" Indie's furious, disbelieving. "After we risked everything to come get you?"

I think of the Outpost. Of the Admiral climbing onto that magnificent, elegant ship to leave it all behind. He walked away from the mess.

I've done that, too. Designed an armor meant to kill and maim that rode upon a ship built to ruin. Set fire to trees where houses hung like cocoons.

It's easier to kill than to save.

It's easier to imagine a new world than to take care of the one you've got.

Did I come all this way just to go back?

I thought I could only love one person. Call. I thought I could only make one thing. The armor, to kill.

But what if there is more.

What if I can make something else.

What if I can love someone again.

If I went back, I could build instead of ruin. I could help the drifters find the children that were taken.

"I'll come with you to the Outpost," I say. "But I'm not going to lead unless people want it."

Indie exhales in frustration. Brig's gaze is steady and straight, holding mine. Trying to understand.

I think he will. The thought flickers hope inside me, and I surprise myself by reaching out my hand to brush my fingers against his.

"Thank you, Captain Blythe," says one of the settlers. I'm taken aback at the relief in his voice and on the faces of most of those around him. Including Laura, who was on my voyage and who knows exactly how badly it went. What cause have I given them to believe so much in me, to ask so much *of* me?

And why do *I* think I can do this? That I should try? That I could change the myth and truth that is both the Outpost's and my own—that we were abandoned, deserted?

Call loved me. That is part but not all. It's the battered hulk, the remains of the *Lily* beneath and behind me. The drifters' houses in trees, their lost children. It's the skeleton crew, who followed me off the ship and into the woods. Naomi might have betrayed me, and Eira is gone, but Tam and I fought shoulder to shoulder. Indie and Brig came back.

It's what's happened, and what's left.

"There's something you need to know," I say to the settlers. "I'm bringing the ship with me."

CHAPTER 52

INDIE IS STILL ANGRY. She's like one of the lamps up in the tree houses. Every time I catch a glimpse of her she's aflame. Illuminating. *Some people always burn.* Naomi was right about that.

If Indie is a lamp, then what is Brig?

Not the Admiral's boy, through and through, but someone who reminds me a bit of the drifters' creations. Bent, bending, in a tree, on the water. Flexing, giving, without breaking.

I stand on the gangway of the ship. Brig and Indie are feet away on the shore with some of the other drifters and settlers. A few are with me on the dredge—Mac from the drifters, Laura from the settlers, a machinist, a drifter who knows how to fix things. There is an uneasy truce as everyone works together to get the *Lily* into the water.

We've taken everything off the ship that we can and given it away. The rest of the drifters met up with us, and they took some. Other people friendly with the drifters took the rest.

I've learned that, in addition to the drifters' permanent settlement farther north, there are several other groups living to the east of the river. They watched as the people with the flying ship came to trade and gather and leave them behind.

They showed me the field where the *Palingenesis* landed. There are burns in the grass and deep ruts where the wheels came down for landing and leaving. Even a ship that graceful, one that can take to the air, leaves scars.

It all seems so small now. The Outpost, the life we lived, what we thought was true. The Admiral refused to share what we had with people around us, wasn't interested in learning from them. But they were out here all along—people who managed to live without coming into the Outpost—something we were told was as good as impossible.

"When the people on the *Palingenesis* came, they were looking for gold," Mac told me. "They'd heard we had it out here. And they were looking for new people to come with them."

The Admiral knew what he was doing. What had proven valuable over time and across cultures? Gold. Even before the Admiral knew exactly what he would use it for, he gathered it in. He accumulated resources however he could. Kill a river. Steal a child.

Laura and the other settlers pieced together more of the story from talking to the other groups. "Once the Admiral heard about the *Palingenesis*, he sent emissaries to learn what he could. He asked what the people on the ship wanted. And it turned out he had everything they needed, not just the gold. The Admiral convinced them that our best people would be better than anyone the drifters or the other small groups could offer."

"What are they called?" I asked. "The group who brought the ship?"

Laura shrugged. "They didn't really seem to have a name. They called themselves the last of the Society."

When Laura said that, Indie walked away without a backward glance or a word of explanation. I called after her, but she didn't break her stride as she headed for one of the drifters' boats, as she piloted it away from us with light, long strokes in the river.

I thought she might have gone for good. But the next morning, she was on our ship, calling out orders, figuring out how we could best get it back in the water.

"*Would* you have gone on the *Palingenesis*?" I ask Mac now.

"I don't know," he says. "I'd have liked to have the chance."

"She might still be in the Outpost," I say.

"I know," he says. But I understand why he hesitates, why he'd even consider going on the ship and leaving the possibility of finding his daughter behind. When your heart has been broken, it's hard to keep looking.

"Something happened when the *Palingenesis* flew away," I say. "Did you see it? When they went past the sun?"

"A few people think they burned up," he says. "Others think it was a trick of the light—the sun glinting off the metal. I don't know which it was."

I know the Admiral was on board, and the Quorum. I hate them all. But Eira was on that ship, and others from my crew, and I can't help but hope that they all made it to wherever they were going.

And that they never come back.

Mac presses something into my hand. I unfold my fingers to find a piece of paper with a name on it.

Eva.

"If you can find her," he says, "let me know."

"I will," I say. "I'll send word."

It's time to go.

Mac and the others who've been helping ready the dredge walk from the gangway to the shore. I glance up at the *Lily*. It looms behind me, a working shell, bereft both of what it used to hold and what once protected it.

All that's left on board are the things I'll need to survive the journey back to the Outpost. Tools to fix the motor if it breaks down. Some food. A few blankets and pallets.

The ship is stripped. And now's the time to find out if it's light enough to get home.

The settlers hitched up the dredge to the horses and to the mechanized wagons. They'll pull it along the bank downriver to a place where the water swells in to the shore. Then they'll cut me loose and I'll start the motor. I hope the plan works. It might.

The river has been rising.

"I'll see you in the Outpost," I call to Laura and the others on the bank, and my heart races. Can I do this? Bring the *Lily* back alone? Can I walk away from the drifters and Mac and Brig and Indie, maybe forever?

I walk up the gangway and start to pull it closed.

Footsteps behind me. I turn. It's Brig, his boots leaving dusty prints on the metal.

"I thought you were staying with the drifters."

"I was thinking I might," Brig says. "If you did." The light from the sun reflects off the water, the metal around us. His eyes seem to dance, to hope.

What is he saying? Are there words behind his words? I think there might be. But I don't know what to do about it. Within my chest there is a seed sprouting, a leaf uncurling.

I'm afraid to let the roots take hold.

"Of course," I say, my voice flat. "You have family in the Outpost."

"That's not—" he begins.

And then Indie is there, too, almost stomping up the ramp.

"Why are you doing this?" Indie asks. "Who's to say they still won't kill you when you get there?" She glares at me, hands on her hips.

"It's your fault," I say, glaring in return. "I wouldn't be going to the Outpost if you hadn't come back for me. No one ever did that before."

"We did," Brig says. "When you were setting the fires in the woods. We came back then, too."

He's right. They did.

"So our helping you made *you* want to help the settlers?" Indie rolls her eyes. "They're not innocent, you know."

"Neither am I."

"None of us are," Brig says. I can't bring myself to look at him, to see or not see something there. But his voice resonates around me, sends a hum from the soles of my feet to the top of my head. As if the ship's running, but it's quiet. I haven't started it yet.

Indie folds her arms. "This still doesn't make sense to me."

"You don't have to come," I tell her. "You belong to the drifters."

"I don't belong to anyone."

"You know what I mean," I say. "They care about you. You care about them." She's found a place to belong, in spite of everything. Why would she leave? "And with Porter gone, they'll need you to lead."

"They have Mac," she says. "And I've started over again more than once." She pauses. "I used to think that was sad. And it is. But it also means that I know I can do it again. I'm not afraid to keep seeing what is out there." Indie shrugs. "I need to find out what I can about the children. I can go back if I don't like it."

She could. She knows where the drifters live. But she also can't return and have it be exactly as it was. And she knows that, too.

"You should both go," I say. "Run." There's more I have inside, more words and thoughts and feelings, but I can't say them around the lump in my throat, the roots unfurling around my heart without permission.

"You're going to need help." Indie takes a deep breath. She knocks on the side of the ship next to her. "Besides, this thing is named after me."

The three of us are up on the bridge, me steering with my bandaged hands, Indie and Brig calling out to the settlers as they drag our ship along the bank to the swell. At first, I think the water won't take us, though I can hear it against the metal of the dredge, can feel it underneath. But then—wagons and horses straining, settlers and drifters calling out—the back of the ship scrapes away from the shore and we are buoyed up.

The three of us break into cheers. Brig wraps an arm around me. Without thinking, I lean into him, my forehead almost resting on his shoulder. The motion surprises him—I feel him start—and it surprises me. I don't allow myself to be vulnerable. I don't let myself touch others.

"Indie, can you steer the ship?" I ask, pulling away.

"Of course I can." She's indignant. "I used to pilot machines much more complicated than *this*. Steering the *Lily*'ll be like controlling a whale instead of a hummingbird."

"All right," I say, not sure what she means.

"A hummingbird's harder. They're fast. On the *Lily*, I can see what's coming a mile away." She gestures down the river.

We didn't see the drifters coming. But I don't point that out. She knows.

"Brig, go and get us the map from the captain's quarters," I say. "It's the best one. Bring it up to the bridge. I'm going to get the motor started."

Neither one of them ask if I need any help, or if they should come with me.

They understand. I want to be alone.

Down on the mining deck, I flip the switch. The motor powers up, begins its mechanical hum. Even without the mining equipment, it's loud in the belly of the ship as the motor's refrain echoes from the metal walls. It's not a beautiful tune, an easy one, a lullaby by any stretch of the imagination. It's the kind of low hymn you find yourself making to keep moving when you're tired, or to hold on to calm when there is terror, or simply to remind yourself that you still have a voice, even if you are the only one who hears it.

I sit down next to the motor. There's a hole in the right knee of my pants. Tam's blood is still on my shirt. My own blood, too.

No gold. No armor. No Tam. No Call.

Just me and the ship, singing.

"Motor's sounding good," Indie says, when I get up to the bridge. Brig looks over his shoulder from where he's tacking the map on the wall. I don't know if either of them can hear the residue of tears in my voice. I took care to scrub any traces of salt from my face.

Indie gestures for me to take her place. "Your turn," she says. "I'm hungry." Her long red hair is wild, her clothes almost as dirty as mine. Brig's finished with the map and he comes over to join us at the helm.

"Mac gave me this," I say, pulling out the scrap of paper to show them.

"Eva." Indie touches the paper. "Mac's daughter."

"Whatever else happens, we'll try to find them," I say.

She nods, rubbing a hand across her eyes, before walking out through the blackened door frame. Neither Brig nor I calls or follows after her. It's Indie's turn to be alone.

I put my hands on the helm to steer. The three of us will take turns keeping to our course. "We'll have to find Tam's family, too," I say to Brig, without looking at him. "Tell them what happened."

Brig walks to the window near me. He looks out at the river in front of us, kneading the back of his neck with his strong, smudged hand. There are cuts and burns all over the back of it, and on his wrist and forearm. My eyes run over his hand, his neck, the curl of his hair, the square of his shoulders, and I'm caught when he turns.

I swallow.

"This was in the captain's quarters," he says, reaching into his shirt pocket. "Someone must have found it and put it back for you."

I tear my gaze from his face and look at what he's holding. Call's ruler.

I take it in my hand. When I do, my fingertips touch Brig's. I slip the ruler into my pocket. My breath catches when I look up. There is a flash in his eyes, a flicker in my heart.

CHAPTER 53

"**PROMISE ME,**" I whisper to Brig and Indie. "*Promise me that if we need to, we can run.*"

"I promise," Brig says. Indie nods.

We are nearing the Outpost. Its lights flicker in the distance. Tomorrow, we will be upon it. I shut down the motor so we could come up and hear the quiet and try to see a last star or two.

I breathe the air. I taste the river in it, and the forest beyond.

I have a taste for you.

Call said that, and more.

Finish it for me.

It's the only way you're going to see the world, Poe.

Go on, he said to me. *Then you can come back up here.*

My heart pounds.

Would you have wanted this for me, Call? I think, as I stand cold on the deck of a ship empty of gold. As I count the stars up high. As I feel Brig warm right next to me, see Indie a few feet away.

Yes.

Call.

I wanted to finish your dreams for you.

But that's part of the tragedy of being gone too soon.

You don't get to finish them and no one else can do it for you, no matter how much they might try.

But do you still live on, if someone you loved, someone who loves you, goes on to live their own dreams?

I think so. I think you live on best that way.

You are in my heart when it soars. In my hands when they make something new. In my breath when I run.

And someday, even that will be gone.

You will be deep in my blood and bones, part of me, but I will have moved past you.

Even as I carry you with me, I will have left you behind.

ACKNOWLEDGMENTS

First and foremost, my gratitude to my husband, Scott, and our four children: Calvin, Ian, Truman, and Lainey. You all have your own stories and ways of being in the world, and I learn from each of you every day. It is a privilege and honor to be part of this family. Thank you for your patience, support, and love.

I also owe a great debt to my parents, Robert and Arlene Braithwaite, who have always taken me to wild and beautiful places and asked me to look closely.

Jodi Reamer has been my agent since the beginning, and I'm thankful every day for her wisdom and humor. Jodi has changed my life for the better in so many ways, and she is one of the wisest people I know. It's an honor to be associated with her and to have convinced her to ride the Matterhorn at Disneyland. I am also very grateful to Alec Shane and Cecilia de la Campa at Writers House for their help and advocacy over the years.

This is my sixth book with my editor Julie Strauss-Gabel, and each time the process is a revelation. No one asks questions like Julie. She makes me think about the heart of my story and find the best words to tell it. I am thankful for her brilliance and her generosity. I am also indebted to Anna Booth, Venessa Carson, Maggie Edkins, Theresa Evangelista, Melissa Faulner, Felicia Frazier, Alex Garber, Carmela Iaria, Jen Loja, Shanta Newlin, Emily Romero, Felicity Vallence, Natalie Vielkind, and everyone at Penguin Young Readers. I'm lucky to work with all of you.

One of the true pleasures of my career is getting to know wonderful teachers, librarians, and booksellers. Rose Brock, Gene Nelson, Anne Holman, and Margaret Neville, thank you for your tireless efforts on behalf of readers and your communities.

Writing this book required me to go outside of my comfort zone in many ways. I was lucky to have experts to offer advice and input. Any mistakes that remain are mine alone. Corwin Revis helped me figure out mechanics and logistics for a futuristic ship based on mining dredges from the past and present, and he was unfailingly smart, patient, and interesting in his comments and suggestions. James Worthington answered many random texts about how the gunfight scenes might work best, and never once laughed at me (at least, not when I could hear). Huge thanks to him, his wife, Amy, and their wonderful kids for being fantastic neighbors and friends.

Since my last novel with Penguin was released, I went back to school to get an MFA in creative writing, and it was one of the best things I've ever done. My beloved classmates at the Vermont College of Fine Arts were a surprise and a gift. I knew I would love going to school at VCFA; I could never have anticipated exactly how much. The Dead Post-It Society has a special place in my heart. Extra thanks to Salima Alikhan, Robin Galbraith, and Brendan Reichs, my housemates while I was at school. You picked me up when I was down and made me laugh hard, think big thoughts, and stay up way too late. I'll be forever grateful. My gratitude also to the advisers and mentors I had at VCFA. It was a complete honor to work with such talented teachers, writers, and human beings. Special thanks to An Na, Kekla Magoon, and Susan Fletcher.

Ash Allan, Mikayla Kirkby, and Mylee Edwards: you took such care for my kids while I worked, and we are all enriched by having you in our lives.

It is dangerous to list beloved author friends, because I am afraid I will miss someone, but their support and friendship have meant the world. I owe Renée Ahdieh and Sabaa Tahir a great deal for their support and encouragement on this manuscript in particular. Ally Carter and Jenny Han, thank you for inviting me on retreats where I could soak up your genius and work on this novel. To my local writing friends—Ann Dee Ellis, Shannon Hale, Veeda Bybee, Lindsey Leavitt Brown, Emily R. King, Bree Despain, Rob Wells, Emily Wing Smith, Brandon Mull, Julie Olson, and Erin Summerill—I owe you big-time for supporting WriteOut, for dinners and lunches at favorite places, and for hiking and talking and laughing with me. We found some silver linings together during some very cloudy times.

Margaret Stohl, thank you for taking me under your wing and teaching me how to give back and keep going. So much of what is good in my life and career are because of you. To the boards of all the Yalls: you're too fun and smart for your own good. Please don't change, ever.

I don't know how I'm lucky enough to have Brendan Reichs and Soman Chainani as my friends, but I'm beyond grateful. Sometimes I think I am out of words, or alone, and you remind me that neither is true. You're two of the best human beings I know. Brendan, writing and working with you is an education and a gift. Soman, you are the Serena Williams of kidlit. Thank you both for everything.

During the writing of this book, I was lucky enough to help start a writing camp for kids in rural Utah. I can't thank the WriteOut Board enough for their countless hours of service and work on the behalf of the camp and the kids who attend. Scott Condie, Ann Dee Ellis, Krista Bulloch, Denise Lund, Brian Jackson, Amy Jackson, and Brandon Jameson—you made it happen. Thank you for figuring out scholarships, hauling boxes around in a golf cart, writing scavenger hunts, putting together schedules, managing finances, designing graphics, and executing a myriad of other tasks with good humor and great ideas. Bridget Lee, thank you for your generosity in coming on board and helping us learn how to make this ship sail. Enormous thanks to all the volunteers on the ground who help us with the nitty-gritty. And my very deep gratitude to our amazing teen campers, who treat one another with such respect, kindness, generosity, and joy.

Finally, and always, a huge thank-you to the readers. You are the why and the how. Thank you for making this job I love possible. Thank you for caring about books, one another, and the world around you.